Office Perks

'What's this about you taking Lucy's knickers off in the street, Niall Flynn?'

'I did that.'

'To get a date with us two and Sophie?'

'That's the size of it, yes.'

He was laughing, cool and confident. She was teasing.

'Well, you may not have Sophie, but you've got us, so can you handle it?'

'Oh, I can handle it.'

'So, what are you going to do about it, big man?'

'Take the pair of you home and do you both at the same time.'

'Oh my!'

Other books by Monica Belle:

Noble Vices
Valentina's Rules
Wild in the Country
Wild by Nature

Office Perks
Monica Belle

BLACK LACE

Black Lace books contain sexual fantasies.
In real life, always practise safe sex.

First published in 2005 by
Black Lace
Thames Wharf Studios
Rainville Road
London W6 9HA

The right of Monica Belle to be identified as the Author of
the Work has been asserted in accordance with the Copyright,
Designs and Patents Act 1988.

Design by Smith & Gilmour, London
Printed and bound by Mackays of Chatham PLC

ISBN 0 352 33939 X

1

19 July, 10.45 a.m. – Lucy Doyle arrives at St Bernold's Parochial House.

19 July, 2.40 p.m. – Father Donald Jessop delivers a lecture on morality, with particular emphasis on the impropriety of accepting the lingam in the oral cavity.

19 July, 2.41 p.m. – Lucy Doyle is advised to seek alternative employment.

'"Accepting the lingam in the oral cavity!" Pompous old fart. If he doesn't want me to give the gardener blowjobs, why can't he just say so?'

What else was I supposed to do? The job was beyond boring, and all the stuff they'd given me about developing my spiritual side was just crap. Forty pounds a week, to play skivvy to a bunch of priests! There is such a thing as a minimum wage, and I told Father Jessop this in no uncertain terms. He said I should be honoured to serve God. That was lecture number two. Lecture number one was on being late, because I was supposed to be there from seven-thirty, followed by the unsuitability of wearing a skinny top and low-rise jeans while working for him. Lecture number three was about the cock-sucking.

OK, so if I'd wanted to keep the job perhaps I should have offered to suck Father Jessop off as well – or rather, to take his lingam in my oral cavity – but I'm not that sort of girl. He'd dropped enough hints, in-between lecturing me. Even when he'd told me off for showing too much flesh his eyes had been firmly on what he wanted covered. Then came the compliments. First there was how pretty my curly orange hair looks like against my white skin – or, to put it another way, I look like a partially bleached carrot but he'd still like to get into my knickers. Then there was how 'decorative' I looked, a true 'flower of Erin' – meaning firm little tits and a toned round bum which he would dearly like to get out of my knickers. Lastly there's how fragile and innocent I looked, how naïve; maybe naïve enough to be talked into wanking him off with my knickers?

Maybe not, but that's what Father Emanuel Slynn wanted our Siobhan to do, and she a choir girl, too. I wouldn't, not with either of them, but I would with Todd Byrne, and I did. He was my type of man, six foot and more, with hands so big I could imagine sitting on one and him lifting me up. Strong too, like a bull, all muscle, and mature; mature enough to know what he wanted; mature enough to accept my approach at face value.

I was only supposed to take him a mug of tea, but just the smell of man and earth was enough to get me horny, never mind the sight of him. I was bored. I was pissed off with the way Father Jessop treated me. I wanted to feel like a woman, not an accessory. Todd was nice, too, joking with me and making me feel good about myself. So I took his cock out and sucked him off, with my mouth full of hot tea, which is a great way to get the boys going.

He took it right in his stride, stroking my hair as he grew hard in my mouth, and letting me decide how deep he went. I'd seldom had such a gorgeous cock to play with, so big and smooth and silky. He didn't rush, or try to push me further, but let me take my time, really getting the taste and feel of him into my senses, until I wanted to come. I'd have done it too. One hand down my knickers, a few deft touches and I'd have been there, in heaven. Maybe not Father Jessop's heaven but heaven all the same, with my mouth full of big, hard cock and my fingers well down in the crease of my pussy. I pulled my bra out so I could play with my nipples, and was just unfastening my jeans when Father Jessop came in.

So there I was, standing in a Kilburn back street on a hot summer's afternoon, my pre-university work experience well up the Swanee and wondering what to do with myself. Home was out, because Mum was not going to be pleased, and no doubt Father Jessop would have already been on the phone. I'd get a lecture. I'd get compared with Mary. I'd get compared with Mary and Siobhan. Maybe I'd even get compared with Mary and Siobhan and Tara.

What I needed was to come home with a job that paid real money. That would shut them up. On second thoughts, knowing them it probably wouldn't, but it would make me feel better. Not that I was feeling bad, not really. I knew I should have felt guilty, but I didn't. Guilt just isn't my thing, which is odd, because my family do guilt like we do drink. I guess it's the Irish Catholic prerogative.

Instead I felt happy and excited, with the memory of sucking Todd Byrne's cock fresh in my mind and the prospect of freedom ahead of me. I could do anything, anything at all ... well, almost anything. Well, not a lot really, but I didn't care. Flipping burgers was better than Father Jessop.

Maybe a McJob was the answer. I wanted a slice of life, to meet new people, different people, fun girls, sexy men. Working in a burger bar, a pub, a restaurant, I'd get plenty. On the other hand, I wouldn't get much money and I'd be at work in the evenings. I wanted my evenings to myself, and the insultingly small amount I'd been offered at the parochial house had made me want to earn more.

I'd been wandering aimlessly down Maida Vale, and stopped at a newsagents to buy a notebook and a pen. There was a coffee bar nearby, but one look at the price of an espresso and I'd decided against it. A low wall and a can of something cold served instead of the coffee and fancy-looking tables and chairs, and after a moment's thought I opened my notebook and began writing.

What does Lucy want to do?

The answer was, laze around, get pissed with my girlfriends and shag lots of cute men, so I crossed it out very carefully and wrote:

What can Lucy do?

Cook, sort of.

Use a computer, just about.

Dance, better than most.

Drink, more than most without falling over.

Discuss James Joyce, pointillism or glacial features well enough to earn me three As.

After another moment's thought I wrote:

What can't Lucy do?

Work hard.

Get up in the morning.

As she's told.

That seemed to narrow it down nicely, so I made three columns and filled them in slowly as I sipped my drink.

Job	Good	Bad
McJob	Lots of people	Not much money
		No evenings
		Bosses
Office job	More money	Bosses
	Evenings	Boring
Stripping	Lots of money	Family freak
	Lots of people	No evenings
		Bosses

4

There was one big problem – the bosses. It didn't matter if it was a little Hitler in a burger bar, a stuffed shirt in an office or a sleazeball in a lap dancing club. A boss is a boss, and bosses and I are a bad mixture. A few other options flicked through my mind – librarian? Mime-artist? Pickpocket? All of them had drawbacks. I also needed to be able to return home within three hours with the triumphant announcement of my new job. Telling Mum that I'd decided to become a pickpocket was really going to be popular.

I walked on, up to the Edgware Road. I ate a doughnut and let serendipity take its course. I had just about finished it when I realised I was standing under a sign for a temp agency – Super Staff. It had to be worth a shot. Cramming the remains of the doughnut into my mouth, I pushed the intercom bell. A woman's voice answered and I was let up, into a small room with five blue plastic seats and a potted plant. The voice, now coming through a slightly open door, told me to wait. A second voice sounded, male, nervous and addressed to the first.

'. . . anything, really. You see, I'm really just waiting to see what comes up in my field. My PhD's on cultural assimilation among the peoples of . . .'

'Yes, Mr Robins.'

'Dr Robins.'

'Quite, Dr Robins, but unfortunately your qualifications are not suitable for us. Here at Super Staff we need commitment, a willingness to work to a flexible, efficient timetable. Personal presentation is also important.'

I quickly wiped my mouth in case there were any stray doughnut crumbs, simultaneously wishing it was as easy to put my bra back on as it had been to get it off. It was in my bag, where I'd stuffed it hastily after being caught by Father Jessop. I was very glad indeed that I hadn't worn lippy. The guy had a PhD and they didn't want him. What hope did I have?

Two minutes later he'd been bundled out, looking crestfallen, and I was face to face with the voice, a middle-aged woman called Mrs Maryam Smith, because that was what it said on her desk. She didn't have glasses to peer at me over, but she should have done. Instead she looked down a long nose, then opened a file.

'Miss Davenport?'

'No. Miss Doyle.'.

'I have Miss Davenport for four o'clock.'

'It's only five to.'

She gave a click of her tongue and began to sort through a heap of files. I decided I ought to say something.

'I don't have an appointment.'

She looked at me as if I'd just confessed to being a serial killer.

'I was just hoping to sign up with you, for temporary work.'

She gave a heartfelt sigh and shook her head. A brief flurry of paper and she was ready.

'What experience do you have, Miss Doyle?'

Secretary to Father Donald Jessop of St Bernold's Parochial House sounded good.

'Until recently I was secretary to Father Donald Jessop of St Bernold's Parochial House.'

'Indeed? And why did you leave?'

'Sadly Father Jessop passed away.'

'I see. My condolences. Presumably Father Jessop's successors will be able to provide references?'

Not good at all.

'No, er . . . I'm afraid not. The er . . . the parochial house burnt down.'

'How awful!'

'I'd rather not talk about it.'

'I understand, of course.'

The intercom buzzed. She spoke into it, then to me.

'That is Miss Davenport. Please fill in these forms and I will be with you shortly.'

I took the forms, a white one, a pink one and a green one. In the outer room, a girl with long brown hair and serious heels – evidently Miss Davenport – was sitting on one of the blue chairs. We exchanged smiles as we swapped places and I began to do the forms. The white one wanted to know all about me, so I told them. The pink one wanted to know what I'd done and with whom, so I made it up. The green one had lots of boxes to tick, so I ticked them.

Miss Davenport had shut the door so I didn't get a chance to earwig her conversation, although I'd caught a few words. She had a cut glass accent, public school for sure, which went with her appearance: a two-piece skirt suit of fine dove-grey wool, crisp white blouse with a thin black ribbon at her throat, silk tights, maybe even stockings. Little-Miss-Snooty all through, except for the heels. Her heels were four-inch stilettos in shiny black patent with a tiny scarlet logo at the outside, what looked like a burning H.

She came out not long after I'd finished doing my forms, gave me a glance I'd swear was pity, and left. I looked after her, thinking what a stuck-up bitch she was, before answering Mrs Maryam Smith's call. Back in her inner sanctum she took my forms, glancing over them. By the time she'd got to the bottom of the one with all the little boxes, her frosty, formal expression had faded to something approaching affability. She nodded as she put them down.

'Well, Miss Doyle, you're certainly very well qualified, remarkably well for your age.'

'The Church set very exacting standards.'

'So I see. But still, with us you will be working in a business environment, under pressure, often called on to work unusual hours, and in general to maintain a proactive attitude to both ourselves and our clients.'

I nodded and smiled. I didn't know what the fuck she was talking about, except for the bit about unusual hours.

'I was required to start work at the parochial house at seven-thirty in the morning.'

Her eyebrows rose a fraction.

'I doubt that will be necessary. But let us say, for the sake of example, a client were to ask you to accompany him for a weekend conference?'

I hesitated. The answer was that it depended how horny he was, but that didn't seem likely to be what she wanted to hear. On top of Miss Davenport's folder was a stapled sheaf of paper headed – Guidelines for Staff.

'Naturally I'd follow the Super Staff guidelines.'

Her smile grew broader. It was the correct answer. She handed me a copy of the guidelines, three pages of small, closely spaced print. I bit down a grimace as she went on.

'One last question, Miss Doyle. What would you bring to us here at Super Staff?'

I was ready for that one.

'First and foremost, commitment, also good personal presentation and a willingness to work to a flexible, efficient timetable.'

She gave another pleased smile.

'Well, Miss Doyle, naturally we'll need to check your references, but I think I may fairly say that you will fit in very well with us here at Super Staff.'

'I'm sure I will. Thank you.'

I got up, left and that was it. I had a job, or, rather, I

would have a job if I managed to talk the people I'd given as references into covering for me. That was an itsy-bitsy problem, and something I needed to attend to sharpish. Not that sharpish, because a tot of Power's was called for, to celebrate and to toughen myself up for the inevitable blow-up when I got home.

There was a pub directly over the road, the Bull. They didn't have Powers, but they did have Jameson's. I ordered a double. After all, for the first time in my life I was going to have some money to spare. As I turned away from the bar I realised that among the few others getting an early drink in was Miss Davenport. She was scowling as she read the document Super Staff had given her. I went towards her, hoping her heels said more about her than her dress, her looks, her accent.

'Hi? You were in Super Staff, over the road?'

'Yeah, daft bitch.'

She scrumpled up the document and dropped it into an ashtray with a motion of fastidious distaste.

'Fuck that for a laugh.'

I was a bit taken aback. To hear her speak she might have been royalty, but she swore like my uncles.

'What was it?'

'First formal warning.'

'Oh, right. What are they like at Super Staff? Strict?'

'The usual bollocks. They expect everything for fuck all.'

'Don't they pay much?'

'Depends. Generally ten or twelve an hour.'

'Ten or twelve pounds an hour?'

'Yes, mean bitch.'

Not in my books she wasn't. Even at ten pounds an hour I would be taking home ten times what the parochial house had meant to pay me. I didn't say anything, not wanting to look totally naïve, and she went on.

'You get a specific rate with each job, depending on the skills you'll be using. Half the time you end up filing anyway, and making tea and coffee. You'll find that wherever you go there's some guy on a power trip who wants you to be his personal tea maid. Women are worse.'

'I can cope. I'm Lucy, by the way.'

'Bobbie. Would you like another?'

'I'd love to, only I'm a bit broke.'

'Whatever. When I get kicked out you can sub me.'

'OK, it's Jameson's.'

She went for the drinks, leaving me a little surprised, and quite pleased. I hadn't expected her to be so friendly, but it was as if working for Super Staff made us instant friends. She seemed to know what she was doing too, which had to help. The moment she got back I put the question which had been uppermost in my mind.

'Could you give me some advice?'

'Sure.'

'How quickly does Mrs Smith check our references?'

She laughed.

'Did you give email addresses?'

'No.'

'Then you've got until maybe Thursday to sort out whatever you've been up to. She never rings, but I wouldn't hang around if I were you.'

I nodded thankfully.

'How does it work then, with jobs?'

'It's simple. You get a call in the morning, telling you where to go and who to see, then at the end of the week, or whenever, you get your boss to sign a time sheet.'

'Sounds OK. What's a "proactive attitude"?'

'It means you have to give the male clients blow-jobs on demand.'

'You're joking!'

She nearly choked on her wine, clutching at her neck in her effort not to laugh before she managed to get herself under control.

'Of course I'm joking! It just means you're expected to volunteer to work late if it would help, that sort of stuff. Basically, be a good little wage slave.'

'Do any of the men hit on you?'

She shrugged, utterly indifferent.

'Sure, sometimes. Sometimes I go for it, if they're cute. You're not supposed to, but then it's none of SS's business.'

'SS as in Super Staff?'

'Yes. It suits them. Don't worry about it, because if you're good they need you a lot more than you need them.'

I picked up the guidelines.

'How about all this?'

'It's churn. Bin it.'

'Churn?'

'Stuff that's forever being rewritten, so there's no point in reading it. The only thing they're really hot on is moonlighting, if you accept private offers for work from their clients.'

'Is that why you got your warning?'

'No, that was for flashing a window cleaner.'

'Flashing a window cleaner?'

'Yes. He was cute too, and he was staring in at me while I was filing. I thought, maybe after work. So I flashed my tits.'

'Couldn't you just have asked him?'

'Don't be silly, he was outside the window on the fifteenth floor. He got the message all right too, only there was CCTV in the room. Nosy bastards.'

I couldn't help but laugh, and warm to her. She was as much of a bad girl as I was, propositioning men and drinking shorts in the afternoon. I just had to top her story.

'I know the feeling,' I casually slipped in. 'I got sacked earlier today, for sucking the gardener off.'

'You dirty bitch!'

It was not a criticism, far from it. She was laughing.

'Tell all, and I want the details.'

My head was already spinning a little. No surprise, with four shots of whiskey on a nearly empty stomach.

'OK. I'm going to university in September. To Edinburgh, and my family had set it up for me to work at this parochial house, that's where priests live. It was dead, and I won't even tell you how much they were going to pay me, but the gardener was huge, hands like spades, and just all man.'

'Rough?'

'Rough, yeah.'

Her eyes were glittering and her hand was tight on the stem of her wine glass. I suppressed a giggle as her tongue flicked out to moisten her lips.

'Just how rough?'

'Rough, but he wasn't a pig about it. You know how some men are, trying to get the whole thing down your throat. He wasn't like that, he stroked my hair and tickled my neck. I love that, with a cock in my mouth and my man's hands holding my head.'

She shook her head.

'That's nice, but I like really rough, the sort of guy who won't think twice about doing it in front of his mates.'

It was my turn to wet my lips, thinking back to Dalkey, and kneeling in the long, warm grass behind my Nan's house with Shaun Cullen's cock in my mouth while his mates watched me suck him off. I nodded.

'I know, but there were only the priests. Father Jessop

caught me at it, so I got kicked out. That's why I was at Super Staff.'

She nodded in turn. Her face was a little flushed, and I could feel the heat at my own neck. My pussy was beginning to feel more than a little in need of attention. I wanted to talk.

'I don't know why I'm telling you this, because I haven't even told my sisters, but last summer, in Ireland, a man I'd been going out with got me to suck him off – with three of his friends watching.'

I giggled. Bobbie had closed her eyes, her face set in dreamy pleasure. When she spoke it was a sigh.

'Yes, please. Where they very rough with you? Did your boyfriend make you take your clothes off?'

'He pulled my top up. I wasn't wearing a bra.'

She purred.

'I wish!'

'Haven't you? Like that?'

Suddenly her tone had changed completely.

'No! Men are such cowards, or else stupidly jealous, or they can't get hard in front of their mates.'

'Shaun Cullen didn't have any trouble. He was well up for it, so he could show off in front of them.'

'He didn't ... make you do them too, did he?'

'No!'

'Pity.'

'You're terrible, worse than me!'

'I want it like that, but I seem to scare them off.'

'Maybe because you're too tall, and you do sound ... you know ...' I'd been going to say stuck up, but decided against it. She made a face.

'It's just me,' she said, anticipating what it was I was going to say. 'I shouldn't complain, I suppose. The window cleaner, Jack, he was good. He still had his overalls on, and he took me down a back alley, right in the middle of the city, behind a church. I went up against the wall. He just picked me up, under my bum, pulled my knickers aside and lifted me onto his cock. All I could do was cling on tight while he had me. It was like being fucked by a bear.'

'How do you know? Do you often get fucked by bears?'

'Very funny.'

'Are you going to see him again?'

'I don't know ... maybe. I don't want him to start thinking I'm his. Do you want another whiskey, or shall we share a bottle of wine? The Sancerre here is OK.'

'Fine, that would be great, yes.'

I'd glanced up to where a list of wines was written on a blackboard, with the names in red and white chalk within a fringe of grape leaves. The Sancerre was a white, and cost twenty-five pounds a bottle. Bobbie wasn't bothered, making sure the barman took a really cold one from the back of the fridge. He brought it back with two glasses on a tray. I knew it was stupid to drink wine on top of whiskey, but I didn't feel I could refuse her. She poured and we chinked glasses.

'Here's to big, rough men.'

My response was a giggle. I felt happy, accepted, and had no desire whatsoever to start for home. Much better to drink with my new friend, and talk dirty, only the pub was beginning to fill up as people came out of work. A group of young men had sat down at the table beside us, five of them, talking in loud, brash voices about money, cars, girls. I caught a snatch of conversation.

'... and the girls go down under the table, right. Blow-jobs all round, right, and afterwards, they get up on the stage to do a strip, only one of them's a tranny!'

The others burst into raucous laughter and I found myself giggling, imagining the men he was talking about, all as pleased as punch because they'd had their cocks sucked, and then finding out one of the girls was really a man. Two of them were quite attractive, in a slick sort of way. I glanced at Bobbie, wondering if she was thinking the same, just as the buzz of general conversation and the music hit a lull at the same instant. The voice of the biggest of the five came to me, clear as a bell.

'Who d'you reckon on, Pinky or Perky?'

It wasn't hard to guess who he was talking about, or why. Talking sex with Bobbie, my nipples had gone stiff, and were sticking up through my top as if making a determined effort to escape, upwards. I could see why Bobbie was Pinky too, because she was flushed from her neck up. So was I, as my temper flared with my embarrassment. I rounded on them, wanting some really biting put-down – just the sort which always comes ten minutes after you need it. Bobbie just laughed.

'Show them what they can't have, Lucy!'

I didn't even think. My hands went to the hem of my top and up it came, tits bare to the room, perky nipples pointing more or less at the ceiling. There was a wonderful moment as the guy's jaw dropped and his eyes went round. The guy next to him saw too, and swore. Their mates realised something was up and jerked around, too late. I'd already covered up, trying to look sweet and innocent as I raised my glass to my lips. Bobbie dissolved in laughter, and so did I, unable to stop myself.

For just an instant all five men looked completely stunned, before they all began to talk at once, the three who hadn't seen demanding to know what had happened and the two who had telling them. I got up, walked slowly around to the big guy who'd called me Perky and put my hands on my hips, looking down at him. I meant to give him a moment to take me in, maybe wonder if I was interested, before telling him he would never, ever, have the least chance of getting his hands on what he'd seen. The barman got in first.

'You two, out!'

I rounded on him.

'What's it to you, you great gobshite? I'll –'

He started around the table. Bobbie was already on her feet, giggling and shaking her head, the bottle of Sancerre clutched in her hand. I made for the door, laughing so hard I tripped and had to clutch on to a lamppost for support as I fell out onto the pavement. Bobbie came after me, stumbling on her heels, and we ended up in each other's arms, laughing too hard to stand properly.

The barman had had enough of us, and didn't follow, leaving us to move off up the road, arm in arm and drinking Sancerre from the bottle. We hadn't gone ten yards when the guy from the pub appeared, overtaking us, to turn and walk backwards . . .

'Hey, girls . . .'

. . . straight into a huge black guy who'd just come out of a doorway. Both of them went down, and Bobbie and I were clutching onto each other for support. The guy from the pub was babbling apologies immediately and the black guy didn't look best pleased, but when he did manage to get up it was Bobbie and me he rounded on.

'What's so fucking funny?'

Bobby made a little purring noise in her throat.

'Ooh, big man!'

'Are you taking the piss, 'cause . . .'

I'd stepped in-between them, sure he was going to hit her. I caught the scent of him, totally male, my face level with a heavily muscled chest half covered by a vest.

'Sh! Cool down!'

He was going to push me aside, until I squeezed his crotch, filling my hand with his cock and balls, or rather, not filling my hand, because he was packing more meat than a steak house. A shiver ran right through me as I stepped back, my tummy fluttering, a little scared, but hoping he was man enough to react to me the way a man should. He gave a sharp shake of his head.

'You want to watch who you tease, girl!'

'Who says I'm teasing?'

He just picked me up, one big hand under my bum, one on my back, pressing his lips to mine. For just an instant I was fighting, shocked, before I melted. My mouth came open under his, our tongues met and we were kissing. His hand was kneading my bottom, my body right off the ground, and all I could do was cling to him, my legs up around his huge hips, the bulge of his cock pushing up against my pussy, already growing hard. I wanted to be fucked, then and there, on the pavement of the Edgware Road, my clothes ripped off and my legs spread wide, his lovely big cock in my mouth and up my pussy, filling my body right completely.

I was drunk. I was horny. I'd have done it if he'd made me, maybe. Not really, no, because no man is that much of an animal, more's the pity. He put me down and I let go of him, my legs shaking as my feet met the pavement. Bobbie was staring at me. She looked as flushed as I felt. The guy from the pub had stepped back a little, and glanced between us, hopeful but unsure of himself.

Something inside me wanted to tell the black guy to fuck off. Maybe it was social conscience. Bollocks. I took his arm.

'Well, are we going?'

He looked down, and just nodded. Bobbie took his other arm and the three of us had started up the street, with the guy from the pub trailing along behind. I had no idea where we were going; maybe to another pub, maybe to somewhere our new friend could fuck our brains out, only I was leading them, so . . .

'Where the fuck are we going?' I blurted out.

The black guy answered me.

'If you want what I think you want, that's my rig. Otherwise, you'd better run, girl.'

He'd nodded to where a huge great articulated lorry was blocking half the road. Bobbie looked towards it, her mouth a little open, her eyes wide, just creaming herself as she spoke.

'You're a trucker?'

He nodded and said something under his breath, maybe "posh skirt". My stomach was fluttering terribly as we made for the cab of his lorry, with Mum's warnings about not going with strange men fighting the raw lust in my head. Lust won hands down, and a moment later he was pushing me up into the cab with a hand on my bum. The rig was spacious, with a flat shelf behind the seats where he could sleep. The smell of him – and the diesel of the truck – was thick in my nostrils as I climbed in. Bobbie followed and he went to the far side, leaving the guy from the pub standing on the pavement.

'Hey, do I get to come?' he asked.

Truck man was going to speak, probably to put him down, but Bobbie already had a hand out. He climbed in, and the black guy kissed his teeth as he took his seat, but said nothing. I felt better, because they couldn't both be psychos, surely?

As the engine rumbled to life, I made myself comfortable on my tummy in his sleeping space, looking forward between a pair of tatty orange and brown curtains. Bobbie was in front of me, between the men, and spoke as we began to move.

'Where are we going?' I asked again.

The driver took a moment to concentrate on pulling out into the evening traffic before he answered, his voice full of lust and laughter.

'Never mind that. You just keep yourselves warm.'

The guy from the pub turned to us, his voice very different, eager and nervous, as he spoke.

'What are your names? I'm Luke.'

I answered.

'Lucy.'

And on a whim, 'But you can call me Miss Doyle.'

It was right, for him, not for the driver, who answered with a grunt.

'Frazer.'

Bobbie didn't answer at all, because she was trying to get Frazer's zip down. He slapped her hand.

'You want it, girl, you've got it, but not here, yeah?'

She stopped, giggling happily as she stretched. The bottle was still in her hand, and I took it, swallowing down a big gulp of wine, cold and sharp in my throat. We were moving north, slowly, the cars stretching in front of us in a multi-coloured metal line as far as we could see. Bobbie sighed, almost whining.

'Nobody can see, let me play with you!'

Frazer grunted and glanced out at the ranks of windows to his side, most of them with a prime view into his cab, including those of Super Staff. The first bus we passed was going to get an even better view. Bobbie didn't care, burrowing for his fly as he tried to fight her off, one handed. He was getting hard in his trousers, a wide ridge extending down one leg, extending a long way, I noticed to my delight. I swallowed, imagining how he'd look with it out, thick and dark and proud in Bobbie's hand, in her mouth, in my mouth . . .

I had to have him, and Luke just wasn't the same. He

was cute maybe, but too much the lad. The way things were going he'd have Bobbie and I'd end up with second best, or nothing at all. I had to stick my oar in.

'Wait, you greedy cow, you'll get us arrested,' I warned her, careless as to how she might react. She seemed like a good sport but I'd known her less than a couple of hours. I wasn't sure how she'd react to criticism.

Too late. His zip was down. Her hand burrowed in and closed on his cock. He grunted in pleasure and she was purring as she began to rub on him, heedless to my protestations. The other guy, Luke, was staring, his mouth open, one hand on his own crotch. I could smell the musky scent of Frazer's cock, and I reached down, determined to get my share. His trouser button popped open as I tried to force my hand in beside Bobbie's, and suddenly he was out: a thick, dark column of meat over two fat balls pushed up where she'd shoved his briefs down to get him out. I took it, wanking him, as she was, and we were both giggling hysterically.

'Ladies! Somebody's going to see! Shit!'

The traffic had loosened up and we were moving, Frazer struggling to shift gear as we tossed at his cock. We'd punctured his cool, shocking him, and the last of my doubts just vanished. I wanted his cock in me, to ride him and let him ride me, to be lifted and popped on the way the window cleaner had fucked Bobbie up against the wall. I wanted to be bent over and have it slid up me from behind, good and deep with his hard six-pack pressed to my bare bum; to go down on my knees with him on my back, doggy style.

If I didn't watch what I was doing all I would get would be a charge for riotous behaviour, or whatever it's called when a girl gets caught tossing off her boyfriend in public. I stopped, and slapped Bobbie's hand for her.

'Bad girl! Put him down!'

There was a rug at the back, over Frazer's makeshift bed, and I pulled it away, to cover his lap. He shook his head, grinning as he sped up. Luke let out his breath.

'You girls are hot,' he said.

I answered him, eager to get my own back, to turn him on and make him beg.

'And you're a cheeky git. Pinky and Perky, is it?'

Bobbie laughed. 'It suits you,' she said

'Hey,' I cried. 'You're supposed to be on my side! Anyway, it's better than Pinky!'

Luke laughed, just a little forced.

'I like it.'

'Miss Doyle, I said, if you want . . .'

'OK, Miss Doyle, Miss Perky Doyle!'

'Oi!'

I gave him a clip on one ear, not hard. He had to suffer. Frazer held his peace, very much the man in charge, guiding his huge rig skilfully through Maida Vale with the rest of us joking and laughing, drinking too, the bottle quickly finished to leave me relaxed and eager to go.

We were barely through Kilburn when he turned off onto some sort of service road, between blocks of flats, red-brown brick and several stories high, out into a huge open lorry park, something I'd never even guessed existed so close to home. It was perfect, hardly a soul in view, save for a bored security guard in a hut by the gates and a cluster of truckers idling by a hot dog van.

My insides were tight in anticipation of what was coming to me as we drove down between ranks of parked lorries to the far end, where a few cabless trailers stood beside the high spiked fence. Frazer parked, grinning as the lorry hissed and the hydraulics calmed down before it shuddered to a stop. Luke gave me a nervous glance. Bobbie twitched the rug away from Frazer's lap, exposing our plaything.

His cock had gone soft, but it was still impressive. I like big cocks, and I don't care what anyone says. Big is nice, thick especially, to look at, to hold, to suck, and if it won't all go in, I just have to do my best. Frazer had it all, and I was wriggling forward immediately, my body half off the shelf of his sleeping compartment in my eagerness to get my fill. He sat back laughing as Bobbie took him in hand to feed him straight into my mouth.

My senses filled with the taste of cock and I was sucking him, mouthing on the fat, meaty head before trying to get as much in as I could, with Bobbie wanking him into my mouth. He was getting hard, swelling in my mouth, longer and fatter, enough to fill me right up. Bobbie's voice cut into my mounting bliss.

'Now who's a greedy pig?'

I was nearly off the shelf, and she smacked my bottom, but I ignored her, revelling in the in the big, hard thing in my mouth, now rock solid. Bobbie smacked me again, harder, and this time he took me by the hair, gently disengaging my mouth as he spoke, his voice now hoarse and low.

'Up in the back, yeah?'

I nodded and scrambled quickly back, rolling onto his bed as Bobbie climbed in after me. Frazer followed, Luke waiting, hesitant. I didn't have time to worry about him, as I was pulling my top off to let Frazer take my tits in hand; his big, rough thumbs were on my already stiff nipples. Bobbie had his cock, tossing him as he played with my tits, and guiding it between them for a tit-wank. I took hold, making a slide for him and kissing at his cock head as it bobbed up and down in my cleavage.

Bobbie had begun to strip as Frazer gave me my titty fucking. Her smart jacket shrugged off, her blouse tweaked open, and her bra lifted over small, firm breasts. Her skirt came up and I saw that she was in stay-ups with lacy tops, and tiny silk knickers with the wet crotch pulled tight over her pussy lips. Frazer had seen this too, and gave a pleased grunt as he pulled her close, still fucking my tits as he slid a hand around her bum. She gasped and her face went slack with pleasure as a finger found her pussy hole.

He moved back, sitting on his bed with his long, powerful legs splayed out and his cock rearing up from his open fly, beckoning to us. We came, crawling in, to lick and suck and kiss at his erection. Bobbie took his balls in her mouth, her jaw as wide as it would go, and I was on his cock alone, taking as much as I could fit in. He settled back, his hands folded behind his head, cool and easy as the two of us worked on his cock and balls. I heard Luke's voice from behind me, weak and pleading, an eager puppy.

'How about me?' he whined.

Bobbie's bum was right in his face, silky white knickers stretched taut over her neat cheeks. A man would have pulled them down and fucked her. I answered him, cool and mocking, as I pulled up from Frazer's cock.

'You get to watch, if you're a good boy, but you keep your hands to yourself.'

Frazer gave a chuckle and reached out to tweak Bobbie's knickers down at the back, leaving her bare to Luke's wide-eyed gaze. I could see the lust and jealousy in his eyes, so strong, and a truly gloriously wicked thought hit me.

'I'll make a deal,' I said. 'I'll suck you, all the way, but only if you suck Frazer.'

Bobbie had come off Frazer's balls, and burst into laughter. I took his cock, waggling it at Luke, who had gone bright pink and was stammering something about how he wasn't gay but would I suck him anyway. I wagged my finger.

'Uh, uh, no blow-job from Lucy, not until you've found out how it feels to have a great big cock stuck in your mouth!'

'Yeah, but you're a girl. You like it. Come on!'

'I love it, but it's hard work. Now come on, open wide, Lukey baby.'

I'll swear Luke was going to do it, but Frazer cut in.

'Choh! Will you two mad bitches just shut up and lick?' said Frazer. 'I ain't having no guy suck me.'

I went back down on him, feeling full of mischief as I began to suck again, wishing he'd let Luke suck him, no, made Luke suck him; maybe after he'd fucked us both, and come in his mouth. It was a great thought, and I held on to it as I sat up to undo my jeans, keen to get Frazer inside me. Bobbie stayed down, holding his erection and licking at the shaft and the bulging deep purple sac of his balls. I watched as I pushed my jeans down, taking my knickers with them, kicking it all off. Bare but for my lifted top I crawled close.

Frazer lifted Bobbie off his cock and I mounted up, his big hands on my waist as I felt the firm, round head beneath me, pushing between my cheeks, in the slippery groove of my pussy, and to my hole, third time lucky. I sighed as I felt myself fill, all the way up, as if he was in me right to the top of my head. He took my bum, pulling my cheeks wide as I began to bounce on his cock.

I showed behind, his thick brown cock straining out the mouth of my pussy and the little pink star of my bumhole between my spread cheeks. Luke was staring, I knew, and he could see just about everything too. I didn't care. I wanted him to. I wanted him to watch and wish it was him. I wanted to laugh at him while he sucked Frazer's cock, then deny him after all. I wanted to come, and I was going to.

My hands were around his neck, touching the thick,

heavy muscles of his back and shoulders. He held me like a doll, gripping my hips and bottom as he bounced me on his cock, in full control of my body. I put a hand to my pussy, spreading my lips to show him what I was doing, and Luke, rubbing myself to the ecstasy of being fucked. Bobbie gave a delighted gasp as she saw I was masturbating, and I was there, thinking of the two of them watching me as I was fucked.

It was so good, long and tight and lovely, after building it up nearly all day. I was so full of cock, moving in me to a steady rhythm as I rubbed at my bump, and so full of delicious, dirty thoughts. There I was, near nude, mounted up on a big, big man, his hands on my body, his erection inside me, my new friend watching, another man watching, and wishing he could have me too, both of them, in me together, pussy and mouth, but with Luke's own mouth still full of the taste of Frazer's cock.

Bobbie was pulling me off before I'd even really finished. I tried to protest, but I was dizzy with pleasure and drink, and off balance. I went over, legs wide on the floor of the compartment, and banged my head on the wall. By the time I managed to focus she was on his cock, just like I'd been, only the other way around, with her bum stuck out into his lap. He obviously didn't care who he was in, fucking away merrily with his huge hands covering her tits.

Luke was still staring, knelt up on the middle seat, only Bobbie had taken her knickers off at some point and he had them held up to his face, sniffing them as he wanked himself indulgently. A moment later I was laughing.

'Look at you, you little pervert! Get off on girls' knickers, do you?'

He looked at me, his face so full of hurt and pleading

that I immediately felt a real bitch. Then he was babbling.

'Please, Lucy ... Miss Doyle ... please, just in your hand. Anything, please!'

I opened my mouth to call him a wanker, but nothing came out. He just looked so sorry for himself. Telling myself I was just being kind, I scrambled down beside him. I didn't want to touch his cock, but I was going to do it, the way Father Slynn had made Siobhan, using a pair of knickers, not mine, Bobbie's.

She tried to say something as I took them and folded them around Luke's straining cock, but Frazer was jamming himself into her hard and fast, and all that came out was a grunt. I began to wank Luke, his cock pushing up and down in the silky knickers, hot and hard beneath. Frazer gave a deep, animal growl; Bobbie cried out in delight, and he'd come in her, finishing himself off with a series of furious thrusts that had her gasping and squealing in pleasure.

Her thighs went wide as she lay back on him, her pussy open, his cock dark and thick in her straining pink hole, his hands still kneading her breasts. She started to rub, squirming on him as she brought herself up towards orgasm, with Luke staring enraptured as I wanked him into her knickers. In just seconds she'd come, panting out her lust with her eyes shut tight and her bottom wriggling in Frazer's lap.

She wasn't the only one; my own excitement was rising too high to stop Luke as he began to paw my tits, and to groan, and thank me over and over in a voice thick with lust. One hand found my bum, but I didn't stop him, until his fingers had slipped down between my cheeks and he was tickling my bumhole.

'Get off me, you dirty pig!' I yelped.

Too late. He grunted, and his cock jerked in my hand.

The white silk stretched on his knob went suddenly dark and he'd come in Bobbie's knickers. He'd penetrated my bumhole too, and I squealed in shock and outrage as I felt his finger go in, right in, because I was wet with my own juice.

'You bastard!'

His answer was a long sigh, and broken words tumbling out, maybe an apology, as he pulled me close, too strong to resist, with his finger working deep up my bum. I let go of his cock and slapped him, hard, a lot harder than I would have done if the finger up my bottom hole hadn't felt quite so lovely.

2

21 July – Lucy Doyle persuades her uncle David to pretend to be a priest.

22 July – Lucy Doyle fails to persuade Niall Flynn to provide a reference.

23 July – Lucy Doyle persuades Niall Flynn to provide a reference.

What a bastard! What a conniving, evil gobshite! He's my brother Ryan's best mate. He's known me since I was like seven, six even. And what does he want? He wants his dirty cock sucked just to say I've done a bit of typing for him in his mouldy garage. Flynn's Executive Motors, my arse. More like Flynn's Con Artists and Rip-Off Merchants.

I should have kicked him in the balls. If he wasn't so horny I would have kicked him in the balls. If he wasn't such a blarney-mouthed son-of-a-bitch I would have kicked him in the balls. He is, and I didn't. I sucked them instead. It was what he wanted – him tossing off in my face. That was after I'd got him hard. He came in my eye too, which is always a shocker.

Not that it was exactly the first time, but still.

So I got my references, one from uncle David, who just thought it was funny, and one from gobshite bastard Niall Flynn. He thought it was funny too, but in a different way. Mrs Maryam Smith phoned me the following Monday and I was officially a Super Staff girl, highly recommended by my 'former employers'. I had an engagement, too, at twelve pounds. By lunchtime I'd have more money than Father Jessop would have paid me in a week, and it was just as well, what with Mum and Mary lecturing me on how I'd brought shame to the family and what an ungrateful cow I was.

I had to move myself, with the agency ringing at just after eight to tell me I was supposed to be in Docklands by ten. The only thing I had which was going to make me look even close to the way Bobbie had the week before – that is, the way she'd looked before she started getting her kit off for Frazer – was the black skirt and jacket set I'd bought for Great Uncle Stephen's funeral two years before. A white blouse pinched from Mary, a black velvet ribbon in my hair, dark tights and black court shoes, and I really did look as if I was going to work in an undertaker's. I put on some cherry-red lippy and nail polish on the way, adding a little more each time the train pulled into a station, and by the time I got there I looked at least vaguely businesslike . . .

. . . to find that everyone else was in casual clothes. Some of the girls were even in low-rise jeans with the tops of brightly coloured thongs showing at the back, making me feel seriously overdressed. Two other women were smartly dressed: my boss, a fire-breathing dragon of at least sixty, Mrs Tench; and Ms Roberta Davenport, which is what it said on her desk, anyway. She was acting as Mrs Tench's sidekick, and looked so prim and proper in her perfect grey suit you'd have thought butter wouldn't melt in her mouth. I knew better. I'd seen her rubbing her bump with her pussy full of big black cock. She seemed to be in charge of me.

'What are you doing?' I asked, secretly delighted that we were going to be working together.

'Being your boss, that's what, Miss Perks. Now get to work, before I take my whip to your arse!'

'Yes, but you're a temp!'

'A temp with experience. The company's on a major decruitment drive and we're here to rationalise their personnel overheads.'

'What?'

'They're trying to get rid of expensive full-time staff, so every time one leaves they get a temp. That's so when the whole thing gets cut they don't have to pay out any redundancy money.'

'Oh, right,' I answered. I was beginning to realise that the London employment scene was not exactly worker-friendly. The laws had been changed to favour the bosses all down the line. Gone were the days of the unions and 'out, brothers, out' that I'd read about in my sociology classes.

'What am I doing, anyway?' I ventured, in a half-assed way as I fiddled with one of the desk toys.

'What do you want to do? You can mash data into spreadsheets, file, mail, or go on reception. Smile.'

I smiled.

'You're on reception.'

'What do I do?'

'Look pretty, smile sweetly, say "Good morning, Sir" as if you're really impressed, and oh, don't hit anyone.'

'Hit anyone?'

'Like Luke.'

'Yes, but he –'

'I'm joking, Lucy. The only thing you really need to know is that nobody, but nobody, gets to see Mrs Tench without going through me first. The extension numbers are on the switchboard. You do know how to use a switchboard, don't you?'

'Er . . . no.'

She shook her head.

'You'll learn. Go on, get on with it, or I *will* take a whip to your arse, or at least a ruler. The whip requisitioning procedure around here is just too slow.'

I stuck out my tongue at her and disappeared from her sight, very, very glad it was her I'd had to deal with and not Mrs Tench, or the slight exaggerations on the Super Staff application form would have become evident in double-quick time. OK, not slight exaggerations, blatant lies, but in GCSE business studies they'd always been going on about how important initiative was.

As it went, reception was no big deal. Nearly everyone who came in had a little badge to show me, and I had visitors' passes for the ones who didn't. Not that there were many, in any case. By lunchtime I was bored stiff, and was just wondering if I was going to be allowed to eat anything when Bobbie appeared with another girl; dark and willowy with an olive complexion, maybe Italian or Greek. Bobbie pointed between us as she reached the desk.

'Lucy, Talia. Talia, Lucy. Lunch?'

'Sure. Hi, Talia. You're taking over, then?'

'Sure am.'

Her accent was American, New York maybe, and her manner seriously laid back as she took my place at the desk, as if she could just about be bothered. Bobbie gestured with her eyes as we made for the lift and spoke as the doors swished shut behind us.

'Mouse potato.'

'What?'

'Talia, she's a mouse potato, like a couch potato, only with a computer. She's great on computers, when she can be bothered, but hates anything physical or that means interacting with the general public.'

'Can't say I blame her. She looks fit, though.'

'I don't think she eats.'

'Is she with Super Staff?'

'Sure, nearly as long as me. Fun, but no taste in men.'

'No?'

'Older guys, rich and smooth like cream, she says. Smarmy old gits, I say.'

'I'm with you; young and strong ... and dirty.'

'And rough.'

'I think your rough is my ordinary.'

She didn't answer, as the doors had opened again. A trio of businessmen got in – suits, one white-haired and obviously senior, the others younger. The tallest of the three gave us an admiring glance but his colleagues ignored us completely, and we descended to the ground floor in silence, staring at our shoes and feeling awkward, unsure if we should be trying to strike up conversation. Bobbie only spoke again when we'd come out on the board plaza, with the buildings rising to either side, dizzyingly high.

'You obviously got your references sorted then?'

'Yes, and how!'

'What happened?'

'My Uncle David was OK, no problems, but my brother's mate, Niall, who runs a garage, was a complete bastard about it. He made me suck him off.'

'He didn't!'

'He did, and he was a real pig about it too.'

I broke off, laughing. She looked so eager, like a cat peering into a fish bowl. I'd been going to admit that Niall and I had had that sort of relationship since the day he'd taught me how to suck cock properly. That wasn't what she wanted to hear. What she wanted were rude details, which I was happy to supply, maybe even embellish a little.

'I wouldn't do it the first day, because I thought he'd

back down. After all, he is supposed to be a family friend. He didn't. The letter from Super Staff had arrived, and he had it on his desk in the little office at the back of his main workshop. He'd even done a reply, saying how good I was, punctual, efficient, quick on the uptake, good with computers and accounts – more than I really needed. All he had to do was sign it and send it off. I thought he'd relented, but oh no, not him. He sits down in his chair –'

'What's the place like?'

'A dirty little office, like a wooden shack built into the corner of the workshop.'

'Where there other men around?'

'Yes, six of them. All the guys who work for him.'

She made the same little purring noise in her throat I remembered from before. I decided to embellish a little more.

'Yeah, so six, and the office door doesn't even shut properly. I'm sure they knew. I think they might even have peeped in.'

She sighed.

'While you were doing it?'

'Yes! I think he wanted them to know, 'cause he didn't even bother to try and wedge the door shut, and wasn't exactly quiet about it. Like I said, he sat down in his chair, with his cock bulging up in his overalls, in his dirty, greasy overalls, and he says, "Now there's your letter, young Lucy, what you need and a little more, and cheap at the price too, but if you've a mind to get it sent off you'll pay your fee, and in advance".'

Bobbie made a little whimpering noise in her throat. I was trying not to giggle, and warmed to my task.

'I called him a bastard and told him to go fuck himself. He just smiled, and pulled down the long zip at the front of his overalls, all the way down. All he had underneath was a vest and pair of briefs, little ones which could barely hold in his cock and balls. He was getting hard too. I wasn't going to do it, I really wasn't. I said I'd tell my brothers, but he just laughed. I tried to make him feel ashamed of himself, reminding him how long he'd known me, but he just gives a yawn, like he's getting bored waiting. Then he flops it out over the edge of his briefs so it's all sticking up in the air. I could smell him, even through the oil and grease and exhaust fumes, and he says, "Shut up and get your mouth around me, you little bitch, or I'll have you do all seven of us.".'

'Oh my God!'

'He meant it, too, and so I did it, kneeling on the dirty concrete floor between his knees to take him in my mouth. I could hear the men in the workshop behind me, and I'm sure they knew. I'm sure they saw. Maybe he'd even told them, 'cause he pulled my top and bra up to get my tits out and he told me to stick out my bum. I felt so ashamed, but, I don't know, I just couldn't help myself, because it was really turning me on.'

Bobbie gave an understanding nod. Her lower lip was trembling and her neck had begun to flush. I wasn't exactly immune myself, remembering the taste and feel of Niall's cock in my mouth, as I went on.

'He took ages to get hard, and he made me do dirty things before.'

'What dirty things? Tell me!'

'Like ... like, he has this really thick, meaty foreskin, and he likes it rolled back with my lips so I can suck just the head of his cock, and ... and he made me lick under his balls –'

'His balls? He made you lick his balls?'

'No! Yes he did ... he told me to, and I wouldn't, so he took my hair and rubbed my face against them, until ... until I just had to, and when I did he laughed, and called me a bitch again, and told me my tongue belonged up his arsehole. I thought he was going to make me actually do that, the dirty bastard. Make me put my tongue in, right in, and . . .'

'One touch and I'll come, I mean it,' said Bobbie. 'Go on.'

'He made me take his balls in my mouth again, and suck them while he wanked off. He did it in my face, and in my hair, and he just left me like that, kneeling on the floor of his dirty office with his spunk all over my face and my tits bare. I'm sure the men were watching, I'm sure they were.'

Bobbie gave a single, muted sob. I really thought she had come, touch or no touch, but then she was laughing and smiling, shaking her head. Probably she realised I'd been exaggerating, but she didn't say anything and her eyes were full of happy mischief as we pushed into a sandwich bar.

I stayed at the same place for the rest of the week, on reception, then feeding in data on car and household accidents. We were collecting and processing it for our parent company, Emblem Insurance, but as Bobbie said, when you're a temp, it doesn't matter what the company does, who's who or what's what. All that matters is that you get to the end of the week, because the next week you're likely to be somewhere completely different and all the stuff that was so important just doesn't matter any more.

By Friday I'd got to know the rest of the Super Staff crew on the same job: four girls and one man, or rather, boy. Bobbie was senior, not just in that she'd been made assistant to Mrs Tench, but in experience. Even Talia deferred to her, despite having temped in New York and Boston before coming to England as a PA. I learned her story after work on the Wednesday, over a bottle of cold vino in the big wine bar, Lascar's, that served the cluster of office blocks we were in.

She'd caught the eye of a senior man in one of the big oil companies, and after a lot of spiel from him about how his thirty-year marriage was on the rocks, and a lot of expensive presents, she'd started an affair with him. He'd been very much to her taste; in his fifties, affluent and powerful, and she had seen herself getting well cosy with him, even married. Unfortunately his promises had not only been bullshit, but things had come to a head in London, with what sounded like a serious fight in one of the Park Lane hotels. She'd ended up out on the street, and had gone into an Edgware Road pub with the intention of getting blind drunk before trying to make her way back to the States the next day. She'd met Bobbie, and was still here over a year later.

Kanthi was Indian, shy, strikingly pretty, with lustrous black hair that went all the way down to her knees when she didn't have it piled on top of her head. She never said very much, but seemed to worship Bobbie, while she had a reputation for understanding everything and doing it twice as fast as anyone else. I'd quickly tagged onto her, because half the time I didn't have the foggiest idea what I was doing, and she could always be relied on to help without making an issue of it.

Her opposite was Sophie – petite, with blonde hair cut in a bob, she was full of life and full of mischief. She knew what she was doing, just about, and thought it hilarious that I didn't. Work was something she avoided as far as she possibly could, and she seemed incapable of taking anything seriously. She got away with it because there was something about her that left men with their tongues hanging out of their heads, although she'd fallen in with the wrong boss in Mrs Tench.

The boy was Keith, good-looking in a baby-faced way, with floppy blond hair and pleading eyes. What he was pleading for I could guess, because his eyes followed us about the office constantly, Sophie especially. He was in awe of Bobbie, blushing if she even spoke to him, and barely able to get his words out properly. That was just fine by me, because if Kanthi wasn't around to help me out, he was.

By the Friday I'd got it sorted, at least the basics. I could quantify an accident report and feed it into a spreadsheet so that what came out at the other end didn't cause Mrs Tench to have a hissy fit, and that was good enough for me. By five o'clock I knew I'd made it, a whole week without getting found out, thrown out or even bawled out. I had Bobbie to thank, mainly, but the others too. I also had the prospect of over three hundred pounds in my hand even after the taxman had taken his slice, which was more spending money than I'd had at any time in my entire life. We were aiming to go out for a drink anyway, but I was determined to say thank you, and at least get the first bottle in. Bobbie was last to leave, and I waited for her in the foyer, taking her arm as soon as Mrs Tench had gone on her way.

'How about a bottle of champagne? My treat.'

'You haven't been paid yet!'

'I've got a little, just enough. I insist.'

'You're on, then. Are the others in Lascar's?'

They were, including Keith, which was a pain as I'd been hoping it would be just the girls, and maybe we could meet some worthwhile guys later on. I didn't say anything, because he was one of the gang, sort of, and he had been a lot of help to me. Instead I ordered up six glasses and a bottle of the house champagne. It barely touched the sides as it went down, fresh and cool and enervating; instant resuscitation after a day of feeding endless strings of figures into a computer.

We were talking shop, inevitably; whether we were likely to be back next week, what a pain in the bum Mrs Tench was to work for, if any of the men who worked in the other offices were up to scratch. Talking about men made Keith blush, and it was impossible to resist teasing him – not to his face, but comparing notes with the others on the guys in the bar. I really thought he'd go, but he hung on, through a bottle of white wine bought by Bobbie and he took his share of another, champagne again, sent to us by a group of six suits in the far corner.

They wanted our attention, obviously, but they weren't going to get mine, being too old, too slick. The guy with the silver hair I'd seen around our building was with them. One had a bit of style, very dark with a strong face. The other four were right out of the question. I could see they had Talia's interest, and maybe Kanthi. Not me, and not Bobbie, though. Sophie wasn't bothered either; she was more interested in tormenting Keith.

'So which one do you fancy, Keith? How about the big fat guy with the bald spot?'

His mouth came open like a cod fish.

'Me? None of them! I'm not gay!'

'You accepted their wine.'

'Yeah, but it was sent to this table.'

'Yes, as a present, which is obviously a come on. If you're not interested, you shouldn't have accepted, should you?'

'No, but ... yeah, but ...'

'There are six of them, after all, and six of us, and statistically one of them must be gay, so you'll just have to do your best to accommodate him, won't you? It's only fair.'

'No way!' he spat, his youthful gaucheness obvious and really funny. He was so easily wound up.

'Don't be so ungrateful, Keith, he bought you a present, so put out.'

I couldn't help but join in.

'I bet he'd love it, right up the bum!'

Bobbie shook her head, smiling. Kanthi burst into embarrassed giggles. Talia had made eye contact with the silver-haired man and wasn't even listening. Sophie went on, her tone cool and confident, as if she was stating some well-known fact, and totally at odds with her words.

'It's well known. If you accept a drink from a guy you have to go to bed with him.'

'No way! I bet you don't!'

I decided to chip in.

'Of course she does. We all do, don't we girls?'

Bobbie answered me in her best cut-glass voice.

'It's only good manners.'

Keith glanced between us, surely aware we were teasing but looking in urgent need of reassurance. I shrugged.

'It's very simple. If you're not interested, you refuse the drink. If you are interested you accept, and once you've accepted, well, you have to go through with it, don't you?'

Sophie nodded earnestly.

'It's true. The only question now is, who goes with whom. I think Talia's clicked, and I'm having Mr Moody in the corner. You're little, Kanthi, you take Shortarse, and Bobbie can have Lanky.'

Bobbie laughed.

'That leaves Miss Perks with the guy with the gin blossom nose!'

She was joking, but I had to protest.

'No way! He can have Keith. I'll fight you for Mr Moody, Sophie!'

Both she and Keith were going to reply, but the guy with the silver hair had got up and was walking towards us, his expression affable yet thoroughly in control. I could see that Talia was transfixed, and both Sophie and Kanthi were posing on the instant, flicking their sleek hair about and throwing dazzling smiles. I filled my glass from the bottle he'd sent. I was amused, but no more. He'd figured out how things stood, because he came straight to Talia, addressing her and Bobbie too.

'Perhaps you ladies would care to join us at our table?' he asked, seeming not to care that our status as 'ladies' could be shot to pieces in moments if he plied us with more drink.

Bobbie answered him.

'We're with our friends.'

Talia nodded, just a little hesitant. He gave us a little smarmy smile.

'All five of you, naturally.'

It was obvious who wasn't included: Keith, cut out as if he didn't exist. He was a wimpy kind of bloke, but he was still with us. I felt my temper start to rise, and my mouth came open before I'd engaged my brain.

'There are six of us, now piss off, you old perve.'

He rounded on me, silent for an instant, as if he couldn't believe his ears, before speaking.

'I beg your pardon?'

'Are you deaf as well as blind? There are six of us at this table, not five, and anyway, aren't you getting on a bit to be perving over young girls?'

His mouth came open, then it shut again. Talia was staring daggers at me, and Kanthi too. Bobbie was trying to hide her giggles behind her glass. Sophie wasn't, she laughed so hard she spilt her wine, and could barely get her words out.

'You tell him, Lucy! Go girl!'

He turned away to walk rapidly back to his own table. Talia threw me a single dirty look and followed, tripping on her heels in her eagerness to catch up with him. Suddenly I felt deeply embarrassed, and wanted to be somewhere else, anywhere else. Me and my big mouth was about to make me enemies. Again. Would I never learn?

'Let's go,' I said, sheepishly.

Bobbie nodded and got up, the others following as we trooped out of the wine bar. It was still light, but cool, and as the air hit me I felt a little unsteady, both from the drink and the sudden burst of adrenaline. Kanthi came up beside me as we started across the plaza.

'Actually, you were right to tell him. What a rude man!'

I shrugged and smiled. I wasn't even sure why I'd done it, except maybe that the way he'd approached us had made me feel small. Certainly it wasn't for Keith's sake, because half-an-hour before I'd been thinking he was a dead weight to have around. It had looked that way, obviously, because he came hurrying up to my other side.

'Thank you, Lucy. That was ... that was really nice of you.'

He looked at if he was about to cry. I put my arm around his shoulders.

'Don't worry about it, man. The guy was an arsehole, that's all. Where are we going now?'

I gave him a squeeze and let go. He was embarrassing me, but I didn't want to be nasty. I didn't want him coming on to me either, because I knew I'd have to turn him down. To my relief Bobbie came and rescued me, slapping my bottom as she came up between us.

'Bad girl! You're going to get us in trouble, you are. How about a pub, or several?'

We went, along the shore and down under the river, laughing and joking and growing gradually more drunk and more relaxed. I'd soon forgotten all about the incident in Lascar's, teasing Keith and other men too. He made himself a target, and I couldn't help myself. Nor could Sophie, and we were encouraging each other, getting worse and worse, while he actually seemed to be enjoying it, or at least the female attention.

By the time it was dark I didn't even know where we were, except that it was somewhere along the river bank, near the Thames Barrier. We'd been drinking wine steadily, and I was starting to need to pee, only we seemed to have wandered into some sort of antiquated industrial zone, with tall warehouses of blackened brick rising high to either side of narrow alleys lit yellow by the infrequent streetlights. Trying to hold on until we found another pub was just too much of a pain, and I nipped into an even narrower alley, barely more than a crack between two buildings.

Skirt up, knickers down, and I just let go, with a glorious sense of relief. Only when I'd finished did I realise that Keith had positioned himself so that he could see into the mouth of my alley without it being too obvious. He couldn't have seen much, but he'd watched, and I wasn't going to let that pass.

'You weren't looking, were you, Keith?'

'No, I . . .'

'Oh yes you were, you dirty little boy! He was looking, wasn't he, girls?'

They'd carried on walking, and couldn't possibly know, but Sophie answered immediately.

'Yes you were, you dirty, dirty boy!'

He'd gone crimson, and was stammering desperately, but no words came out. Bobbie came close, her hands on her hips, her expression mock stern as she spoke.

'So, Keith, do you like to watch girls doing private things?' I asked.

All he could do was stand there, his jaw moving up and down mechanically, his face the colour of a beetroot, which was just asking for trouble. He got it, from all three of us, with even Kanthi managing a tut of disapproval.

'I bet he does. I bet he's a Peeping Tom.'

'He is a Peeping Tom! He just watched me pee, didn't he?'

'Dirty boy!'

'Dirty, filthy boy! Do you get off on watching girls go to the toilet then, do you?'

'Oh, he does, you can see it in his eyes!'

'Would you like to watch me too, Keith, would you?'

'Sophie!'

'Oh, but he would, I bet he would!'

I couldn't tell if she meant it or not, and nor could he. The sudden expression of hope in his eyes was a completely betrayal, and she just dissolved in laughter. So did I, and Bobbie, with Kanthi standing back looking shocked and excited. It was Bobbie who finally managed to find her voice.

'Don't tease the poor boy, Sophie, you'll make him cream his pants.'

Sophie turned to her, then to Keith.

'Who says I'm teasing? I'll pee for you, Keith, but only if ... if ... what can I make him do? Come on, girls, help me out!'

I was going to make him strip, but Bobbie answered first.

'Spank his arse for him! That's what dirty little boys deserve!'

Sophie was crowing with glee instantly, and he finally managed to find his voice.

'No, that's not fair.'

He didn't mean it. I could hear the pleasure in his voice, and from that moment he'd had it. He was still babbling denials as Sophie marched quickly into the mouth of the alleyway I'd used, speaking as she squatted down.

'What d'you like best, Keith, front or back view? Back, I bet you like back. Dirty little boys like you are into girls' bums.'

He didn't answer, gaping as she turned her back on us and tweaked up her skirt, showing off her bare pink bottom. She had a Celtic tattoo just above her crease, and a bright-green thong, which came straight down. Keith gave a weak gasp as her pussy came bare, and watched, staring open-mouthed as she let go, her pee splashing on the pavement to trickle down into the gutter.

I could never have been so rude, but she just didn't care, even wiggling her arse to shake off the last few drops. She stood up, bright-eyed and laughing as she adjusted herself, grinning as she came forward.

'And now payback!'

Keith hadn't moved a muscle since she'd asked if he wanted to see her bum. She stepped close, but he was still staring as she cocked her head to one side and spoke, her tone rich with mockery.

'Well? Was that nice? Have you got a hard on? I bet you have!'

She stepped forward and he stepped back, straight into Bobbie, who caught his arms. He gave a little squeak as Sophie squeezed his crotch. Immediately she danced back, giggling in delight.

'Oh, he has, a right stiffy! You dirty little boy! You're right. Bobbie, he deserves a good spanking, but first . . .'

He began to struggle as she stepped forward again. I took his other arm, holding him as she ducked low to unzip his fly and tweak down the front of his pants. A little pink cock sprang free, rock hard. Kanthi gave a little gasp of shock and the rest of us burst into giggles, Sophie crowing.

'Isn't he small!'

I couldn't help but feel sorry for him, but I couldn't help laughing either. It was just too much fun. He wasn't even struggling, much, but he'd given a wonderful groan of half despair and half lust as his cock was exposed. I held on, wondering who was going to do the business, and where. Bobbie gave the order.

'Over there, where we can see what we're doing.'

There was no resistance as she and I hauled Keith down the alley, to where a street lamp cast a yellow pool of light among the shadows. Sophie came scampering behind, Kanthi following further back. Only when we got to the lamppost did Keith start to protest.

'Hey, not here, people will see!'

'Tough. Tie his hands, Lucy.'

'What with?'

'I don't know. His belt, anything.'

'OK. You, stay where you are.'

He obeyed, to my delight, meekly standing against the post as I undid his belt and pulled it free. It was thin, easy to wrap around his wrists, securing them together on the far side of the lamppost to fix him in place. His cock was still rock hard, harder if anything, sticking up out of his pants at a jaunty angle. Sophie took it in her hand, giving a few quick tugs before skipping away laughing and slapping her thighs in glee. Keith had reacted with a low moan, and hung his head, plainly in ecstasy, until he saw what Bobbie had removed from a nearby skip – a three-foot length of bendy hardboard.

'Hey, no, not with that!'

She just laughed.

'Oh yes, Keith, with this. This is what little perverts get, isn't it, girls?'

Sophie gave a cry of encouragement, and in a moment had yanked Keith's trousers and pants down, baring a pair of skinny buttocks. He was looking at Bobbie, his face working between fear and desire, hers full of cruel joy. The board came down with a heavy smack, full across the meat of his cheeks. He gave a pig-like squeal, his cock jerked, and both Sophie and I were clapping and laughing fit to burst as Bobbie laid in, spanking him with the wood to make him jerk and jump and writhe against the lamppost.

His dick was still rock hard, waving wildly about as he was spanked. He began to babble, begging to be let go, his words breaking to the smack of the piece of wood on his bottom and his answering shrieks. She just kept right on spanking, and suddenly he'd stopped complaining, his words breaking to gasps. I saw the spunk erupt from his cock and Bobbie gave a wild and delighted shriek as he started to come. Spurt after spurt erupted as she beat him, laying in the piece of board for all she was worth, to his sobs and our hysterical laughter. Even Kanthi was giggling, with her hands to her mouth and her eyes wide with shock, but pleasure too. I caught the scent of spunk, which went straight to my pussy, but I was right up there with Sophie in taunting him for his behaviour.

'Naughty dirty Keith. Bad boy! Bad, bad boy!'

'Imagine, coming while his bottom's spanked, what a dirty little pig!'

'What a wimp!'

'What a little wanker!'

Bobbie had stopped, and dropped the board. Keith's knees went and he sank down, kneeling at the lamppost with his head hung. His whole body was shaking, and no surprise, because his bottom was a rich red. I thought he was going to cry, but when he finally looked around his expression was rapt adoration. Sophie gave a gleeful crow.

'Ooooh, he likes it. So now we know his dirty little secret, don't we, girls? Oh, boy, am I going to have fun with him.'

She stepped close, and I could stare in amazement as she casually hitched up her skirt, pulled the crotch of her knickers to one side and pulled his head into her crotch.

'Lick me, you little pervert!'

He did it, his eyes closed as he lapped at her pussy. I just watched, shutting my mouth when I realised my jaw was hanging open. I was really shocked, but so horny. She went all the way, holding him firmly in place until the muscles of her bottom and thighs had begun to contract, and she was coming with a long, happy sigh, right in his face. Bobbie began to clap the moment she'd finished, and I joined in. Sophie gave us each a playful curtsey before she even bothered to adjust her skirt, then turned to me.

'Have a go. I reckon he's anyone's.'

I shook my head, wanting it, but unable to make myself do it. She shrugged.

'Bobbie?'

She laughed.

'Not with him, no, but boy do I need a shag!'

So did I, but I needed a drink more. I felt weak at the knees, and dizzy with reaction for what we'd done to Keith, and the way he'd taken it. A dozen different emotions were crowding my head, so I barely knew what to do with myself. Other than get a stiff Powers down my neck. I went to undo Keith's belt. Sophie gave a cruel chuckle.

'Leave him, Lucy. Maybe some big, bad bear will come by and fuck his arse for him. I bet you'd love that, wouldn't you, Keith?'

'No! Please untie me, you lot, please!'

Bobbie gave him an arch look and began to walk away. Sophie made a ring of her fingers and slid another suggestively through it. Keith began to panic, pleading to be released and struggling to get his fingers to where the buckle held his wrists strap tight together. I had to laugh.

'Relax, will you? Nobody's going to bugger you, not really. The worst they'd do is have a good laugh before they let you go.'

'Please just undo me, Lucy, please?'

'All right, you big baby.'

I'd been going to do it anyway, because it really wasn't fair to leave him. The gratitude in his eyes as I worked on the buckle was truly pathetic, and the moment he was loose I went to Bobbie, leaving him to cover himself up. She put her arm around my waist, and Kanthi's, Sophie joining the end of the chain and we set off along the alley once more, kicking in step and for some reason singing 'Summer Holiday'. Keith followed behind.

There was a pub almost immediately around the corner – an odd place, with hardly anyone in it, and a single, grumpy-looking barman staring at a small TV screen while holding a remote control. Bobbie made

Keith get the drinks in, much to the annoyance of the barman, and I downed my whiskey in one as Keith sat down, smiling and blushing. Sophie spoke to him.

'I suppose you expect us to keep your dirty little secret?'

He nodded nervously.

'We will, but only if you do just as you're told. Now go and get Lucy another drink, come on, quick sharp!'

For just a moment he'd hesitated, but he went. Sophie was grinning, enjoying herself hugely. Bobbie was much the same, only cooler. Kanthi seemed rather nervous, and spoke as soon as she'd finished her glass of wine.

'I'd better get back.'

She rummaged in her bag, pulling out first a mobile phone, and then a packet of strong mints, one of which she popped in her mouth, sucking as she retrieved a number from her memory. The moment she'd made the call Keith gave Sophie a single, worried glance, then spoke.

'Could we share, Kanthi? I ought to get back.'

Sophie protested immediately.

'Hey, you're not allowed to go! You're supposed to be paying for us.'

He'd begun to look seriously flustered, but Bobbie spoke up.

'Give him a break, Sophie.'

Sophie grimaced.

'Whatever. This place is dead, let's go back west. Call us one up, Kanthi.'

Kanthi made the call, but I could feel the evening slipping away, my excitement coming to nothing, or a hasty knee-trembler in some West End doorway. I wanted more. Something naughty, something rude.

I'd finished my second drink, and a third, before the first cab came, to take Kanthi and Keith off towards

West London. Sophie spoke the moment the door was closed.

'Men! The moment they're despunked they lose it!'

Bobbie gave a sour nod, but I thought she was being unfair.

'We were pretty hard on him.'

'Nah, he loved it.'

He had come, so I didn't press the point. I'd never even realised it was possible to actually smack the spunk out of a man, but now I'd seen it. However painful it looked it was certainly effective. I thought of Niall Flynn, and how he'd look with his arse bright red and spunk pumping out of his erect cock as I whacked him with a plank, preferably with his lads looking on and laughing. Bobbie caught my expression.

'What's the joke, Miss Perks?'

'I was thinking of Niall Flynn, who I told you about, only like we did Keith.'

'Oh no, not to a guy like that, never!'

'Why not?'

Sophie's ears pricked up, and she got in before I could discover why Bobbie thought Niall should be immune from what she'd just dished out to Keith with such glee. In my view he was a far more deserving case.

'What's this? Who's Niall Flynn?'

I felt a blush start to rise as I struggled to find a good answer, but Bobbie was already talking.

'This guy Lucy knows, a real bastard. He made her suck him off in return for a good reference for the SS, and ... wait for it ... lick his balls and arse!'

Her voice was full of relish, and I found myself blushing hot as Sophie burst into giggles. I was going to admit I'd exaggerated, but Bobbie was obviously envious of me, maybe Sophie too, for all her arch response.

'What a disgrace, Miss Perks. Bribery and corruption, cock-sucking, rimming . . .'

'But he made me, like Bobbie said.'

The expression on her face showed just how much she believed me. I stuck my tongue out at her, just as a squat, balding man appeared in the doorway, glancing around the pub.

'Cab for Chakravathi?'

Sophie answered him.

'That's us.'

He gave her an odd look as we quickly swallowed our drinks. Bobbie spoke to me as we reached the door.

'Where does he go? Niall Flynn, I mean.'

'There's this drinking club above a kebab shop . . . no, Bobbie, we are not going there!'

'Why not?'

'My brother will be there for a start.'

'So?'

'So everything. Ryan doesn't know, and he'd kill Niall.'

'We're not going to tell her brother, are we, Sophie? Call Niall up, tell him to meet us.'

'No! Anyway, why?'

'I want to meet him.'

'I want to watch you go down on him.'

'Sophie!'

The cabby had heard every word we'd said, and turned us a dirty leer as he climbed in. We squeezed into the back, with Bobbie in the middle, and before I'd realised what was happening Sophie had snatched my bag and was rummaging in it.

'What are you doing?'

It was a silly question. I knew. She was going to phone Niall. Whatever happened, it could only mean trouble, and I grabbed out as she pulled my mobile from the bag. Sophie was laughing and talking to herself as I grappled for the phone.

'Niall Flynn ... Niall Flynn ... got him! Hold her down, Bobbie!'

Bobbie grabbed me, trying to pull my arms away as I fought to get at the phone. Sophie was holding it right up against the window, and I couldn't reach. I got her wrist, though, tugging hard even as she pressed the call button. The phone went on the floor, Bobbie let go and I sprawled across her lap as the cab started to move. The next instant I'd been grabbed around the waist and Bobbie was laughing and smacking my bottom. I didn't care, scrabbling for the phone under Sophie's feet. She kicked it away, but I snatched it up from under the chair, pressing the button to cancel the call just as the cabby finally lost patience.

'Leave it out, or you can fucking walk!'

Sophie answered him, telling him to shut up and drive, but she stopped, and Bobbie let me up. I was laughing as I sat back, and flourished the phone at Sophie, only to have to grab at the seat in front to stop myself being thrown back across Bobbie's lap as the cabby took a violent corner.

'Hey, this isn't a fucking speedway!' I shouted.

He ignored us, joining the flow of cars on some highroad or other, just as my phone went. Sensible Lucy would have realised who it was going to be and ignored it, or at least checked the incoming number. Drunken, flustered Lucy answered it – to Niall Flynn, inevitably.

'Hi Niall ... yes, it's me ... no, I'm fine ...'

'No she's not. She wants your cock.'

'Shut up, Sophie. No, nothing Niall, just my drunk friend ... never mind her tits.'

'Big and round and bouncy, Niall! Fancy a grope?'

'Sophie! Sorry, Niall, I ... no she did not say that. OK, she did, but she's pissed.'

'Where are you, Niall? We'll come round.'

'Bobbie!'

She'd said it right into the receiver. I hastened to correct her.

'No, she's just mucking about. Anyway, we're miles away, somewhere in Greenwich, I think. No they are not! They're just pissed, that's all. No, you pervert, I don't care if you've never had a threesome.'

'Ooh, yes please! I'm up for it, Niall, I want to watch her suck on your balls and lick your arsehole.'

'Sophie!'

I tried to hit her, pressing disconnect at the same instant, and we were slapping at each other, both laughing. So was Bobbie, but suddenly she'd stopped, grabbed me around my waist and pulled me down over her lap. Sophie grabbed my hair, and before I could protest my skirt had been yanked up, my knickers had been hauled up my crease and my bare bottom was being spanked. Both of them were laughing uproariously, and louder still as I began to struggle and squeak, because it stung like anything. She wasn't going to stop anytime soon either, and the next thing I knew was that the cab had come to a screeching halt.

'Out!' Bellowed the cab driver.

'Hey, but ...'

'I said out, you mad bitches! Go on with you!'

'Yes, but ...'

'Out!'

'OK, OK, keep your hair on.'

It was not a good thing to say, not when he had quite so much missing on top. Seconds later we were stranded on the pavement, Sophie giggling, Bobbie looking pissed off, me with my knickers still pulled up my bum.

'What a wanker!'

'Yes, you'd think he'd have enjoyed the view. Nice bum, Miss Perks.'

'Yeah, right, but it doesn't half sting. Let's get another cab.'

It was easier said than done. The pubs had started to empty out, and we had to join a queue outside a cab office. It was half-an-hour before we were headed west, now a lot more subdued. As we came into the Blackwall Tunnel I realised Sophie was asleep, or she'd passed out. Bobbie didn't look much better.

'Shall we just get dropped off home?'

'Best get Sophie back. Cabby, forget the West End, go for Archway.'

'You got it.'

We went, first to Archway, where Bobbie helped Sophie from the cab and into a block of red brick flats. She was going to stay, but I had to get back, and got dropped off at the end of my street a few minutes after midnight. It was quiet, as always, and a little scary, the shadows of the terrace and the privet hedges seeming to hold a thousand menaces. When a tall figure stepped out I nearly jumped out of my skin, only to realise who it was, his rich accent and strong voice infinitely soothing.

'Back already then, Lucy?'

'You scared me, Niall!'

I was shaking slightly, and I clung to him by instinct. His hand immediately slipped down to my bottom, squeezing a cheek through my skirt as he went on.

'I thought you'd be around, and I knew you'd not get dropped at the door.'

'Thanks.'

He was pawing my bottom, obviously turned on. I was thinking of what he'd overheard on the phone. So was he.

'What was it your friends were saying back there a while?'

'You know.'

'I do, and it just happens that Ryan and your Ma think I've gone to collect you from Greenwich.'

'They do?'

'They do that, so how about you and I take a little detour, by my place? Then you can show me just what they meant.'

Oh God. I couldn't stop myself. I was too drunk, too horny, too vulnerable to his masculine charm and the way he just knew he was going to get what he wanted. He steered me toward his house, just a few doors from my own, his hand never leaving my bottom, his long, strong fingers stroking and kneading my cheeks. In the doorway he kissed me, lifting me up on tiptoe to meet his mouth, and still fondling. He'd pulled up my skirt, and went on to pat my bare bottom. I was praying none of the neighbours were watching.

We went straight upstairs, without preamble. My knickers came down, then off. A finger was eased up my pussy as I pulled down his zip, and his cock came out. I went down as before, on my knees in front of him, to suck and lick his cock and his balls and, when I was quite ready, to put my tongue to his arsehole.

3

31 July, 11.45 a.m. – Lucy Doyle wakes up next to Niall Flynn.

1 August, all day – Lucy Doyle is lectured by her mother, two sisters and one brother, until she finally admits where she spent the night. Family reaction – delight. Oh shit!

2 August, 7.45 a.m. – Lucy Doyle discovers she is no longer working for Emblem Insurance. Instead she is attaching stickers to crates, in Tilbury.

Not good. Not good at all. OK, so the sex was good, but everything else was crap. Niall was great in bed, no question. The tension inside me had been building up all evening, and I just took it out on him. Let's face it, he didn't make me lick every intimate part of him, he let me, because what with Sophie and Bobbie and what we'd done to Keith, I'd never felt so horny in my life. I'd made him come in my face too, deliberately this time, tossing him off as I sucked his balls with my other hand working hard on my clit.

Most men would have crawled into bed and gone to sleep. Not Niall. He asked for a striptease, and he got one. By the time I was nude he was ready again, and I mounted his cock for a long, leisurely shag session. He made me come, again, and that wasn't the end. Even when I went to wash he came up behind me, held me down over the sink and rubbed himself hard between my cheeks, before giving me another fucking. The last was some time in the dead of night, cuddled together in bed with him on top of me and my thighs spread wide to receive him.

It was good. It was great. I wanted more. I did not want a brief engagement, marriage, and twenty kids, which was what Mum expected of me. So did Mary. Both of them just assumed Niall and I were now an item and would therefore marry. They also assumed I'd drop my place at uni. I didn't even argue, pretending I was tired on the Sunday night and making for bed early.

The discovery that I was on a new assignment, and in Tilbury, really did not help. We'd all assumed we'd have at least another week at Emblem, because there had been loads to do. There still was, as I discovered by ringing Bobbie on the way to Tilbury. She, Sophie, Kanthi and Keith were still there, along with two other temps I didn't know. I'd been moved on, and it was nothing to do with my work. The silver-haired guy I'd called a pervert and told to fuck off was Lucas Sherringham, the Managing Director of Emblem Insurance.

The other person who wasn't there was Talia, and not because she'd been given the boot. She was now shacked up with Lucas Sherringham, apparently in a penthouse flat somewhere in Docklands, with nothing to do but sip champagne and nibble chocolates. Apparently she'd been there all weekend, and he, in her words, was a 'wonderfully sensitive and mature lover'.

I was brooding over it all the way to Tilbury. It's so easy; flirt and flatter and fuck and in no time you've netted yourself a rich man and you no longer have to worry. Lots of girls did it, and more tried. It made sense too, logically, but I knew I could never do it, not me, not Lucy Doyle. I need to want a man, and I'd rather have had Keith than Lucas Sherringham, with all his pent-houses and champagne and cars, but I knew I wouldn't do it. I was too proud, or too stubborn, or too stupid.

The Tilbury job had to be the dullest ever invented. I was in a huge warehouse, and when I say huge, I mean huge. From the outside it looked like an aircraft hanger. Inside it was almost completely occupied by row upon row of gigantic metal shelves, and every one of them stacked with crates, cases, boxes and packages. Lucy's job? Label the fuckers.

With every lorry that came in, and there were plenty, I had to check exactly what was in each case, feed the information into a program, print out the labels and stick them on the correct boxes. It wasn't difficult, but it was endless. To make it worse, my manageress, Mrs Henshaw, could have given Mrs Tench lessons. She never gave me a moment's peace, and even bawled me out for spending a few minutes chatting to one of the forklift operators.

It was the same all week – up at seven, over an hour to get to work, running around like a blue-arsed fly all day, an hour to get back home, and sinking exhausted into bed. It wasn't even well paid, at eight pounds an hour. Other than swapping endless texts and calls with Bobbie and Sophie, only three things came up to break the monotony: Niall, Todd and Keith.

Niall I expected. After all, my mum now seemed to think he was my fiancé, and even Ryan was all right with it. He came round on the Tuesday, by which time I was more than glad of his company. I liked the comfort of being held in his arms and slowly fucked in the back of his car after being filled up with Powers and Beamish. It left me wrecked the next day, but it was worth it.

Todd was far more of a surprise. I'd had no idea what had happened to him after I'd been booted out of the

Parochial House, and was even wondering if he'd been sacked. He hadn't, because Father Jessop was a hypocritical old bastard, but he had enjoyed his blow-job, and he wanted more. I gave in, after just a little hesitation, taking him into Willesden Lane cemetery to have his cock sucked and let him finger me.

Keith I sort of expected, but had hoped he would have the common sense to realise that while I hadn't been as big a bitch to him as Bobbie or Sophie, that didn't mean I was interested in him. Unfortunately, he didn't seem to have any common sense at all, and was bombarding me with texts – first to thank me, presumably because I hadn't left him to be buggered by bears. Then came the request for a date, which arrived as I was kneeling in the shade of a big yew tree, about to unzip Todd Byrne's trousers. I declined as soon as I'd done my business.

Todd was on Thursday. Friday night I was meeting the girls after work, Tina and Leanne, at Charlie's in the West End. It was a riot, getting completely pissed and staggering drunkenly along the embankment in a line, Bobbie, Sophie and I, with the two new girls who were at Emblem with them. A group of lads tagged onto us outside Temple station, passing rude compliments and offering us swigs from their cans of lager. I took one, and drained what was left in it, causing complaints as I handed the empty can back.

'Hey, you greedy cow,' one complained. 'She's only gone and drunk the whole fucking can!'

His mates just laughed at him and, as he opened another one, I made to grab it. He pulled quickly back.

'No way,' he whined.

'Go on, don't be a git,' I said.

He moved back, walking backwards down the pavement.

'You want a drink, love, you can get your tits out for it first!'

'No way!'

Sophie and Bobbie backed me up, calling him a bastard, their voices quickly drowned by the lads' shouting, then as they began to chant.

'Yeah, go for it. Get yer tits, out, carrot top! Get yer tits out! Get yer tits out for the lads!'

They were singing it, really loud, and dozens of passers-by were staring. I'd have done it too, only Bobbie got in first.

'Only if you show us yours.'

'We ain't got none, love!'

'Posh, ain't she?'

'Here, look!'

One of them, the bulkiest, jerked his football top up, spilling out his huge, pasty beer gut. Two others followed suit. Bobbie just laughed.

'I meant your cocks, stupid!'

'No way!'

Sophie chipped in, and so did I.

'You're not seeing our tits, then, you cheeky bastard!'

'Dead right. Get 'em down and I'll get mine up, or no show!'

'You serious?'

It was a tall lanky guy, who'd been the quietest so far. I nodded, suddenly tense, because his hands had gone to his fly. We were in the middle of the street, with people everywhere, and only a big plane tree to provide any cover. He didn't care. Out it came, a fat white cock with a meaty foreskin half rolled back over a bulbous head. We dissolved in laughter. I was about to pull up my top to show him I could give as good as I got, only for Leanne to pull on my arm.

I was running immediately, not knowing why, or

where, but in stitches as the lads followed with angry shouts. We didn't have a hope, in heels and skirts, but it didn't matter. I got caught by the lanky guy, and pulled down onto one of the piers. It was deserted and, before I really knew it, my top was up, and my bra. He was groping my tits as I struggled to get his trousers open, and kissing and licking at them as he yanked my skirt high.

My knickers came down and he'd buried his face in my fur, licking avidly as he wanked himself. I melted at this, clinging on eagerly as he pushed me up against the cold stone blocks of the Embankment wall. His hands went under my bum, pulling my knickers aside. I felt his cock touch my pussy and he was in, deep in, filling me. We were snogging as he began to pump into me, fast and furious, tangled together in a mess of disarranged clothing. He went harder and faster as he let loose a stream of dirty talk in me ear.

'I'm going to give it to you hard, you little slut,' he said. 'And don't think you can get away from me – not until I've shot my load in your tight little cunt.' That seemed to do the trick for him. He finished with a grunt, jamming me against the cold stone. I wondered if he'd spoken quite so roughly to previous conquests, or if it was something about me that brought out the beast in the man.

He gave a long, ecstatic sigh as he came down, lowering me to the wooden deck of the pier. My legs were shaking, my breath was coming hard and fast, and I wanted to come. He stood back, grinning as I began to masturbate, my hips thrust forwards at him.

'Your tits don't half jiggle, love,' was the best he could do by way of an observation. I asked him to repeat his dirty talk to me – to say what he had said to make himself come a few moments earlier.

The filthy sod wasted no time in seizing the opportunity to be as foul-mouthed as possible. I came, as hard
as I'd ever come, thinking how good it felt to be caught
and stripped and fucked, so sudden and so hard. He
watched goggle-eyed, well pleased with himself, his cock
still hanging out of his trousers. I'd closed my eyes, my
ecstasy and the drink singing in my head, in bliss, until
a sudden change of light made me realise something
was wrong. As my eyes jerked open I realised what. A
riverboat was starting in towards the next pier along,
the bright lights from the saloon windows illuminating
me, tits out, one hand down my knickers, and maybe a
hundred thoroughly respectable-looking types in dinner
suits and fancy gowns staring right at me. He was long
gone.

It was funny, especially because I'd got away with it,
and been given a good, rough fucking while the others
had got nothing. Not that I discovered until I called
Bobbie the next day, because I'd managed to lose them,
and ended up going home on my own. I didn't even
know the name of the guy I'd shagged, any more than
he knew mine.

They'd only been another few yards down the
Embankment when a police cruiser had pulled up and
told them to behave, probably more or less at the same
instant I was being filled with cock. It had broken the
moment, and they'd had no idea what had become of
me, so they'd gone on to another bar with the lads.
Nothing had come of it, so Bobbie was well jealous of
me when I told her what I'd been up to.

She was more jealous still when I told her I couldn't
come out with them the next night because I would be
with Niall. They were going to Phatz in Camden Town,
which was having a ladies' night, with free entry and

drinks half-price for girls. I was sorry to miss it, and just a little resentful that I seemed to be getting drawn into a full-on relationship with Niall whether I liked it or not.

I wasn't going to let it happen, but I wanted him; for his easy humour, his stamina and, best of all, the way he made me want to be dirty. Mum seemed to think it was some big first date and, although she knew I was no virgin, she actually cautioned me to play hard to get while I was making up on the Saturday evening. I didn't answer, pretending to concentrate on my eyelashes.

Bobbie had given me the address of the shop where she bought her heels, and I'd treated myself to a pair from my first paycheque. They were shiny black, with the logo in scarlet and also the actual heels, which were four inches high. My shortest black dress, stay-ups and black ribbon to tie back my hair completed the look, unusual and I hoped a little exotic. Siobhan said I looked like a hooker.

Mr Phibbs two doors up had some gorgeous scarlet roses growing in his front garden, and when Niall came to collect me I pinched one for my hair. It had him drooling, Niall, not Mr Phibbs, and pawing my bottom as he hurried me into the car. I felt good, sexy, a little naughty, ready for both mischief and sex, once I'd been suitably wined and dined. Niall looked well pleased with himself, and I wondered if he had a nice surprise for me, perhaps dinner at some posh restaurant.

'Where are you taking me, then?' I asked, fluttering my eyelashes.

'Gogarty's.'

'You're joking.'

'No.'

It was certainly a surprise, but not the sort I'd bargain for. Gogarty's had to be the most Irish of Irish bars east of Dublin. Half the people there would have been to school with me, and nine out of ten would know me or my brothers and sisters. It would be like being paraded, and I wasn't at all sure I liked the idea. In fact, I definitely didn't.

'Why Gogarty's?'

'What's wrong with Gogarty's?'

'Nothing, but it's ... well, it's hardly a romantic night out, is it? I'm not dressed for Gogarty's either.'

He gave me an incurious glance, as if unsure what I was talking about.

'What's this, "romantic night out"? A few pints and we're back to my place, where I aim to fuck the living daylights out of your little arse. How's that for an evening?'

'Charmed, I'm sure.'

He just laughed, knowing full well that when the time came I'd be as keen as he was. We drove in silence for a while before he spoke again.

'So, what's with your friends, then?'

'How d'you mean?'

'The ones you were with in the cab. Said I could grope her tits, she did. I heard. Do you think she'd be up for it?'

I just laughed, hearing the eager lust in his voice.

'Come on, Lucy, I'm serious.'

'I'll bet you are, you dirty bastard!'

'Look who's talking!'

'What are you after, Niall?' I asked.

'What am I after? You have to ask? I'm after the two of you in bed. Three of you, maybe. There was your other mate there too, wasn't there? Bobbie. Three girls in my bed, now that would be something!'

'What makes you think I'd be up for that, Niall Flynn?'

'Wouldn't you? You're a dirty bitch, Lucy Doyle. I thought you'd be up for anything.'

I hit him, but only playfully. We reached Gogarty's,

the front a blaze of green lighting, with the doors thrown open to the warm night air and music blasting out. Inevitably we couldn't park anywhere near it, and ended up well down a side street before we'd found a space. As he parked I was thinking of what he'd said, how it would be to share him, as Bobbie and I had shared Frazer. It turned me on, but it just couldn't be done. He'd be sure to tell somebody, and once a rumour like that got going, my name would be all round town as a Grade A whore.

Ryan would find out first, probably, and he could be pretty protective. Siobhan was sure to, and so Mary, and so my Mum, and then there'd be hell to pay. As we started back towards Gogarty's I was hoping he'd drop the subject. Not Niall Flynn.

'So, with the girls, then. Fix a date with the one with the big tits first, why not, and . . .'

'It won't wash, Niall.'

'Why's that? Don't tell me you've gone jealous on me?'

'I'm not jealous, Niall. I won't do it because you'd be bragging.'

'I would not!'

'Sure, I believe you.'

'Ah, come on with you, how can you say a thing like that? Did I ever tell when you wanted to know the feel of a man's cock in your gob, and to know how it's done, did I now?'

'Well, no, but . . .'

'But nothing! Now come on, say you'll fix a date. We can meet at least.'

'No!'

'Come on, or do I have to make you?'

'Like how?'

'Like I make you ring them.'

'And how do you propose to make me ring them, Niall Flynn?'

'Perhaps by showing your bare arse to the street if you don't.'

I stuck out my tongue, turned round, stuck my bum out and flipped up my dress, showing just about everything, as all I had on was a black thong. It made his eyes pop, and I was laughing as I danced away from his clutching fingers. So was he.

'Your sister's right, you're a slut and more, Lucy Doyle. Now get out that phone.'

'Make me.'

'I will. I'm thinking, perhaps you'll not be so cheeky in the club with no knickers under that pretty dress?'

'You think so, do you?'

'I do. Now out with the phone.'

'In your dreams, Niall Flynn.'

'Come on with you, Lucy, or I'll have those knickers here and now.'

'You haven't the guts!'

'Oh, haven't I just?'

'No, you haven't. You're nothing but a great gobshite, Niall Flynn, all mouth and no action.'

'Am I, by Jesus!'

He dashed forward. I screamed and ran, tripped over my heels and had to clutch onto a lamppost to stop myself landing smack on the pavement. The next instant his hands were on me, my dress had been yanked high and he was groping for my knickers.

'Not here, Niall, no! I was joking, that's all!'

I tried to push him off, but I was laughing far too hard to fight back as his thumbs were stuck in my waistband. My knickers were levered down, our of my crack and down to my knees. I caught hold of them, kicking and cursing him and trying desperately not to laugh, but failing. My dress had stayed up, rucked high around my waist, bum and pussy bare to the street. I covered myself by instinct and he'd immediately jerked my knickers right down to my ankles, and off, one foot at a time, with me thumping at his head and calling him every bastard under the sun.

'You great gobshite pervert,' I howled. 'Now you'll give those back this instant!'

He didn't answer me, but was laughing as he danced back, waving my knickers above his head in triumph before putting them to his face and drawing deep on my scent.

'Now that's grand, as any man'll tell you – the smell of cunt in the evening air.'

'Give them back, or you're a dead man, Niall Flynn!'

'I'll give them back just as soon as you've made that call.'

'No!'

I tried to snatch for them, but he jumped backed, holding them as high as he could, well beyond my reach. An elderly couple had emerged from one of the doorways in the terrace by our sides, and gave first me, then Niall a set of dirty looks as if we'd been fucking in the road. Niall took no notice at all, his face full of impish joy as he held out my knickers at arm's length, dangled between forefinger and thumb, beckoning.

'Come on with you now, Lucy Doyle, make that call.'

I started for him, determined, but he leapt, agile, to the side. Even without my heels I didn't have a hope in hell of outrunning him, and he knew it, wagging his finger disapprovingly.

'None of that now,' he teased. 'And you should mind your tongue. No way for a young lady to talk, that isn't. Now best to make that call, 'cause with that little dress you'll be showing your bare arse to half of Gogarty's every time you bend, you will, and you'll need to keep your knees close. You're a bad girl, but you wouldn't want to go flashing your cunt to your old schoolmates now, would you?'

'You fucking bastard!'

'Make that call, Lucy Doyle.'

I dug into my bag, glaring at him as I rummaged for my phone. He just laughed, perhaps knowing as well as I did what he was doing to me, because deep down what I wanted was to be bent over the bonnet of the nearest car and fucked till I screamed. Not even Niall Flynn had the balls for that, not sober anyway, but he continued to hold out my knickers so that anyone who passed by could see, and would know I was bare under my dress. I kept my eyes firmly on his, trying to look accusing as I called up Bobbie's number. She answered almost immediately, with a blare of noise in the background.

'Bobbie?' I started. 'It's Lucy. I can't hear you very well but I'm in Kilburn, with Niall Flynn. He's been molesting me again. He's taken my knickers off and he won't give them back unless I make a date with the two of us and you and Sophie. He wants a threesome. I'm serious. I said you wouldn't, you would? Ha, ha, great, I'll tell him! Have a good time, and don't do anything I wouldn't do.'

Niall was all ears.

'What'd she say? She up for it?'

'She says that you'll have to try a lot harder than that if you want to get three girls in sack with you all at the same time.'

It was a great answer, the perfect answer, winding him up to think he might just get it, but with nothing promised and no idea of how. She'd turned it around on him completely, leaving him with his tongue hanging out as he quickly gave me my knickers back. I pulled them on, back in control and full of mischief as we started up the street once more.

He was well steamed up, and when I gave his crotch

a friendly squeeze in the shadow of a big van he turned out to be half stiff. I gave him another flash of my bum, quickly, because we were almost at the corner of the High Road. His response was to smack me, leaving my cheeks tingling as we walked into Gogarty's to find it packed, with the press two and three deep at bar and every table taken. Some of my old friends were at one of the big round tables by the open doors, and they waved as they saw me. I made to join them, only to be hustled on by Niall, with my arm firmly gripped in one big hand.

'Hey, Niall!'

Whatever his answer, it was lost under the music, and an instant later I realised where he was steering me, and why. Burning embarrassment rose up, but it was nothing to the thrill of being frog-marched into the loos, with Niall completely unable to contain his lust for me. He chose the gents. Three men looked around as he kicked the door wide, their faces showing surprise, amusement, envy, as Niall pushed me into a cubicle and slammed the door.

'Down you go, and get this in your gob, you little tease.'

He'd sat down, his long, lean thighs spread wide as he pushed his trousers and briefs to his ankles. I caught the scent of his cock, mixed with the male tang of the cubicle, at once sickening and compelling. His cock and balls were on display, pale and fat and turgid, ready for my mouth, and soon to be ready for my pussy. I got down on my knees in my pretty dress to suck, eager and dirty, thinking not just of the man I was with, but of the three others who knew what I was doing. I didn't know any of them, but he did, and they seemed to know who I was.

'That's little Lucy Doyle he's got in there, it is.'
'It's never!'

'It is.'

'Fuck me! Hey, Niall, pass her on when you've finished, would you?'

'Fuck off!'

The door was jammed shut against my bum, and not coming open in a hurry, but it was impossible not to feel vulnerable as Niall began to stiffen in my mouth. All anyone had to do was cram themselves in behind me. My dress would come up, my knickers would come down and they'd do me while I tongued Niall's big, beautiful erection. It was such a dirty thought, so good to get off on. My hands went down into my panties, stroking and rubbing at my clit as the big cock in my mouth came to full erection.

He was already groaning, and he caught hold of his shaft, tossing himself into my mouth as I sucked on his helmet. I was going to come, maybe before he did, my body urgent and tight, thoughts of being gang-banged racing through my head. They'd just take me, four at once, unable to hold down their lust, sticking their cocks in wherever they'd go, in my mouth and my pussy, maybe even up my bum, all in a welter of uncontrollable male lust.

'Fuck me,' someone said.

'Get a load of that! She's frigging herself, the dirty bitch.'

I realised they were looking over the top, but it was too late. Neil came with a grunt, full in my mouth and I was there myself, swallowing as best as I could as my body jerked and shook in orgasm with all three of them staring down at me, and no doubt wishing for just what I was. My climax was so hard, so long, one of the best, but even as I took Neil deep to suck down the last of his come, my thoughts had turned to the downside.

What is it with guys? They can never take their pleasure with a girl and appreciate her for what she's given them. No, they have to boast about it, or start putting her down. OK, so I hadn't actually done anything with the guys who'd watched me with Neil, and if they'd treated it as a peep-show, then they were the dirty ones. Unfortunately, they weren't going to see it like that. To them it would be the old story – when a guy does something filthy, he's cool, but let a girl do the same and she gets it in the neck.

I was not hanging around in Gogarty's; not for anything. Niall just thought it was a laugh and wanted to stay so he could bask in his mates' envy. I wasn't having it. Gogarty's, everyone in it and everything about my old social life, was beginning to make me feel stifled. Unfortunately, there was only one way I could think of to get him to leave, and that was to persuade him there was more fun to be had at Phatz. He went for it.

We drove over to Camden Town and made our way to Phatz. Neil complained at having to pay when I didn't, but soon brightened up when he set eyes on Bobbie. She was at a table on the balcony, wearing a red mini-dress that left just about every inch of her long, elegant legs on show from below. She was also wearing stockings and a serious pair of heels. Sophie was with her, across the table, and Leanne too, with a cluster of men talking to them and a third leaning back on his chair at an adjacent table. I shouted and waved, but there was no way they were going to hear over the music.

The guys with my friends were slick city types, and I caught Niall's glance of uncertainty and aggression as I pulled him towards the stairs. I wondered if I should flirt, maybe soothe my feelings a little for what had happened in Gogarty's. Pulling myself up on his shoulder, I yelled into his ear.

'Get some drinks in. I'll see you up there. Mine's a Powers.'

He nodded and pushed his way towards the bar. I climbed the stairs, fought my way around to the table, greeting the girls with hugs and kisses and quickly pinched a chair from some guy who'd gone to the bar. Four girls, seven guys, two well fixed on Sophie and Leanne – that left five in the running. One was told to go off and get drinks as I sat down and leant across to speak to Bobbie.

'Niall's here with me.'

'Oh, yes?'

'Yeah, tease him a bit, OK?'

She smiled and nodded, glancing around to seek him out.

'Tell me that's him, Lucy.'

I looked round. It was, and I had to see her point. Big and rough, and putting it on a bit in front of us and the city guys, he looked all man. I felt a touch of pride as he pushed his over way to us. He put the drinks down and set his back to the balustrade over the dance floor as I yelled out an introduction. Bobbie immediately reached out, and for a second I thought she was going to grab his crotch, but she settled for squeezing the muscle of his thigh. As he looked down in surprise her tongue flicked out to wet her lips.

'Prime steak, you lucky thing!' she said in my direction.

'Don't flatter him, he's already getting ideas,' I laughed.

Niall looked down at me.

'More lip from you and I'll give you more than ideas. And your friend too.'

I stuck my tongue out at him and Bobbie made a little purring noise. I shook my head. It was hopeless. He was already basking in her admiration, preening himself, and she was no better. OK, so he wasn't like Keith or Luke, to be teased and cajoled for a laugh, but she might have made some effort. I downed my Powers and went for another, leaving them to it.

It was my first drink, but I already felt light-headed. I knew it could happen: Niall with Bobbie and me, and maybe Sophie too, that very night. Maybe all I needed to do was go with the flow and it would. The idea filled me with all sorts of confusing feelings. There was jealousy, uncertainty, and the sure knowledge of disapproval. There was also a strong sense of mischief, of anticipation for something so naughty and which I'd never done before, and raw lust for Niall and to see him with her.

They were well into each other by the time I got back. Bobbie's eyes were sparkling as she took him in, the others forgotten. He'd pinched my chair, and for one awful moment I thought I was simply going to get cut out, but there was nothing but warmth in his welcoming smile, and he drew me straight down onto his knee, making it quite plain that I was his number one, first and foremost.

I relaxed, enjoying it all, the pang of annoyance at the consequences of sucking him off at Gogarty's quickly fading in a haze of whiskey and pleasure. It was good to be with Niall, and to enjoy Bobbie's undisguised eagerness, and the stifled desire of the other men there, who'd turned to Sophie and Leanne but were giving the three of us ever more envious glances as the atmosphere slowly warmed.

It was only when Sophie disappeared with two of the men that I began to think it really might happen between Bobbie, Niall and me. She'd had her arms around them both, and from what I knew of her I was sure she'd let them share her. Whether they could handle it I didn't know, but it was impossible not to think of her on her hands and knees, enjoying a spit-roasting. I was still a little unsure of myself, but incredibly turned on.

By the time we left, Niall was clearly sure he was going to get his way. He put his arms around our shoulders as we walked up the High Street, and lower as we entered the dim side street where he'd parked the car. By this time he had one hand on my bum, and one on Bobbie's. She didn't complain, and nor did I, letting him squeeze and stroke, stopping him only when he began to inch my dress up to get at my bare flesh. He laid off, but gave me an admonishing pat, just as Bobbie spoke.

'What's this about you taking Lucy's knickers off in the street, Niall?'

'I did that.'

'To get a date with us two and Sophie?'

'That's the size of it, yes.'

He was laughing, cool and confident. She was teasing.

'Well, you may not have Sophie, but you've got us, so can you handle it?'

'Oh I can handle it.'

'So, what are you going to do about it, big man?'

'Take the pair of you home and fuck you.'

'Oh my!'

'You pig, Niall! Do you really think we'll let you?'

I couldn't help it. He was so conceited, but my body was giving a very different message. I wanted him, together with Bobbie, for his sex and the delicious naughtiness of sharing with my friend. He didn't answer, but gave my bottom a firmer slap as we reached the car. I climbed in, full of resentment for his sheer arrogance but with my feelings at fever pitch.

We'd let Frazer have us both, so why not Niall? For one reason Frazer hadn't been my boyfriend, and Niall was ... sort of. Luke had been there too, balancing the sex. Now there were three of us – two girls, one man. No excuses. We'd be sharing, allowing him to have us both together, for his pleasure.

He never even asked if we'd like to be dropped off; he just drove, fast, to his house. We had to park well down the road, and I was terrified somebody – my family, friends, any one of the dozens who knew me – would see as I scuttled quickly to his door. Bobbie was giggling with drink and sex as he kneaded her bottom through her dress. Indoors I hesitated, knowing it was my last chance to back out. Niall locked the front door behind us.

'Upstairs with the pair of you!'

He slapped our bottoms, sending us towards the stairs. I felt one last strand of resistance break and I was running up after Bobbie, giggling and stumbling drunkenly, into Niall's bedroom. He followed, grinning as the two of us bounced down on the bed, and he'd begun to strip. It was going to happen, for real. My heart was in my mouth, my pulse hammering as we watched him undress, so casual, as if stripping for sex with two girls was something he did every night of the week. Bobbie just stared at him, admiring his body as it came bare; lean, hard torso and muscular arms, long, powerful legs, and at last his cock and balls. He was already half stiff, and as he climbed onto the bed he was grinning and hefting it in his hand, ready for us.

'Who's first, girls?'

We just went together, crawling quickly forward so urgently we banged our heads in our eagerness to get at him, and ended up in giggles as we began to kiss and lick at him. He lay back, thighs up and open, his hands ruffling our hair and tickling our necks as we worked. I took his cock in my mouth, Bobbie went for his balls, and we were both sucking deeply to make him sigh and tense, pushing his crotch into our faces. In just seconds he was rock hard in my mouth, and as Bobbie lifted her head from his balls I guided his penis all the way in.

It was so horny watching her suck, her pretty face set in bliss as she mouthed on his thick, heavy erection. I wanted to be nude, and began to pull on my clothes, peeling my dress up and off, pushing my knickers down and kicking them free. In just my stockings I got back down on Niall's dick, taking the bulging sac of his balls in my mouth as Bobbie sucked him. Her arm came around my shoulder, hugging me as we indulged ourselves in Niall's body, then higher, pushing my head gently down.

I knew what she wanted, and I did it, letting his balls slip free of my mouth, to have my face pushed close, my lips puckered, to kiss his arsehole as Bobbie dissolved into delighted giggles. She wasn't the only one giggling as I pulled back, feeling wonderfully naughty and ready for anything.

'Fuck us, Niall, side by side.'

He didn't waste time, climbing onto me even as I rolled over with my thighs spread in welcome. I sighed as he found me, pushing up, deep, and we were doing it as Bobbie stripped off her dress and bounced down beside us, watching with her hands between her thighs. Our eyes met briefly, hers full of laughter and of lust, before Niall's mouth found mine and we were kissing, even as he pumped into me, and knowing he was about to mount my friend, by my own invitation.

'Now the other one ... stay as you are, Lucy.'

I didn't need telling. Even as he slid free I was masturbating, my head to the side to watch as he mounted Bobbie, coming into her arms as he drove his cock deep inside her. It looked so good, watching her being fucked, her face in ecstasy as he pumped himself into her, his buttocks pushing up and down, the muscles of his shoulders and back and legs working as he increased his pleasure. I would have come, then and there, under my fingers as I watched them, with the memory of how it felt to have him inside me still fresh in my head. He stopped suddenly, though, and pulled back, kneeling up, his erection glistening wet with our mingled juices as he spoke.

'Now for doggy style. Get over, the pair of you, and let's see those fine arses.'

I was giggling hysterically at his words, but I didn't hesitate, nor did Bobbie. We rolled over, arms around each other as we got on our knees, bare bottoms lifted to offer our pussies to him, a thoroughly rude view we didn't mind giving in the slightest. All our inhibitions had given way to the urgent demands of pleasure. He gave a contented sigh at the sight, his cock in his hand, his eyes flicking between Bobbie's bottom and mine, unsure which eager pussy to fill.

She got it first, eased in deep with his hands on her hips as he began to fuck her. She was gasping instantly, and I could feel the shudders passing through her body every time he thrust in. At least seven or eight times I thought he'd come, but his stamina was admirable. He pulled out, got quickly behind me, and then I was getting the same treatment, being fucked on my knees with my friend cuddled tight beside me.

He did it hard, until I was panting and clutching at the bedclothes, totally abandoned to my pleasure. When he slipped free I heard my own groan of disappointment, but as I felt Bobbie tighten in reaction as she was once more filled with him he'd pushed a finger into me. I splayed my legs, eager to come, while he fucked her, and

77

while I held onto her. My fingers went back, rubbing myself as he worked my clit, clutching and groping and fingering.

Bobbie was panting, her skin wet with sweat, her scent mixed with his. It was all perfume and girl and man, a wonderful combination of sexual aromas. Niall had us both, bottoms up on his bed, surrendered to him side by side, nude but for our stockings and heels – his to enjoy as he pleased. We'd done the lot. We'd licked and sucked his cock and balls, I'd kissed his anus, we'd been fucked side by side, on our backs and on our knees.

I was coming, and at the exact moment my muscles started to go tight in orgasm he did it, entering me again, his hands closing on my hips and his cock pushing into me with a single, deep thrust. My breath came out in one long, ecstatic groan and I was there, in heaven, coming hard as he fucked me. I was still clinging to Bobbie as I rode it. At the very highest peak Niall grunted, and I knew he'd come too, deep inside me, adding a final glorious jolt to my pleasure.

He held it in, as deep as he could go, as I finished off, rubbing at myself and wriggling my body against his until at last it was over. As I slumped down on the bed he slipped free, his penis still rock hard, rearing up from his belly. Bobbie twisted around to look at him, this fit, rough bloke with a still-tumescent but spent member, revelling in his wantonness.

An instant later we both dissolved in relief, lying together, thoroughly pleased with ourselves, but not half as much as Niall. He was grinning from ear to ear, a cat who not only had just had the cream, but the canary and the goldfish too. Not that we'd finished, because I knew how quickly he'd be ready again, and with two naked girls on his bed it would be faster than ever. In due course.

'Fetch us a drink, Niall,' we demanded.

He went, content to play the host now that he'd come, and that he had us firmly where he wanted us. I settled back, adjusting the pillows to make myself comfy, naked and content on his bed with Bobbie beside me, ready for a night of sex. She stretched, her hands on her taut little breasts, stroking. I knew she hadn't come, and it looked like she needed to. As she began to lazily toy with herself I felt a twinge of embarrassment, but I couldn't help watching fascinated as she played with her nipples and gently stroked her belly and inner thighs.

Niall was soon back, and Bobbie stopped playing with herself as she heard him approach. He had a bottle of Jameson's and three tumblers, all brimful of ice. I accepted one and we chinked them together in a toast. He'd sat down at the far end of the bed, his cock lying heavy and flaccid on one thigh. It stirred slightly as he eyed our naked bodies. He took a swallow of whiskey and nodded.

'Now that was just grand, and I've a mind for more of the same, or perhaps something a little different.'

'Oh yes, what?'

'How about you two get together?'

I just laughed.

'You wish, Niall Flynn!'

'Why not? You held on, didn't you, just now?'

'That's different. Get away with you, Niall. I know it's every man's fantasy to see two girls together, but . . . hey, Bobbie!'

She'd moved up a little on the bed, and suddenly put a hand on my thigh, stroking upwards.

'Come on, Miss Perks, let's give him his show,' she whispered.

Niall's eyes were like saucers and his cock had already begun to move up his leg as it swelled. I hesitated, not wanting to stop Bobbie, telling myself I was no lesbian, but unable not to react to the gentle caress of her fingers, not knowing what I wanted and what I didn't.

He shifted, taking himself in hand to tug gently at the shaft, his eyes fixed on where Bobbie's hand was tickling in the groove of my firmly closed thighs.

'Open up, pretty please?'

She was so eager, even a little hurt. Still I hesitated, not wanting to admit to myself that it felt nice, not sure I could cope with the implication. Bobbie spoke again.

'Come on, Lucy, it's just for him.'

Niall nodded in agreement.

'That's right, Lucy. No harm in it, not when it's for your man.'

Bobbie's finger had reached my tummy, tickling in my bellybutton, and lower.

'Be fair, Lucy, you wanted to watch one man suck another off.'

Niall flinched, but he didn't speak, perhaps sensing that I was right on the brink, the urge to open my legs building in my head. They were right, it was for a show, so it wasn't like it made me a lesbian or anything. Only I knew full well that Bobbie wouldn't just be putting on a show, that she'd probably fancied me from the start. I didn't fancy her, but she was a friend, and there was no denying how stiff my nipples felt, and how strong the urge was to let my thighs come apart, especially after I'd witnessed the hardness of Niall's now erect cock.

I caught the sound of my own sob as my legs came open. Niall swore softly, and Bobbie had begun to masturbate me, rubbing in the groove of my fur. She'd make me come, I knew, and I didn't want it to go that far, to surrender so much of myself. But I told myself it was a show, bums and tits for the boys, no different to flashing a friend's tits for a laugh, not really . . .

'OK, you dirty bastard,' I said. 'What would you like to see best?'

'Get in a sixty-nine.'

He sounded like he was going to choke with lust, and for all my misgivings it was impossible not to giggle. I was still uncertain, and might have demanded something not quite so intimate, only Bobbie had already scrambled around, mounting me with her bits right in my face before I could give more than a squeak of protest. Suddenly all I could see was her open thighs, the swell of her bottom and her open, ready pussy, but I caught Niall's voice from beyond.

'Fuck me, that's good. Now lick each other. Go on, get dirty.'

Bobbie didn't need to be asked, her arms already curling around my thighs, to pull them wide and immediately bury her face between. Her tongue found my clit and, despite myself, I was gasping in pleasure. Still I held back, the scent of her sex strong in my nostrils, not sure if I could do it.

I never even realised Niall had moved until he took me by the ankles. An instant later the head of his cock was at my entrance, and in, deep in me. Bobbie kept licking, awkwardly, for just a moment, and then she'd sat up. Niall was already moving in me, thrusting deep to make me pant, even as Bobbie's bottom settled into my face, her pussy right on my mouth. I couldn't speak. I could barely breathe. Niall was in me, now holding my thighs, fucking me hard and deep. His voice came again, thick with passion, harsh and commanding.

'Lick her, Lucy. I've got to see it.'

Bobbie giggled, wiggling her bum in my face, and I was doing it, licking her, my tongue on her sex, lapping at her clit. He groaned in ecstasy, she gave a little happy sigh, and I just gave in, showing off as I lapped at her, to give him the dirty lesbian show he wanted, even as he fucked me.

They rode me, all the way, both coming to orgasm over my body. Bobbie first, with her thighs and bottom cheeks contracting right in my face, then Niall, all over my belly as he pulled out at the last instant. By then I no longer cared, and as Bobbie's fingers found my sex and her mouth my breasts I simply let her get on with it, soaking up physical ecstasy as she brought me off.

4

8 August, 11.45 a.m. – Lucy Doyle wakes up next to Niall Flynn *and* Bobbie Davenport.

What had I done? Three in a bed and sex with another girl, on the same night!

What I'd done was enjoy myself, and there was no getting away from it. It had been good, great, brilliant. I was still there too, snuggled onto Niall's chest with Bobbie on the far side, all three of us well content. It was late morning, according to the clock on Niall's beside table, and the sun was streaming in the room as we hadn't even bothered to close the curtains before falling asleep. As I pulled myself out of bed I was thinking vague thoughts about Mrs Peabody and the Simms family across the road, both of whom would have had a prime view of our threesome if they'd been watching. If so, it would be round the district in seconds, but I found it hard to care.

As it was, every person I'd ever known was soon going to know that I'd sucked Niall off in the loos at Gogarty's. The additional news, that I'd slept three in a bed and had sex with my mate would make it worse, but only so much worse. If anything, it was what I needed. It was an excuse to get out, to find myself, and a life of my own where I didn't have to be what other people wanted me to be.

That was all very well, but for the time being I had practicalities to deal with. I didn't have enough money to raise a deposit for a flat, and I didn't want to rely on favours. There was going to be some serious disapproval if I moved in with Niall; and if I seemed to be heading that way in the fast lane in any case, it was at least an excuse not to. Play was one thing, but I wasn't ready for settling down.

I was ready for more sex, and I got it on the Sunday; first on the bed with Bobbie watching, again when Niall caught me in the shower, and a third time after she'd gone, leaving him with his well-sucked dick sticking out of his trousers. He wanted me to stay, but I was too nervous of the reception I'd get at home, and I left in the early afternoon. Fortunately, it wasn't as bad as I'd expected. Siobhan and Tara both knew what had happened at Gogarty's, but they'd kept it to themselves, while if either Mrs Peabody or the Simmses had seen me with Niall and Bobbie they'd presumably dropped dead from shock. It was short of eight o'clock when I collapsed gratefully into bed.

The prospect of a return to Tilbury was less than thrilling, but I knew they wanted me for another week at the least and there was nothing to be done about it. At least, so I thought until shortly before eight o'clock on the Tuesday morning, when Mrs Maryam Smith rang to ask if I'd take a different assignment, somewhere out near Watford. I accepted like a shot, sure that whatever it was it couldn't possibly be duller than the Tilbury job.

My first thought was that somebody, probably Bobbie, had put in a good word for me and that I'd be back with the girls. I wasn't, which I found out after arriving a huge, sprawling factory built in 1930s style and painted pastel green. They made customised motorbikes, with lines of gleaming machines ranked outside ready for delivery, and the huge entrance hall was a shrine to the successes of their products over the years. The reception desk seemed tiny, the girl behind it tinier still, but neat and cool, well in keeping with her surroundings. I approached her, feeling slightly awed.

'Hi. I'm Lucy Doyle, from Super Staff.'

She looked at me over her glasses, her expression suggesting that I was cluttering up the hall. With a faint click of her tongue she began to consult her computer screen, her expression growing puzzled, then irritable.

'For Mr Drake?'

'That's right.'

'He is expecting a Miss Cherwell.'

I shrugged.

'He's got me.'

'So I see.'

She sighed and shook her head, lifted her telephone and quickly tapped in what was obviously the number of an extension.

'Mr Drake? There's a Ms Doyle here for you, from Super Staff . . . in her place, apparently. I'll send her up.'

She put the phone down and looked up at me.

'You can go up. First floor, right of centre.'

'Thank you.'

She didn't bother to respond, and I made for the stairs, a great double zigzag fully in keeping with the imposing architecture of the place. At the top was a broad corridor, completely empty with doors opening from it at wide intervals. The central ones were tall, veneered wood, and opened on to what looked like a committee room, with a long central table around which were ranged a good two dozen elegant, high-backed chairs. The next to the right, presumably the one she meant, was firmly closed. I knocked. A voice answered, male, controlled and a little stern. I opened the door to find a man looking at me from behind a huge keyhole-shaped desk of polished wood. He was youngish, maybe thirty or thirty-five, clean-cut, smartly dressed, very much at ease with himself, and not particularly pleased to see me.

'You've been sent in place of Miss Cherwell?'

'Yes.'

'Is there a reason for this? I had specifically asked for Miss Cherwell.'

'I'm sorry. I'm sure I can cope with anything she can, but if you'd rather I went...'

'You've spoken to her, then?'

His voice had softened considerably. I decided to lie, or at least to bend the truth.

'Briefly, yes, on Saturday night.'

'She's not ill then?'

She'd been in the best of health, her arms around two men, but I was sure the detail was irrelevant.

'Er ... no, not at all.'

'Hmm. I wonder what the matter is.'

I had no idea, but I could see what had happened. He'd wanted Sophie, and for whatever reason, she'd convinced Mrs Maryam Smith that I should go instead. Possibly she really was ill, and I'd been chosen at random, but unlikely, when I'd been in the middle of another assignment. Mr Drake was looking at me thoughtfully. I smiled sweetly, meanwhile silently cursing Sophie for not telling me what was going on. His next remark provided a hint.

'You'll be joining me at Interconference, then, in her place?'

I hesitated, unsure what to say. It looked as if Sophie had dropped me into one of 'those' assignments, where the girl's not wanted for her work skills, but for her looks, maybe more. I'd heard the stories, and seen the results. Talia was with Lucas Sherringham, living the life of Riley, for however long. Bobbie had done it, and

Sophie, evidently. Mr Drake was good-looking, young enough, hopefully man enough . . .

'Yes, of course.'

I'd spoken before I'd really thought about it, eager to break the uncomfortable atmosphere. He smiled. I thought of Niall, but I was one hundred percent determined that he would not possess me, nor any other man. If I wanted to take Mr Drake up on his offer, I would, and it would be my choice, nobody else's, whatever that offer might be. He gestured to a seat, now relaxed.

'It had better be Richard, then, and you are?'

'Lucy.'

'Lucy, cute name. So you're a friend of Sophie's . . . well, you must be.'

'Sure, yes, we er . . . go around together all the time.'

'Great. She's explained, then?'

'Er, no, not really. Just that . . . that she couldn't come for the Interwhatsit thing, and could I go instead.'

I smiled, praying that whatever reason Sophie had for dropping me in it, it wasn't that Mr Drake was into something weird, like the stuff they have on late night cable TV. If he expected to dress up as a woman, or be led around on a dog lead, or have me put him in nappies, I was going to run, and when I caught up with Sophie I wouldn't be responsible for my actions. Then again, maybe he just wanted to show me off in front of his colleagues, with no strings attached. Fat chance, but I could always quit.

'You're rather early, of course. Do you play golf?'

'Golf? No.'

'You should. There's no more useful accomplishment if you want to get on in business, except maybe holding your drink.'

'That I can do.'

He laughed, sure and easy, and I felt myself relax just that little bit more.

'I'll teach you, come on.'

'What, now?'

'Certainly.'

I made a vague gesture, taking in the office and the factory in general.

'Don't you have any work to do? Or for me to do, maybe?'

'Work? Not today, no. My position's largely a sinecure, but I have the name.'

I had no idea what he was talking about, but nodded faithfully. If he'd suggested bonking me across the desk without preliminaries I probably would have freaked, or maybe not. If he wanted to teach me golf, then fair enough. I was still getting paid, and it was a whole lot better than Tilbury. He'd gone to a cupboard, and produced a huge red and black leather bag bristling with clubs of various shapes and sizes. For one awful moment I thought he was going to expect me to carry the wretched thing, but he heaved it onto his shoulder, really quite casually. As he came towards me he made a polite gesture to the door. I went out first and he followed, locking it behind him.

We went out the way I'd come in, down the staircase and across the hall. The receptionist gave him an obsequious 'Good morning, Mr Drake', and me a knowing and haughty glance. As I was a step behind him I stuck my tongue out at the snotty little bitch.

Outside he led me past the gleaming ranks of motorbikes, and I finally twigged. Each and every one had a bold, cursive 'Drake' on the petrol tank. I'd seen it before, but simply hadn't made the connection. He owned the place, or at least had a senior place, and one that meant he could spend his day playing golf or anything else if he wanted to.

The few people we saw as we made our way to the car park were as polite as the receptionist. Most of them gave me no more than a glance, and I didn't care if they knew, or what they thought. I was only going to play golf, anyway. His car was a top of the range, brand new Merc, and as I settled into the black leather upholstered front seat I was thinking that I could get used to the life. If I was a good girl, I could file and type and stack and sort, and make coffee, and get shouted at for making some trivial mistake. If I was a bad girl, the possibilities were endless.

We drove for maybe twenty minutes, out into the open country, to a mansion, now a golf club. It was hard not to stare – at the ranks of expensive cars, and the ranks of expensive men and women. They might have been playing golf, but they were showing off too, in obviously expensive and presumably designer kit that made me feel very tatty indeed in my little blue office suit. As I stood nervously in the reception area I was already wondering what a man like Richard Drake would want with me when he could presumably pick and choose from among so many elegant, beautiful women. More than one I recognised from TV, and even the waitresses looked smarter and more with it than I did. I had to ask, and spoke as soon as Richard had finished signing me in and we wouldn't be overheard.

'Why me?'

'I beg your pardon?'

'Why me, here?

'The agency sent you.'

'Yes, but you'd asked for Sophie, and she and I are not so very different. I'm sure some of these women would love to play with you, and I don't just mean golf.'

He laughed.

'They're plastic, false. Everything about them is contrived. You, you're as fresh as a daisy, free and uncomplicated.'

I couldn't help but smile, although I wasn't one hundred percent happy with the implications of what he'd said. Still, I could be free, certainly, and perhaps uncomplicated, if that was what he wanted.

He found me a pair of shoes and we went outside, to a long, flat meadow behind the house, presumably once the main lawn but now a practice range. They were taking no chances, with a twenty foot high net behind us and trees and bushes to either side, creating a long aisle of grass. A row of flags stood at the far end. Richard tossed a couple of balls down on the turf and selected a club.

'The aim, basically, is to get the ball in the hole,' he began.

'I know that. Let me have a go,' I said impatiently.

'It's not quite that simple,' said Drake, with a smile, 'but OK.'

How hard could it be? I'd seen people playing golf on TV, and it had to at least be a lot easier than football or tennis, where you've got somebody trying to stop you doing what you want. I took the club from Richard and waited while he balanced a ball on a little plastic peg. There were other people around, and I imitated the way they were standing, legs braced apart, body slightly bent. The position left my bum stuck out and I gave Richard a little wiggle, just to tease him, lifted the club, and brought it down on the ball as hard as I possibly could.

I missed, completely, but let go of the club, sending it flying and leaving Richard trying not to laugh.

'Here, let me show you,' he said with smooth authority.

I nodded. He retrieved the club, and this time came to stand behind me, his arms around me and his hands on mine as he guided me. My bum was now stuck right in his crotch, and I could feel the bulge of his cock, firm and urgent under his suit trousers. Clearly there was more to golf practice than met the eye. I gave the same little wiggle I had before, but now against his cock, and was rewarded with a sharp intake of breath. He kept his cool, though, helping me lift the club and bring it down on the ball, nice and smooth, to send it maybe thirty feet, but at least in a straight line.

'Good, well done. You see, it's all in the stance.'

'Sure, but I'd take forever to get to the hole like that.'

'The green. First the green, then the hole. These things have to be done in stages.'

I raised an eyebrow, wondering how many stages he was planning. Not too many, to judge by the state of his crotch, which was making a large bulge in the front of his trousers. I made a point of bending over as I adjusted the little peg and balanced the second ball on it, sure his eyes would be firmly fixed to the round swell of my bum. He was going to come close again, making me imagine how it could be, me bent, skirt up, knickers down, and his cock slid right up. But not right outside the windows of a Super golf club, presumably. I'm sure they have rules about that sort of thing.

'Let me try again,' I said, aiming to look as cute as possible.

'OK.'

He stood back, watching me with his mouth set in a slight smile, just a little smug. I got into position, determined to show him I wasn't completely useless, positioned the club against the ball, wiggled to get my pose just right, lifted the club, and brought it down, to send the ball belting off, high in air and too fast to follow.

It went almost at right angles to where we were standing and straight in among the tress. It hit, bounced back in a high arch which I followed with my mouth wide open, up, up, over the net and down, clean through the restaurant window. I closed my eyes, waiting for the tirade.

It never came, just laughter, and with that I was sold. I'd been flirting, just enjoying the possibility that I might go to bed with him. If he'd been pushy, demanding, treated me as if he'd bought me, it would have been right out. He was just the opposite, a bit condescending, maybe, but mucking about and up for fun, even when I managed to smash up his golf club. He was still trying not to laugh as he moved off towards the club house.

'I'd better square that with somebody on the committee. Get in a bit more practice, but gently!'

He disappeared around the corner of the house and I was left to play with his clubs, trying my best to reach the little flags at the far end and failing miserably. Whoever he'd gone to speak to must have been giving him a hard time about the window because he took ages. I was bored by the time he got back, and half expecting him to be pissed off after sorting things out, but he'd kept his humour, settling for a pat of my bottom as he came up behind me.

'Enough for now, I think. How about a spot of lunch?'

'Sure. What's actually happening, by the way? Sorry to have to ask, but Sophie didn't tell me all that much.'

'We're going to Interconference.'

'Well yes, but how long for, where is it, what is it, what should ...'

I'd been going to ask what I should do, but that seemed pretty obvious and I didn't want to seem totally naïve. He looked slightly puzzled.

'Interconference, this afternoon, in Ealing.'

'Ealing? Oh, right … and just this afternoon?'

'Of course. Weren't you given any details at all?'

'No, not really.'

I held back a bit because I was blushing and I didn't want him to see. There I was, imagining myself being whisked away to some remote part of country and carefully seduced, while all the time he just wanted me to hang on his arm for the afternoon. I'd been bringing myself around to accept sex, even to want it, and it wasn't going to happen. He'd never intended that it should. I could see the funny side, but I was still feeling embarrassed as he guided me to the dining-room.

It was beautiful, if somewhat spoiled by the men cleaning up broken glass in one corner of a big, high-ceilinged room that was wood-panelled and hung with paintings. Every table was set with a glittering array of crystal, crockery and cutlery, also flowers and white linen napkins in silver rings. I immediately felt out of place, sure everyone was looking at me, and that everyone knew I was the one who'd smashed the window.

Richard took no notice, allowing the waiters to help us into our seats and frowning over the menu and a wine list a good two inches thick. I was more than a little distracted, and still embarrassed but amused at myself, unable to get the thought of how the bump of his cock had felt pressed between the cheeks of my bottom, and what I'd expected in consequence. He paid no attention, asking what I wanted to eat before making a careful selection from the wine list. Champagne, then something red.

The champagne had soon arrived, presented in a bucket of ice with a napkin laid carefully around the neck. The waiter made a great show of opening the bottle and pouring a tiny amount into Richard's glass for his approval. It was given and our glasses were filled. I

93

downed mine, grateful for the refreshment and in need of a shot of alcohol. Richard took a single, delicate sip, then refilled my glass.

'This is excellent; a pity I'm driving.'

I nodded, considering the prospect of most of two bottles. Our food arrived, some fancy dish involving king prawns for him and whitebait for me. We fell to talking, quite easily really, with Richard asking the questions and me answering as best I could. He seemed genuinely interested – in Ireland, in what I did as a temp, in my prospects at university, and not at all in a hurry.

Steaks and salad washed down with strong red wine followed, and chocolate cake, with which he insisted on getting me yet another wine, this time sweet and maybe even stronger than the red. By the time we'd finished I could barely get up. My stomach was a hard, round ball and my head was swimming with drink. I'm used to it, though, and managed to leave the club without doing anything stupid, either in the way of falling on my arse or offering Richard a blow-job in the loos.

I wanted it, though, just as soon as I could move; to be laid down and very gently undressed, all the way, until I was stark naked, then slowly teased to readiness, and fucked. If he had any idea of the state he'd got me in he didn't show it, merely offering an arm and helping me into his car, smiling all the while. He'd barely drunk anything, and drove back towards London with an easy confidence. I'd got two bottles inside me, and spent the journey staring out of the window with my mind drifting lazily between the thought of having sex with him and the growing tension in my bladder.

The sex could wait. My need to pee couldn't. The moment we got to our destination and through the check-in I was making for the Ladies. Interconference turned out to be a vast and brand new centre, the main area a great airy space beneath a dome not much smaller than the one at Greenwich. It was packed with stands, all to do with technical stuff, engineering, computers, even lubricant technology, whatever that was.

I made my way across the concourse, following a little green sign suspended from the ceiling on wires. It wasn't at all obvious where I was actually supposed to go, and still less so when I'd got in behind the stands. The first door I tried opened into some kind of storeroom, stuffed with bits of display stand and hoardings advertising everything from timeshare to rolled steel. After a very brief nose about I tried the next, and struck luck.

Relieved, I went to find Richard, wanting to be with him, and vaguely aware that I should be doing what he was paying me for. If I wasn't to be taken to a hotel, seduced and shagged, I was presumably just supposed to smile and pass the odd compliment, maybe flirt a little. I was too drunk to care much anyway, full of lust and mischief too.

He was at a stall, involved in a highly technical discussion about suspension systems. I joined him, taking his arm, was introduced, complimented on my hair, and then they went back to suspension systems. It was the same at the next stand, only involving magnetic oils, and the next, chromatics, and the next, rubber technology. By the time they'd finished with rubber technology I was bored silly and beginning to feel I was really and truly earning my money. My feet hurt, I was beginning to regret the amount of drink I'd put back, and my sense of erotic mischief had given way to a dull frustration and a slight headache.

Richard was consulting his catalogue as we moved away from the stall, and nipped in to the space between them and the outer wall to take a short cut. One more bike tech stall and my brain was going to explode, so I didn't hesitate, but took him firmly by his tie. He looked around, surprised. I smiled, looking up into his bright blue-grey eyes.

'I think you'd better come with me.'

'Yes? Is there something you particularly wanted to see?'

'Yes, there is.'

'What's that?'

'Your cock.'

He never even broke his stride, but let me lead him, smiling gently, to the storeroom I'd found earlier. We pushed quickly inside and I closed the door, jamming it with a big piece of red and yellow painted chipboard under the handle. My need was coming back, hot and strong, and I went straight to him, leaning up to kiss him, letting my mouth open to his as he took me in his arms. He wasted no time, one hand coming quickly round to cup a breast, the other moving lower, onto my bottom. I held on, letting him explore as we kissed, enjoying the taste of him and the feel of his strong hands on my body.

I was pressed tight to him, his cock swelling against my flesh, the cock that would shortly be mine, to touch, to suck, to take inside myself. My hand went down, his zip came low and I pulled it out, thick and heavy in my hand. I began to tug on him, kissing more fervently than ever, my body shivering with need as he expanded in my hand. He was nearly stiff when I went down, to take him in my mouth, sucking to let the male taste fill my senses and set me shaking harder still. As I took the head of his cock into my throat he sighed.

'Yes ... like that ... that's beautiful. Make me come, Lucy.'

'Uh, uh, I want it all, inside me,' I said.

I pulled back, looking up, as his penis reared above my face. He nodded and glanced around the room.

'You'd better bend over, then, young lady.'

I nodded in turn, more than happy to comply, thinking of him between my bottom cheeks. There was a stool in the corner, just comfy enough to bend over for a good fucking. I went, bum up, tugging at my skirt even as I got into position. Richard watched, cock in hand, his eyes lingering on my rear as I showed off first my knickers and then my bare bum, ready to take him.

He came forward, and as he pushed his rock-hard erection down between my cheeks I was fumbling with the buttons of my blouse. They came open, and I pulled up my bra to free my breasts, even as the head of his cock found my hole and he was inside me, filling me up with two long, firm pushes. He caught me by the hips, fucking me hard and jamming me against the stool, so that I was forced to cling on, panting and gasping as he drove himself into me, hard and fast. I lost control, shaking my head in my ecstasy, my body quivering to his thrusts.

For a long moment I could do nothing but cling on and take it, a rough, powerful fucking, as hard as Niall gave me, or even Todd. It didn't matter. Only when he slowed down for a moment could I get my fingers where they were needed, to my clit, to touch the hard shaft of his erection where it entered my body; to stroke the lips of my open sex as he began to pump more firmly once more. I was going to come in moments, bent over, stripped and fucked in the storeroom of an exhibition hall with hundreds of people just yards away. It was from behind too, as I'd imagined it, and as his thrusting grew faster and more urgent still I thought of how he had first pressed between my bottom cheeks and how inappropriate the whole situation was.

He should have taken me then and there on the green, and balls (literally) to the golf committee. They could have watched from the windows as he lost control with me, me with my skirt high, him ripping my blouse open, tearing my knickers off, and stuffing the full, glorious length of himself up me from the rear with several hundred people watching in shock or delight, in lust or envy, utterly horrified or keen to take their turn with me.

I groaned as I came, because I couldn't help myself. Richard immediately snatched at my mouth, holding my jaw shut, to leave me writhing on his cock, helpless in my orgasm, barely able to breathe, shuddering and biting at his fingers. He held on tight, until at last I'd finished and he was ramming into me again, harder than ever. I clutched onto the stool, determined to take it, gasping out my reaction as his hard belly slapped onto my bottom and his cock drove in, harder and deeper, fully taking advantage of the saucy little temp who'd crossed his path and wriggled herself against him.

It stopped, suddenly. His cock came free and he was groaning and grunting out my name as he finished himself off over my upturned bottom. I let him, too exhausted to protest, too well-fucked. He even apologised when he was done, and passed me a handkerchief – monogrammed, naturally – to clean up. I did it quickly, sure that we'd be interrupted at any moment, and terrified of being caught with my knickers down despite the jammed door.

That was that, the end of my day and my first shagging by a suit. I was really rather pleased with myself. I'd coped. I'd done more than cope. In fact, I was well pleased with myself, because I'd done what I wanted to do, and enjoyed myself without letting anything get in the way or picking up any emotional baggage. Not only that, but I'd done it without having the faintest idea what was going on. However pleased with myself I might be, Sophie had some questions to answer.

I tried to call her on my way home from Watford, but her mobile was off. It looked like I was going to be back at Tilbury the next day too, which was a serious pain. Egg and chips for tea didn't help any either. As I ate I was thinking of my three-course lunch, and of how easy and pleasant Richard Drake's life was. Maybe Talia was right, and the best thing to do was find a wealthy lover and take it easy. It made sense, yet the idea grated against my pride.

When the phone went on the Wednesday morning I had my fingers firmly crossed, praying it would be Mrs Maryam Smith and that she wouldn't be sending me to Tilbury. It was, and she wasn't. I had an assignment in the West End, at a theatre. I went in full of anticipation, imagining myself doing something exciting, even glamorous, helping out backstage, perhaps even with costumes or make-up, even meeting the stars . . .

The job involved sitting at a table in a dusty room in a shed built on at the back of the theatre, putting perforations in ten thousand tickets which had been delivered without them. It also involved Sophie, who turned up ten minutes after I'd been put to work, greeting me with a hug and a kiss that drew a look of disapproval from the woman who'd been set to watch over us, presumably to make sure we didn't pinch any tickets. I had to ask.

'So, yesterday?'

'Yeah, thanks, Lucy, that was so good of you. I'd dropped myself right in the shit.'

'Good of me? You didn't give me a lot of choice.'

She gave me a puzzled look.

'Sure I did. You could have just told him to fuck off, couldn't you?'

'Yes, but, it might have been nice to know what was going on!'

'Yeah, yeah, I should've rung, sorry. The thing is, I got two at the same time, you know how it is, and –'

'Would you two please concentrate on your work. It is very important.'

The supervisor had spoken, and I bit back my responses, both to Sophie, asking if 'how it is' involved shagging clients of Super Staff, and to the woman, asking why if it was so important she wasn't doing it herself. I knew the answers anyway. Richard Drake hadn't expected to be dragged into the store room, but he hadn't been that surprised either. The supervisor was far too important to lower herself to manual labour.

We weren't, but we were being paid for a full day, regardless, and so it made sense to work as fast as we could and hope that if we managed to finish early we'd be given the rest of the day to ourselves, or at least a more interesting task than making perforations. It was hard work too, tedious and tough on the muscles and the skin, leaving my arms and shoulders aching and a blister on my thumb by lunchtime. We'd done more than half, and the supervisor grudgingly let us out for a half-hour break. I had a dozen questions to ask Sophie the moment we were out of earshot, but she got in first.

'So what's this, Miss Perks? You shagged Bobbie, and this guy Niall, and you didn't invite me?'

'You were with two other guys.'

It was the first answer that came into my head, and a pretty good one, I thought, but I was blushing, as much for what she'd said as that I was sure we could still be overheard. She didn't care.

'Oh, them. Idiots! They got into a fight over me, would you believe it?'

'Yes. Now what happened on Tuesday? I didn't know what was going on at all. I had to bullshit my way through the day.'

'You didn't shag him, did you?'

'Richard Drake? No ... yes.'

'Cheeky cow! He's mine.'

'What do you mean, yours?'

'I always get Richard Drake; he's one of the best. Where'd he have you, in the boardroom?'

'No, in a storeroom at ... never mind that, what do you mean, he's yours? If he's special, why didn't you go?'

'I couldn't. Anyway, I want to know about you and Bobbie. Did you lick each other...'

'Sophie!'

'Come on, did you?'

'Sh!'

We were out in the street, but there was no shortage of people, ears flapping for a juicy bit of scandal. There was a pub a little way down, The Cross Keys, and we made for it, Sophie still talking.

'I bet you did, dirty bitch.'

'Sh, will you!'

She laughed.

'You did, didn't you? I bet he got off on that, they always do.'

'What do you mean, always?'

'Oh, come on, you're not the first.'

'Have you?'

'Sure, twice. You know how it is, you get pissed and there're no decent guys around, so ...'

She trailed off with a shrug, leaving me gaping for just how casual she was about it. I didn't want to sound naïve or shocked by what I'd done so I answered just as casually.

'You're right. No big deal.'

'Fun, though, which is why I want the details. Spit it out, Miss Perks, all of it.'

The pub was crowded, but so noisy that once we were installed in the corner with our drinks in our hands, nobody could possibly hear what we were saying. I told her everything, from leaving Phatz to the morning after. She soaked it up, just glowing with pleasure as I told her how Bobbie and I had shared his cock and balls, how we'd lain side by side, then knelt, arms around each other as we were fucked doggy style. How we'd gone head to tail, how she'd sat up on my face as Niall fucked me. That made her eyes go round and her lips come apart, giving me a flush of pleasure at her reaction.

'She sat in your face? What, properly?'

'What do you mean properly?'

'With her bum in your face.'

'Sure.'

She gave a little shiver. I knew I couldn't lie, because she was sure to make Bobbie retell the story, but that was no reason not to milk Sophie's surprise and delight in my behaviour. She blew her breath out and swallowed about half her drink in one go.

'Gorgeous! One up you with Bobbie's bum in your face, you dirty bitch! You didn't mind, yeah?'

'No ... it was, you know, no big deal.'

She nodded, accepting what I was saying, but I could tell she was impressed. I wondered if I could add any further details and get away with it, but held back. She spoke again.

'And it was your first time, with a girl?'

I just shrugged.

'You can really handle it. Most people get freaked.

Richard Drake too. I mean, I knew you could handle him, or I would have suggested you take my place, but I never thought you'd fuck him. And not in a storeroom at an exhibition!'

Again I shrugged.

'So what were you doing, better than Richard Drake?'

'Hilary Chalmers, who owns...'

She stopped, looking over my shoulder.

'Talk of the devil.'

I turned, expecting to see Richard. I didn't, but in the doorway was Niall, looking out over the heads of the crowd. Our eyes met and he began to push towards us. Sophie gave me an arch look, to which I returned a puzzled one, then addressed Niall.

'What are you doing here?'

'That's a great way for a girl to address her boyfriend when he comes to take her out for a surprise lunch. You're Sophie, yes? Hi.'

Sophie gave him an appraising look as I answered.

'That's very sweet, Niall, but we're supposed to be back in eighteen minutes. How did you find me anyway?'

'It didn't take a detective. Your Siobhan told me where you were working, and when you weren't there I tried the nearest pub. So what's with the long hours? I thought you were just a temp?'

'I am a temp, but I still have to work. What about you, anyway?'

'It's a quiet day, and I'm the boss.'

'Lazy bastard. I should be finished by two, half-two at the latest, if you want to hang around?'

'I can do that.'

He went for drinks, leaving me feeling ever so slightly irritated and Sophie looking amused.

'Getting serious, is he?'

'I don't know.'

'All the way down here to take you to lunch and no chance of a shag? That's serious.'

I shrugged, trying to put my annoyance aside. It was a nice thing to do, and I knew I should have felt grateful. I didn't. Instead I felt as if by coming to my work place he was being possessive. He'd called me his girlfriend too.

It took so long for Niall to get served that Sophie and I had to go back almost immediately, after draining our drinks in one. We were still a couple of minutes late after waiting to have the double security gates at the back of the theatre opened for us, and earned a sharp look from the supervisor. I got back to work as fast as I could, but I was preoccupied with Niall.

I thought I should possibly say something – perhaps point out that he shouldn't be possessive if he was up for three-in-a-bed romps. After all, I could just see his reaction if I suggested bringing one of his friends in to share me. He might like them to know he was shagging me, maybe even catch a peak, but touching would be a very different matter, let alone full-on sex like we'd had with Bobbie. As for the idea of him getting in a sixty-nine with another guy to help me get off...

It was so outrageous, so impossible, that it made me laugh aloud. I could just imagine his reaction – disbelief, then fury, then hurt at the implication that he might be anything other than one hundred per cent straight, that I could even think such a thing. Yet he expected me to lick Bobbie's pussy and fuck me while she sat her bare arse in my face.

My amusement turned to an irritation when I could almost hear his word by word aggrieved explanation of how it was different for girls. It was completely unreasonable, and yet it was hard to imagine the sort of man I liked taking a different attitude. Frazer had been far from amused at the idea of Luke being made to suck his cock in return for Bobbie and my favours, and with Todd Byrne the idea was more ridiculous than with Niall.

I was still mulling over the situation when we finished. As we'd anticipated, we were allowed to go, if only because the supervisor evidently didn't think us competent to do anything else, and seemed to regard our very presence in the theatre as somehow inappropriate. It was actually quite funny, and Sophie was imitating her pompous manner as we were let out.

Niall was still in the Cross Keys, pint of Guinness in hand. Sophie stuck with me and I didn't complain, keen not to stress a strong bond between Niall and myself. He didn't protest either, and we ordered food then and there. I wanted to relax, to enjoy my afternoon, but I couldn't help scheming. Niall was great, and I wanted him, but on my terms. Sophie would flirt, because she was Sophie. Maybe I could let it happen, encourage them a little, steer things so that he might become a plaything for Sophie and Bobbie and myself, impartially. It was worth a try.

At three o'clock we'd eaten and put back another couple of drinks apiece, leaving us laughing and swapping rude stories.

By four o'clock we were drunk, well drunk, with Niall describing in detail how it had felt to do Bobbie and I side by side.

Five o'clock and we'd been thrown out of the Cross Keys, leaving us staggering up Endell Street with Niall's arms around Sophie and me.

Something was going to happen, it had to. It did.

Niall didn't need to be asked. His hands were on our bums as he steered us along and neither I nor Sophie were protesting. Her flat was in an estate at the top of the Hampstead Road, high up in a tower block. We'd barely closed the door before Niall was kissing me and fumbling at my clothes. My jacket came off, my blouse was tugged open, my bra lifted and his hands were on my breasts. I let him grope, still kissing as my desire rose. Sophie had her arms around him, working on his trousers. They came open, and down, briefs and all.

He was tugging my skirt up as she began to play with his cock, and as my knickers were pushed rudely down she'd taken him in her mouth. I wanted it, then and there, my schemes forgotten except in that I needed sex and didn't care if Sophie joined in or not. I broke away, to quickly pull Niall's top off. She had his trousers right down, then off and we quickly had him stripped. I went down beside her, to take his balls in my mouth, sharing him just as I had with Bobbie even as I shrugged my blouse and bra away.

Sophie was being greedy, and I pulled her off him by her hair, eager for my share of his erection in my mouth. She stood back and began to strip, not dancing, not a tease, just rude. He was watching, his eyes fixed on her body. First she bared her breasts, cupping them in her hands with her blouse open and her bra pulled up, holding them out in open invitation and playing with her nipples to get them hard.

I was watching from the corner of my eye, and licking Niall's cock like an oversized lollipop as she turned to slowly lift her skirt and ease her knickers down over her pushed-out bum like a lap dancer. The pose left her pussy lips peeping out behind, moist and ready. He gave a lustful grunt at the sight and I pulled back.

'Go on, Niall, fuck her, and me.'

He didn't need telling any further. Sophie gave a squeak of surprise and delight as she was grabbed by the waist and pushed down over the back of her sofa. His hand went to his cock, guiding it between her bum cheeks, to rub quickly in her crease before sliding into her. She was panting immediately as he began to get into a rhythmn. I stood up, kicking my knickers off and bending over the sofa next to her, putting my bottom on offer in the same rude pose as she was in. Niall's hand found my bum and a thick finger slid into me.

'Gorgeous. But aren't I the lucky bastard?'

Sophie gave a disappointed sigh as he pulled out to come behind me, replacing his finger with the full thick length of his erection. I was instantly dizzy with pleasure and panting out my ecstasy just as she had been. It was good, wonderful, in fact, but it lasted just seconds before he'd gone back to her. A few hard shoves and he was in me again, pushing slowly in so I could feel the mouth of my pussy spread to his helmet, then back to her, entering us turn and turn about, until I felt I would go crazy if I didn't get a proper seeing-to.

I was going to come anyway, one way or another. I had to. As he eased himself up Sophie one more time, I cocked my leg up to spread myself onto the smooth firm plastic of the sofa. Niall gave a soft grunt at the sight and pulled out, to grab my thighs and stuff my open sex as I began to rub myself. I closed my eyes, my feelings building towards orgasm, thinking of how I was spread open to his cock, totally uninhibited, with Sophie watching.

It stopped, and he pulled free to leave me on the brink of orgasm. I heard my own groan of disappointment, but I was still squirming myself on the sofa top, too close to orgasm to care. So was Sophie, up on tiptoe, rubbing herself as Niall entered her one more time. I saw her face change as her pussy filled and her pleasure tipped over into orgasm. As Niall began to push into her she was babbling.

'Harder, Niall ... do it in me ... please, Niall ... now.'

His mouth was set in a hard line, his teeth gritted with his won ecstasy, but he answered her.

'Not that one, doll, that's for Lucy, that's for the girl.'

Sophie didn't answer, coming on his cock, which he held in until she'd finished, his face set in pleasure, and in satisfaction for the state he'd got her into; got us both into. I was ready, rubbing my pussy on the smooth, firm plastic, too close to orgasm to care for anything but having him inside me as I came. He obliged, slipping himself free of Sophie's body as she went limp, twisting around to slide himself easily into me.

I went frantic, bucking my body on the sofa top the instant I was full. He was fucking me, and my head was full of images of the way I was, spread bare for entry, rubbing myself in wild abandon as he fucked me, deep and hard, and side by side with a friend who he'd fucked too.

Sophie was watching, and giggling, as I came, which made it all the better, long and tight and high, with Niall's cock moving fast inside me all the time. He'd said he was going to keep his come for me, and he obliged. He shot his load deep inside me at the perfect moment, the very peak of my ecstasy, so that we came together. Sophie saw, and gave a little mew, maybe excitement, maybe disappointment. Niall responded only when he had pulled himself free of my body.

'Sorry, love, but you see how it is. If I was to get you pregnant there'd be hell to pay, but if it's Lucy, well, it just brings things forward a little bit, and no harm done.'

'You cheeky bastard,' was all I could manage, and he just laughed and slapped my bum for me. I was safe, but that wasn't the point. He'd come in me, happy to leave me pregnant, maybe even intending to. So one thing was very clear. I was Niall's girlfriend. He had decided.

5

19 August, 7.30 p.m. – Lucy Doyle wakes up in the arms of Niall Flynn.

19 August – 7.30 a.m. + 1 second – Lucy Doyle realises her head hurts.

19 August – 7.30 a.m. + 2 seconds – Lucy Doyle realises that she is in Sophie's bed, at Sophie's flat, but that Sophie is on the sofa.

Not good.

I wanted Niall Flynn. I did not want to be his wife, fiancée, little woman, whatever. I mean, at my age? Sod that!

He had a cheek, for one thing – happily shagging my friends and expecting me to be his girlfriend, and his alone. It was not going to happen. He still turned me on, and I'm a stubborn little cow when I want to be. I wasn't giving in, and I wasn't going to chuck him either. There had to be some way of working it so that I got my way.

Mrs Maryam Smith rang just before eight to give Sophie her assignment, and by good luck I was on the same one. Niall had left by then, needing to get the garage open and make sure his lads had done what they were supposed to the day before. Sophie and I went together, by tube, to a mail room in Wandsworth where we and several other temps were supposed to process a huge pile of responses to some big competition. It was simply tedious work, opening envelopes and sorting the enclosed forms into piles. We had a table to ourselves, and once the supervisors had decided we'd got the hang of it we were left alone. Sophie picked up the conversation where we'd left it on our way in, with me pondering how to bend Niall to my will.

'So, what are you going to do?'

'I haven't decided. There's no point in trying to explain how I feel. He'll either laugh at me and make me go down on his cock or get angry about it.'

'What if you tell him you've been going with other guys and that he's got the wrong end of the stick?'

'I don't know. He'll probably tell me it's time I stopped. He might lose it completely.'

'Yeah, but he's been with Bobbie, and me. He can hardly complain if you . . . no, forget I said that.'

I gave her a wry smile. She spoke again.

'How about a bit of reverse psychology? Start going on about the wedding, and how many kids you want, and how you'll need a big house. Tell him he needs to start saving, and to cut down on drink and see a mortgage advisor. Anything like that. I bet he'll be back-peddling in seconds.'

'That's a thought. But what if it backfires?'

'You could even tell him he has to commit, and that means no more bonking your friends. Pity, but . . .'

'Maybe you're right. I could give him a choice – full commitment or an open relationship.'

'Go for it, girl.'

I went back to my envelopes, thinking about what she'd said. It had to work. I'm not naïve, and I don't see the world through rose-tinted specs. Niall was so keen to make me his because it promised a good supply of hot sex, with me and with my friends. I didn't suppose for a minute he was in love with me, for all that we got on well and worked together. He presumably saw the future as sex on tap from me, with the occasional added spice when a friend joined in. It seemed highly unlikely he would be ready for full-on commitment if it meant accepting an ordinary relationship.

One thing was for sure, I couldn't just let things drift. The longer I waited, the harder it would be, so I had to act. All day I tried to think of an alternative, but when it came down to it there were three options – do it his way, dump him, or Sophie's choice.

Sophie's choice was the only choice. I really didn't want to do it, but I had to, and at the right moment. There was no point in giving him the big 'we need to talk' routine. It would just piss him off. He had to understand that I meant it too, or he would react the way he always had, by treating me as a wilful child. It had to appear casual, and it had to be done when he was horny.

I called him up, suggesting a drink, and spent the rest of the day worrying about it, and why relationships always have to get complicated. Sophie was up for coming with me, but I turned her down. It was good to know she was game for more, because that was crucial to my plan and gave me the perfect in once Niall and I were sitting in the back bar of the Lord Ranleagh with our drinks in our hands.

'Sophie says hi, and thanks for last night.'

He gave a low chuckle and I went on.

'She'd be up for more, if you are, and so would I.'

'Am I? I am, and no question.'

'Maybe Bobbie too, all three of us together, like you first wanted.'

He blew his breath out.

'All three? Oh yes ... now when would this be? This weekend, perhaps?'

'Perhaps, yes.'

I took a sip of whiskey, feigning nervousness, before I spoke again.

'What would you like best? Perhaps, to watch two of us while –'

'Jesus, yes, the two them together, while we fuck, now wouldn't that be something?'

'Yes it would. Of course, what we really need is another guy.'

'Another guy? When you have Niall Flynn, lover, you don't need another guy.'

'No? Would you like to watch somebody fuck Sophie or Bobbie?'

'Not on your life! What would I want to see another guy for?'

'No more than I'd want to see another girl. It's still sex.'

'What's that? You were well off on Bobbie.'

I shrugged, not wanting to deny it, cautious of the edge of distaste in his voice. He took a mouthful of Guinness, and was going to say something, but I got in first, determined to carry on.

'It would be fairer with more than one guy, and that's the thing. It's a lot better with more guys than girls. I mean, it's easy for a girl to keep two guys happy, but not so easy the other way around. Just think, Bobbie and Sophie and I could have you and five mates, all at once. Nobody need lose out. Wouldn't that be good, Niall, fucking me while I sucked on one of your mates' cocks? I'd like that.'

I saw him hesitate. He wanted to say something, maybe to point out that nobody else was allowed to touch me, even see me, but he knew my temper, and wasn't going to spoil his chances of three girls in bed together. When he did answer, it was in an uncomfortable mutter.

'You're mine, that's all. Do you not want it to be that way?'

I back-peddled hastily, then went for the big one.

'Of course! You get to call the shots, always, but you've got to admit, it's hardly fair if you're allowed to play with my friends but I'm not allowed to play with yours.'

'Ah, that's the same. You girls, you're well into each other. It's natural.'

'Natural? Says who?'

'Ah, but come on, you see it all the time, girls together. You think nothing of doing stuff together and that.'

'What stuff?'

'Stuff. Kissing and that, and you're always on about how so and so has a pretty face, or nice knockers, or a neat arse. You won't see me saying your Ryan's got a nice arse now, will you?'

I had to laugh, and that made him laugh too, breaking the tension.

'No, I suppose not, but that's not the point. I'm not saying you should play with other guys, just that if you want to shag my girlfriends, then I should be allowed a free choice too. Isn't that fair?'

He nodded thoughtfully, took another swallow of Guinness and then spoke.

'I see how it is, then. You're not happy with me putting it to your friends, and I respect that. So what say, you go with them, and I'll get my kicks from watching, but when it comes to cock time, I'm yours, and you're mine.'

It was not the outcome I'd intended.

'No, really, I don't mind you shagging them. I like it. I just think it should work both ways, that's all.'

He shook his head.

'I can't. You know I can't, Lucy. It's not that I don't want to please you, but you have to understand, that's the way men are. It's the same with gorillas, and lions and that. I was watching this nature programme, the other night, and . . .'

The word 'bollocks' was trembling on my lips as he went on to explain why it was perfectly OK for females to share their men but not the other way around. I could feel my temper rising, because he was being completely and utterly unfair, but for once in my life I held back, biting my lip as he finished.

'So you see,' he rounded up. 'It's not my choice. It's nature.'

I nodded and swallowed the rest of my whiskey. He emptied his own and picked both up, began to stand and then turned to me.

'You're not sore at Niall, now, are you? Not my Lucy?'

He kissed me, and as I responded he licked the tip of my nose and darted quickly back out of reach. I kicked out, missing his leg by an inch, but I was laughing, and I couldn't help myself.

'You bastard!'

Niall responded with one of his best looks, humorous but masterful too, then he turned and made for the bar. Clearly he was well pleased with himself, convinced he'd got me just where he wanted me. He was right too, in a way, because for all my determination, at an emotional level I didn't want to lose him. That didn't mean I had to give up. I was ready for him when he came back.

'OK, you great pig, you get your way, for now. I'll see if Bobbie and Sophie are up for Saturday. Just a shame these things can't last, isn't't?'

'Can't last? And why would that be? I can last, and no trouble there.'

'No, not like that, but you know how people are. Now we're serious, and not using precautions, we'll have to make it official. Everyone'll know, and we'll have to watch what we do.'

'Sure. I'm not suggesting an orgy round at your mam's!'

'You know what I mean, Niall. There's no way we could get up to that stuff, not with a family. You'd need a bigger house too, because I want at least three kids, maybe more.'

'Hold up there a minute, love. Aren't we getting a bit ahead of ourselves here?'

'Not really, no. If I'm pregnant, we'll have to get married before I start to show, say in October or November at the latest, and obviously we'd want to move straight into the new house, as soon as it's properly decorated anyway. Just think, we can have everything we want ... a huge bathroom with a power shower, and a Jacuzzi. I'll design everything, of course, 'cos you're sure to make a mess. We'll need a complete new kitchen as well, 'cos my family are sure to be around all the time, and yours too. You know what your Mum's like.'

As I'd suspected, he hadn't thought it through and, if I was exaggerating, then not by much.

'Hold on! Holy Jesus, Lucy, will you take it a step at a time? I've a mortgage to pay on my place as it is, and the prices they're asking you wouldn't believe.'

'Oh, come on, Niall! You've your own business to borrow against, and interest rates are low. We can afford it. You want to make me happy, don't you, Niall?'

'Of course I do, my lover, but we have to go slowly, that's all.'

I nodded thoughtfully.

'You're right. I'm sorry. Best to take it slowly. Once I'm through uni we'll have a double income and we can do it properly. For now, let's stay as free spirits, and not make a big deal of it to the families. That means you get to play with my friends, too.'

He grinned and ruffled my hair. I hadn't actually said it meant I got to play with other men too, but the implication was there, because I'd never back off from the idea that he wasn't being fair. I'd won, sort of. I certainly hadn't lost.

I nuzzled up against him, sipping my whiskey and thinking of Saturday night.

I was happy for it to happen, more than happy. There was something deliciously improper about sex with more than one person at the same time, which added a lot to the pleasure. OK, so in an ideal world it would have been three men and me, or maybe six men, Bobbie, Sophie and me, but only an idiot leaves a fiver on the ground because there's a tenner in the bank.

Friday morning I was hoping I'd be with Sophie again, and perhaps with Bobbie too. I'd stayed late at Niall's after a quick knee-trembler in the park on the way home from the pub, with me pushed up against a tree with my skirt up and my knickers pulled aside. He'd come, I hadn't, and I'd wanted it, so gave him a long, slow striptease and a longer, slower suck back at his house. He had me on his lap, sitting on him, naked with his cock inside me as I played with myself. We'd had an attack of the munchies afterwards and made ourselves bacon sarnies and, by the time he'd walked me home, it had been nearly two.

Mrs Maryam Smith rang at eight to tell me I was back in Tilbury. There wasn't a hope in hell of making it on time, and the rest of the morning was pure panic, rushing around madly. Once I'd got there, I was desperately trying to catch up with the work that needed to be done. The job in Wandsworth had boring but OK because I'd been with Sophie. Tilbury was far harder, and no fun at all, except for flirting with the warehouse men.

I rang Sophie at lunchtime, to tell her what had happened and suggest going out on the Saturday, drinking in the West End, then back to her place or Bobbie's, if it felt right. She agreed, giggling happily at the prospect of another session with Niall, and promised to tell Bobbie too. I ended the call feeling excited, but just a little put out. It was going to be good, but it could have been so much better if only Niall had been less stuffy about other men.

After lunch, work continued as before, only made easier by the warm glow of a double Bushmills inside me. A lorry had come in during my break, and half the cargo was already stacked, meaning that once I'd done my labels I had to scale a huge ladder on wheels to get at the crates. I knew full well that when I was on top the lads could see up my skirt, but they seemed to appreciate the view and there wasn't a lot I could do about it anyway, except keep my knees together. What I didn't expect was for all six of them to gather round at the bottom of the ladder with mugs of tea, adding the chance of a peep at my knickers to the perquisites of their three o'clock break. I picked up one of the smaller packages, heavy, though, with 'Fragile – China' printed on every side, and poised it above their heads.

'Oi, you boys, bugger off or I'll drop it,' I threatened.

Three moved back, the others held their ground. The foreman, Dave, answered, half serious, half mocking.

'Careful, love, they'll take that off your wages.'

I stuck my tongue out, but put it back. They knew full well I wouldn't have dropped it. All six of them were now looking up, a half circle of grinning idiots. One of them spoke up, Paul, a hefty ginger-haired guy with tats on both arms.

'Come on, love, give us a peep. You're skirt's too tight to see properly.'

'Just as well, you cheeky bastard! Fuck off, the lot of you!'

'Go on, just a peep,' he persisted.

'What you got on, one of them thongs?'

'I like thongs, right up the bum, eh?'

'Nah, those big white ones, like what schoolgirls wear.'

'You're a pervert, John.'

'You're all perverts,' I protested. 'Now fuck off, the lot of you!'

They just laughed. Paul spoke again.

'Give us a flash, then we'll go.'

I responded with the finger, but eventually I was going to have to climb onto the shelf and they'd get a flash anyway. With a deliberate sigh I turned around and quickly twitched up the back of my skirt, flashing the seat of my knickers for just a second. There was an immediate chorus of approval.

'Nice!'

'Red, I like red.'

'Nice arse, love.'

'Yeah, cheeky.'

'Show us some more, yeah?'

'No, you said you'd go!'

Paul just laughed, but Dave responded, turning to the others.

'Fair's fair, lads, we did say. Time to get back to work anyway.'

They nodded, reluctant, but began to disperse, with

only the youngest, George, pausing to throw up a final comment.

'They're going to love that in security, Luce.'

I instantly realised what he meant. Every one of the long isles between the shelving had a security camera pointed down it, and I'd just given ours a prime view of my knickers, which would have been transmitted directly to the bank of screens in the security booth. For some weird reason it was far more embarrassing than showing off to the warehouse men, and I found myself blushing, which drew a laugh from Paul as George shared the joke.

As I climbed onto the shelving I was feeling very odd, embarrassed but turned on, and powerful too, with six men, eight including security, with their tongues lolling out of their heads just for a glimpse of my underwear. It was amusing, and quite horny, while I could tell myself that my reaction to the camera was just silly, especially as I couldn't see the two hulking oafs employed as security guards reporting me for flashing.

I got on with my work, quickly bored by the routine of searching out each case according to its reference number and fixing the appropriate label to the side. It wasn't the first time I'd had to work on the upper shelves, but it was the first time I'd had to actually climb in among the crates, which felt weird. I was completely isolated, working in gaps between the crates, invisible to everybody and inaccessible except by ladder. The top level was the loneliest of all, with the roof just a few feet above my head.

It was dusty, and strangely quiet, both things adding to my sense of isolation. By the time I was halfway through the labelling I was even wondering if it might not be fun to have a sneaky wank, which would be deliciously naughty, and rebellious too. Mrs Henshaw had been giving me a hard time all day, and the thought of her outrage alone was almost enough to make me do it. I nearly did, but a noise from somewhere below made me chicken out.

I finished the labelling, which I was beginning to get down to a fine art, and made my way back through the huge wooden crates I'd been working on, to find the ladder gone. There was an immediate sense of vertigo, which left me clinging onto a stanchion with my stomach fluttering. It had to be nearly thirty feet to the ground, and no way was I climbing down.

My first thought was that somebody else had needed the ladder and had rolled it away not realising that I was among the crates, before I saw it, at the end of the row. I also saw Paul and George standing by it, grinning. I shook my head.

'Very funny. Now could your bring the ladder back, please?'

They exchanged a look and shook their heads, still grinning.

'Come on, guys, stop clowning around!'

George sniggered. Paul spoke.

'First you've got to show us your tits.'

'Yeah, right, with the security guys ogling me? I don't think so.'

George responded.

'You're up for it, then?'

'No, I am not!'

'You said, if the security guys weren't watching . . .'

'No, I . . .'

'Come on, love, just a peek.'

'Just put the ladder back, you bastards! I'll . . .'

I was going to say I'd tell Mrs Henshaw, but I didn't want to. The miserable old cow was sure to have a go at me as well as them, and it would leave me seriously unpopular. I tried another tactic.

'Come on, guys, be fair. I'm getting dizzy up here.'

George was going to push the ladder forward. Not Paul.

'Quick flash then you get the ladder, not much to ask, eh?'

'Oh, for goodness sake. You're a pervert, Paul, you know that, don't you?'

As I'd spoken I'd been tugging the front of my blouse out of my skirt, after stepping back between the crates to make sure I was clear of the camera. Their eyes went wide with satisfaction as they realised I was going to do it, and George's tongue flicked out to moisten his lips as I tugged my blouse up. Taking hold of my bra I cocked my head to one side, doing my best to sound disapproving as I spoke.

'OK, you little perverts, here you are.'

I flipped my bra up and held it, letting them drink in the sight of my bare breasts. They were staring, Paul open mouthed, George biting his lip, to bring back my sense of power. They might have the ladder, but I had the tits. I was laughing at them when I finally covered up, after making sure they'd both had a good stare. George turned a lewd grin to Paul.

'Nice, huh?'

'Nice. I knew she'd do it.'

'Yes, she did it. Now could you push the ladder back, please?'

It was my best school ma'm imitation, patient yet firm. I might as well have tried to give orders to a pair of bricks. Paul sucked his breath in. George smirked.

'One more time.'

'Oh, for goodness sake!'

I flipped my bra up again, putting on an expression of

patient suffering somewhat given the lie by my erect nipples. They noticed, inevitably.

'Perky, ain't she?'

'And some. Getting horny, are we love?'

'No I am not! Now come on, I've kept my side of the bargain, so bring me the ladder.'

Again George was going to push the ladder forward, but stopped as Paul tugged on his shirt. Paul whispered something, too quiet for me to catch. George returned a doubtful look, then shrugged. Paul grinned. Both glanced up at me. I quickly put my breasts away. George gave a muted snigger as Paul whispered something else. Paul looked up at me.

'How about a blow-job then?'

For a moment I couldn't speak for sheer indignation. Then I threw a shoe at him.

'Put that ladder back now, you bastard! What, you think I'm going to suck you off, on camera!'

'You'd do it if we weren't on camera then, yeah?'

'No I wouldn't, you dirty sod!'

Unfortunately I couldn't keep the giggles out of my voice. He held his ground, grinning as he spoke again.

'Come on, love, in among the crates where nobody can see. You've got me so horny you wouldn't believe.'

'Oh, so just because you get horny over me I have to satisfy you?'

He shrugged. George pushed his hips forward, showing off the substantial bulge in his trousers.

'It ain't going to be so bad for you either, girl.'

'In your dreams!'

Paul spoke again.

'If you want to come down from there . . .'

'Don't be stupid, if you're going to come up here you have to put the ladder back, don't you?'

'No.'

What was impossible for a small woman in heels was not impossible for a large man in work boots, especially one who seemed to have the climbing skills of a gibbon, or perhaps an orang-utan, which was what he resembled as he swung himself up from level to level. He was taking a hell of a risk, because he was sure to be on camera, and if security couldn't hear, they could see, and it wasn't going to take a genius to figure out what was going on. I moved hastily back as he reached the top level, letting him into the gap between the crates, more worried by the prospect of getting caught than having to suck him off. He took my action for assent, grinning from ear to ear as we came into the space at the centre of the shelf, moving a crate to make himself a seat and spreading his thighs wide as he took his place. I put my hands on my hips.

'And what, exactly, do you think is going to happen?' I asked.

'You're going to give me a blow-job.'

I held my ground, but I knew I was going to do it. He'd got me turned on, but he was just so sure of himself, and that I wanted to suck his cock. Like Niall, like Todd Byrne, he had the guts to demand what he wanted, without begging, without resorting to force, a man's way. I shook my head.

'OK, if you insist, but you're a real pig, you know that, don't you?'

He just nodded, happy to be a pig as long as he got his cock sucked. I stepped close and went down on my knees, catching the scent of fresh male sweat, then cock as he casually unzipped himself and flopped a fat, pale penis out of his underpants.

'Take your balls out too,' I demanded.

As he adjusted himself I was tugging my blouse up over my breasts, which I pulled out, cupping one in each hand, to show him, and to tease my nipples. Both were achingly stiff, raising my desire as I let my fingers brush over them. His penis was stirring as he watched, and on sudden impulse I moved closer, to fold my breasts around the meaty bulk of his prick. He gave a pleased sigh, and began to push it up and down in my cleavage, making his open trousers rub on my nipples and squashing his balls onto my flesh. I squeezed tighter, making his foreskin roll back as he thrust up into the fleshy slide I'd made for him. He gave a groan of pleasure and I kissed the tip of his cock as it popped up, before moving back to take him deep in my mouth.

'I knew you'd do it, Lucy, you little witch.'

I didn't answer, too busy sucking cock. He was growing in my mouth, almost stiff, the taste and smell of him thick in my senses. I wanted more, much more, and I was going to get it. When I was done with Paul, he'd send George up, another man to enjoy, without favour, the way I wanted it. I snuggled closer, to take Paul in my hand, tugging at his erection as I began to lick the firm, rough flesh of his balls, tasting salt and man. He was mumbling under his breath in between little gasps, his dirty words making me feel ruder still.

'That is good, Lucy, fucking good, yeah, right in your mouth. Suck them. Oh, yeah, you are such a good cocksucker, Lucy, a great cocksucker, tits out and all.'

It was crude, dirty, urgent, just the way I felt. I took him back in my mouth, sucking eagerly as I jerked at his shaft and squeezed his balls. He stopped talking, grunted, then flooded my mouth full of come. I swallowed, keen to take it in, down my throat as I sucked hard and pulled as fast as I could. Again and again he erupted down my throat, but I took it, every drop, until at last he was finished. I rocked back on my heels, my head swimming with lust, and smiling.

'There, was that what you wanted?'

'Oh yeah, and some. You are good, Lucy, fucking great!'

'Just you remember it. Now send George up, and you can watch if you like.'

He went, and I sat back, my eyes closed, just letting my feelings build. I could feel the huge metal frame shaking to his weight. It stopped, began again, and I knew George was climbing up. I swallowed hard, my whole body trembling from what I'd done and what I was about to do, kneeling bare-chested in the dust while men came up for me to suck their cocks. I opened my eyes as I heard George's voice.

'That good, was it, girl?'

I managed a weak nod.

'You ain't seen nothing yet. Ever sucked a black guy?'

Again I nodded, shuffling close as he sat down. I didn't want to talk, I wanted to suck. My hands went straight to his fly, peeling it down to burrow inside and pull him out. His cock was long and very dark, except for the head, which was fat and pink with a heavy foreskin already peeled back. I took him in my mouth even as I pulled his balls free, sucking and squeezing to make him gasp with pleasure before he spoke again.

'Do you need this?' he asked. 'Not getting it at home, huh?'

I didn't answer, lost in the pleasure of cock sucking. My hands went to my breasts, to feel their weight and stroke my skin, running my fingers over my stiff nipples as the urge to touch myself between my legs became more urgent. I wanted fucking, good and hard, with a cock in my mouth at the same time, stripped down for action on all fours with a man to pleasure me at either end.

Paul hadn't come back to watch, which was a shame,

and this alone kept my fingers off my pussy as I mouthed and licked at George's long, deep-purple dick. I'd have done it anyway, and had soon reached back to tug my skirt up over my hips, showing my knickers once more as I imagined them being torn aside for rear entry. Unfortunately the sight of my bum on show was too much for George, who came in my mouth. I just caught it, and took him deep to swallow what he had to give me, sucking it down to leave me dizzier still.

I was going to masturbate in front of him, badly in need of my orgasm and wanting to salvage what I could of male attention. He was grinning, well pleased with himself for the state he'd got me in, and would have stayed had not the foreman's voice called for him, abrupt and a little angry, and right next to us. I looked around, to find Dave standing between the boxes, his expression working between lust and annoyance. I was babbling immediately.

'Don't be cross, please. I'll do you too. Come on, let me suck your cock.'

He didn't need asking twice. A jerk of his thumb had dismissed George and he'd taken his place on the packing case. I went to him, crawling, to unzip him and take him in my mouth. He was older, still soft. Maybe he'd take longer, long enough to let me get my rocks off properly with him still in my mouth. I had to do it, for all I needed two men. As he began to swell I was pushing my knickers down at the back, right down, to leave them taut between my knees, the feel of the cotton cutting into my flesh keeping me aware of what I was showing behind – my swollen cunt ready for penetration.

I thought Dave might respond, and I'd have let him, but he just watched, cool and quiet as his cock grew slowly to erection in my mouth. He had to be hard before I came, and I was teasing myself, stroking the soft bulge of my pussy mound, my tits, my bottom and thighs, bringing myself higher and higher until I could bear it no more. My fingers found the wet crease of my sex. I was masturbating as I sucked cock, with Dave wanking himself into my mouth, faster and faster still.

He was going to come, and I held off, right on the brink, thinking of what I'd done, what I was doing, cocksucking on my knees as I played with myself, three men in a row, so naughty, so dirty, so good. I was taking it from them and pleasing them with my dirty antics. It always gave me such a thrill to turn guys on to the point where they couldn't hold back, had to have me, desperate to spurt into me.

Dave shot in my mouth and I pressed hard on my clit at the same instant. I was vaguely aware of voices, but I didn't care, rubbing myself as I swallowed down his spunk with my orgasm singing in my head and throbbing between my legs. It was only at the very peak I realised I was being watched. A pair of scuffed work boots appeared at the edge of my vision, another man admiring my naked body as I wriggled in orgasm and struggled to swallow down the foreman's come.

I pulled back. Words were exchanged, quite crossly, but I wasn't really listening. John was there, sitting himself down with his cock already flopped out of his trousers, right in my face. My muscles were still twitching in orgasm, and as he took me by the hair and pulled me down I took him in without arguing. I could hear others too, and knew I'd be expected to suck them all, six men, the fourth now in my mouth. I was tired, my jaw aching, my knees sore, but I was determined to go through with it, to milk every last drop of pleasure from my experience and every last drop of come from their cocks.

John took no time at all, holding me by the hair and

fucking my mouth. I was off balance, still horny but starting to lose control. Not that it mattered, they were going to have me and that was that. John came in my mouth and I struggled to swallow, gasping for breath as the next man replaced him, my fifth, with the sixth watching, his cock in his hand as I went down on his mate. I didn't even know his name, but it didn't matter. We were not about to have polite conversation.

I was going to be made to do it, to suck and fuck at the same time, just as I'd wanted. It was too good to miss, and as the man I was sucking began to wank into my mouth, I gave my bottom an encouraging wiggle to show I was ready and willing. He wasn't, his cock was limp in his hand, and I pulled back, to take him in, praying his mate would know what to do. He just laughed, tugging at himself as I began to kiss and lick at the other's cock and balls, determined to get him stiff.

The first guy moved behind me, and the most delicious melting sensation ran through me as I realised he was going to put it in me. The head of his dick touched between my bum cheeks. I pulled back, teasing him before he grabbed me and then shoved it right in, filling me and pushing my breath out in one long gasp. He grunted, thrusting hard as I struggled to get his mate's still limp equipment in my mouth. The cheeky sod had come, deep up me, jammed in against my bottom as he emptied his balls into my body.

Disappointment filled me even as I took the other man's cock back in my mouth. It was so close, but they'd failed to give me what I so badly needed, and I was left to suck off one last man before it would be otherwise. I'd still do it, so as not to hurt his feelings, but as I mouthed on his cock and tickled under his balls I was thinking of how pathetic men can be about performing in front of each other. Again I caught the sound of voices, the security men, and I realised we'd been caught. It was over.

The guy I was sucking swore and pulled quickly away, darting off between the cases even as the biggest of the two security men, Mike, shouldered his way into the space. He took one look at me and his mouth came open in surprise and lust. I had to offer, because I wanted it, because he was one of the biggest, roughest men I'd ever seen; and it was the only way of keeping myself from being sacked.

'You can have a go too, come on.'

I didn't wait for an answer, pulling at his fly. His hands went to mine, just briefly, but I could feel his cock bulging in his trousers, and he could feel me. I pulled him out, straight into my mouth, sucking on his thick, fleshy prick even as his mate arrived.

'What are you-?'

'Shut up, Ismael, wait your fucking turn!'

Ismael didn't answer, but just stood staring as I guided the security guard down onto the packing case. I took his balls out to suck them, eager to oblige and to keep my job. My bum was sticking up behind me, available, my pussy open and ready – surely a tempting target? I half turned, to give Ismael a nod of encouragement before taking Mike's cock back in. Still he stood watching. I wiggled my bum, willing him to take me, and before Mike came in my mouth. Still he failed to react, gaping like a fish. I pulled back, gasping.

'Just fuck me, will you, you dozy git!'

His mouth fell open, but the next instant he was snatching at the buckle of his belt. As it came loose I'd taken Mike back in my mouth, now sucking contentedly with my bottom well lifted for entry, and watching from the corner of my eye. Mike laughed as Ismael nearly fell in his urgency to get his trousers down, but there was not going to be a problem. His long, dark cock was already half stiff, and he got straight down behind me.

I closed my eyes in bliss as I moved my pursed lips slowly up and down on Mike's shaft, acutely aware of every sensation my body was bringing me as I was prepared for my fucking. Ismael's cock settled between my bum cheeks, rubbing in my crease. I could feel it stiffening and growing to make a long, hard bar, before he pushed it down. Big hands closed in the flesh of my hips. His cock pushed at my entrance, in among the wet folds, to send a jolt of ecstasy right through me as he touched my clit, and then up me.

It was happening, what I'd imagined so many times: two men inside me, my body held in big, strong hands, rocking between them on their cocks. Mike had taken hold of my head, while Ismael's fingers were locked deep in the flesh of my hips. I couldn't have escaped if I'd wanted to. But I didn't. Anything but. What I wanted was to be fucked, long and hard, mouth and pussy full of cock, my breasts naked, Ismael's solid body pushing onto my bare bum over and over as his erection slid in and out inside me.

I had to come again, and my fingers flew back to my pussy as I fought to keep my balance. They found the wet flesh, mine soft, then Ismael's hard as he eased himself in and out. These guys had full control, enjoying my body, and I could let go completely, concentrating on the feeling of a double fucking as I began to rub. It was perfect, so naughty, so rude – me on my knees with my clothes dishevelled to show my breasts and my bottom, my pussy too; kneeling to suck man after man after man.

It was too much to take in without coming, which was what I was going to do. I should have held off, teased myself, waiting until they were ready and I could have had my body filled as I came. I couldn't, my need was too strong to hold back as I went wild, squirming my body on their erections, sucking frantically on Mike, wiggling my bum on Ismael, desperate for more contact as my body went tight, and I was there.

I would have screamed. I would have screamed the warehouse down if I'd hadn't had several inches of thick, hard penis in my mouth to keep me quiet. Mainly I'd have screamed for the sheer ecstasy I was in, but also because at the exact moment I hit my peak so did they, together, and as my body jerked and shook in orgasm I was being pumped full of thick, hot spunk, the perfect detail to a perfect climax.

Just possibly – just – I might not have indulged myself with the entire male staff of the Tilbury bond if it hadn't been for my sense of pique at Niall expecting to shag my friends without allowing me the same latitude. Then again, probably not, but perhaps I might have felt a teeny bit guilty. As it was, I was absolutely singing, and the only bad thing about it was that I'd have liked to be able to share my experience with Niall, describing what had happened in glowing detail until he'd been fit to burst and then getting down to business ourselves.

I couldn't do that, sadly, although it was nearly as much fun describing what had happened on the phone to Bobbie and Sophie, both of whom were creaming themselves by the time I'd finished. As well as being desperate to tell them, I'd called to make sure we were on for Saturday night. I now felt good about it, having disposed of my reservations, and was up for just about anything Niall could think up, along with a few ideas of my own.

Sadly it was not to be. Aside from drooling over my experience, Sophie was not on good form, in bed with a nasty cold and not up for anything. Bobbie didn't want to play without Sophie, and was also due on, souring her mood and making her insecure about enjoying herself in front of Niall. We agreed to postpone, setting a firm date for the following week, when with luck all three of us would be on form.

Niall was less than happy, and took a lot of convincing that we hadn't simply chickened out. We went out anyway, just the two of us, drinking in the West End because I couldn't face Gogarty's, then back to his house for whiskey and sex. I did my best, and it was good. The first time we'd barely got the door closed behind us, and he had me on the floor in the hall, on my back with my jeans and knickers pulled down and my legs rolled up to let him get into me. He'd been getting wound up to it all evening, and he'd come in moments, leaving me more in need than ever.

It took me a short while to tease him back into action. I put the Prodigy on and stripped for him, fast and rude, making a show of my bum, right in his face and when I was nude pouring Jameson's down my tits so that he could lick it off. He'd left his cock out and I went down as soon as the music had finished, naked on my knees to him as I slowly sucked him back to erection. As soon as he was ready I mounted up in his lap, thighs spread wide so he could play with my breasts as I stroked myself and felt his balls and his cock where his shaft filled me out. I came like that, rubbing at myself and snatching at his balls while he bounced me on his erection.

Even as I came I was imagining how much better it would have been with a second man to slip his cock into my mouth as Niall and I fucked, and it was the same later. Niall had me on the bed after I'd showered, kneeling with my bottom up for rear entry and his thumbs holding my cheeks spread wide. It felt glorious, and it was him I wanted in me, no question; but even with his hand tucked in under myself to bring me off I was imagining how it would be to have him fuck me while one man after another enjoyed my mouth.

I'd learned how it feels to have two men attend to me at once, and I wasn't going back.

6

23 August, 7.30 a.m. – Lucy Doyle wakes to the sound of her radio alarm, ready for another day.

23 August, 7.58 a.m. – the telephone rings, presumably Mrs Maryam Smith with the weekly assignment.

23 August, 7.59 a.m. – Lucy Doyle is no longer ready for another day.

It was Maryam Smith, and she wanted me in at Super Staff, preferably half-an-hour ago. She didn't say why, and she sounded so pissed off I didn't dare ask. I was close to panic as I struggled to make-up and get my shit together, and it didn't get any better. As I sat on the tube, all the things that might have gone wrong were going round and round in my head.

Maybe Lucas Sherringham had finally discovered who had called him a pervert? I'd be sacked on the spot.

Maybe my little escapade at the Tilbury bond had been caught on camera after all? I'd be sacked on the spot.

Maybe she'd found out that my application was a load of bollocks? I'd be sacked on the spot.

Maybe she'd reported it to the police? I'd be arrested for fraud the instant I set foot in the building.

Come to think of it, it was probably best if Lucas Sherringham and Mrs Henshaw had both complained, in spades. At least I could walk away.

By the time I reached Edgware Road tube I was biting my lip and wondering how I could have gone to the loo, drunk nothing, and still feel as if I was about to wet my knickers. I stopped outside the Bull, wishing it was open, just to make sure Super Staff wasn't occupied by the fraud squad.

It wasn't, or if it was they were being remarkably discreet about it, and I finally plucked up the courage to cross the street, press the intercom, mount the stairs and present myself at Mrs Smith's office. She was looking at me down her nose, my file open on the desk in front of her. I found myself scowling, prepared to defend my conduct, because even if it was pointless I would go down fighting. She began.

'You were supposed to go to Tilbury today,' she began.

I went pink. It was the Tilbury thing, and doubtless half-an-hour or more of video you could have offered in any porno shop from Bangkok to Birmingham and no questions asked. Lucy does London. Lucy takes six, no, eight.

'... but Miss Cherwell is ill and she suggests you take her place. It's a higher rate, and Mrs Henshaw is prepared to accept Miss Chakravathi in your place. Is that acceptable?'

All my tension had drained away in the time she'd taken to speak, leaving me weak at the knees and so, so relieved. If she'd suggested I take an assignment stoking Satan's furnaces I'd have jumped at it, and I was nodding my head immediately. She went on.

'Good. You'd better hurry then. Here's your assignment sheet, and thank you for being flexible.'

I nodded and took the sheet. Leanne had just come into the outside office and I made way for her, exchanging smiles as we passed. My sense of relief continued as I made my way down to the street. It was like after having a close call in a car, or finding that the home pregnancy test is negative. I needed a drink, but it was too early and I had to content myself with a can of ginger beer as I made for the tube.

It was only when I was on the platform that I read my assignment, assuming I was headed for Watford and Richard Drake, maybe a spot of golf, perhaps sex over the office desk. I wasn't. Instead I was to go to right out to Henley-on-Thames, where Hilary Chalmers would meet me at the station.

Hilary Chalmers was the one Sophie had taken rather than go to Richard Drake. He had to be something else: either seriously rich and generous, or seriously horny. Perhaps both. Either way, I was well up for it. It was twenty-four pounds an hour too – so much more than I normally got that I had to double-check the assignment sheet to make sure I'd read it properly.

Meeting me at the station suggested that something dubious was going on, and as I sat on the train out from Paddington I was more than a little apprehensive. Maybe he'd be cute, maybe he wouldn't, and I knew I could never, ever allow myself to go with somebody I didn't fancy. Still, Richard Drake had been OK, better than OK, and Sophie had preferred Hilary Chalmers.

My thoughts were going round and round all the way to Henley and, by the time I'd arrived, I was quietly determined to do what suited me – nothing more, and nothing less. After building myself up it was a bit of a knock to find nobody there to meet me. There were plenty of people being dropped off and picked up, so I waited at what seemed the most sensible place, expecting something fancy, a big Merc or a Beamer 7, maybe even a Roller. When a silver S-Type Jag appeared I found myself straightening up and quickly adjusting my skirt, but when it stopped a woman got out, evidently wealthy, in a designer suit of deep-blue wool, perfectly accessorised and made up just so, her face set in an aloof sneer.

There was nobody else in the car, so I went back to inspecting the road and trying to look winsome and efficient at the same time. The rich bitch came to stand near me, glancing at her watch in an irritable manner, then at me as if I was personally responsible for her woes, then at the train as it pulled out. After another moment she went for her phone, dialled, stood tapping her foot for a space and then spoke.

'You're late ... you assured me you would come anyway.'

She went quiet, listening with increasing irritation, then glanced at me before speaking again.

'She had better be, that's all. Could you speak, please?'

It took me a moment to react, because she was holding the phone out to me. I took it, totally astonished.

'Hello? Sophie! Yes, thanks a bunch! Yes, OK, but you owe me big time!'

My smile as I handed the phone back to the woman was more than a little nervous. Hilary Chalmers was a woman, and by the look of it a real gorgon. I immediately felt a complete idiot, more so even than when I'd discovered that Richard Drake didn't expect to whisk me straight off to a hotel room. Also, Sophie's final instruction was less than reassuring – 'Whatever happens, humour the mad bitch.'

She spoke as she took the phone, her voice marginally more friendly.

'You are Lucy Doyle?'

'Yes, hi. Hilary Chalmers?'

'Ms Chalmers will do, I think. Follow me.'

As she turned to the car I made a face at her behind her back, because if there's one thing I hate it's people who expect to be 'Mr A' and 'Mrs B', while I'm plain old Lucy.

I got in to the Jag, which was top of the range, with leather upholstered seats, satellite navigation and every luxury and gadget on the market. She didn't seem inclined to conversation, and drove at breakneck speed, leaving me clutching the seat and thinking evil thoughts about Sophie. Why she'd turned down a day with Richard Drake in favour of Hilary Chalmers I couldn't imagine, unless she was simply too terrified to make the choice she wanted. Nothing else made sense, but if 'Ms' Chalmers thought she could treat me like that, then she'd picked the wrong girl.

We drove up a big hill, and in among woods, down a minor road and then a track, to a big house set well back among trees and behind an automatic security gate. There were two other cars parked on the gravel in front of the house, a Z5 and a monster Range Rover, both brand new. Evidently we had company, and I wondered if I was expected to act as secretary for some meeting of big nobs. That couldn't be too hard, and if she wanted to be formal, then so could I, and the pay was good. As I climbed from the car I made of point of standing very straight and prim. Finally Ms Chalmers condescended to speak.

'Sophie assures me that you understand the need for discretion?'

I nodded.

'Absolutely.'

'Very well. You will find your clothes laid out in the Blue Room. Change and be down in ten minutes.'

'Yes, Ms Chalmers.'

She opened the front door onto a square hallway panelled in dark wood. Various doors led off it, and a staircase, which I took, wondering why I was supposed to change and how I should identify the Blue Room. It was easy. Two short corridors led from the landing, with doors opening from then. All but one of the doors bore a discreet glazed plaque of one colour or another. I chose the blue and entered a big, high-ceilinged room furnished in muted tones. The bed was huge, a massive wooden four poster polished dark with time and spread with an embroidered blue coverlet on which were set out my clothes: a dress of plain blue wool, strapless, pleated at the waist, flaring at the skirt, and so short it wouldn't have been decent on a dwarf.

A pair of knickers, full cut, see-through white, and frilly. Ridiculously frilly.

A white suspender belt in the same OTT style.

A pair of stockings, white fishnet.

A pair of heels, white and a good four inches high.

A hat.

The hat was the final touch, a flouncy thing such as a waitress from the 1920s might wear. I just stood there, staring at what I was supposed to put on, with my temper slowly bubbling. Now I could see the game. There would be men downstairs, whoever owned the others cars, and maybe more. I would have to serve them, simpering and pouting in my ridiculous outfit, just so they, and obviously Ms Bitch-Queen Chalmers, could get off on some weird power trip.

I'd promised Sophie I'd do as I was told, and there was the twenty-four pounds an hour to be taken into consideration, but there are limits. After just a moment of reflection I'd decided what I would do. I'd serve drinks, smile politely, clear up, and whatever else seemed reasonable, but if they thought I was dressed as a sleazy French maid they had another thought coming. First I needed to make my position clear to Ms Chalmers.

A few deep breaths and I started back down the stairs.

One of the doors was open, and she must have heard the click of my heels on the wood, because she called out.

'There's a tray in the kitchen. Bring it.'

I hesitated, wondering if I should make my stand first, but deciding against it. There was no point in antagonising her more than was necessary. I found the kitchen on the second attempt, where there was a tray set out on the polished granite work surface. On it was an ice bucket with the neck of a champagne bottle sticking out, and a single glass. Slightly puzzled, I picked it up, bracing myself for the confrontation as I swept out of the kitchen and into the room with the open door . . .

. . . and dropped the tray. Ms Chalmers was there all right, but she was on her own. She was also wearing nothing but a black silk body, black stockings and shiny black high-heeled boots. I could only stare, standing in a mess of ice and broken glass as the champagne bottle rolled under the black velvet couch she was lying on.

'Stupid girl!'

She spat the words out, her face twisted in anger, and she kept going, at the top of her voice.

'How could you be so bloody stupid! That is not how it is done. You do not break things and you do not disobey me! I'm quite capable of giving you what you need without that sort of idiotic provocation, and I ought to just throw you out, here and now, but seeing as you're determined to get it . . .'

I didn't have the faintest idea what she was talking about, but she'd stood up, and was coming towards me with murder in her eyes. My hands came up automatically, and I took a step back. She snatched for my wrist but I jerked it away.

'What do you think you're going to do?' I wailed.

'I'm going to spank your naughty bottom, that's what I'm going to do!'

'What! Get off!' I yelled.

She'd caught my other wrist, pulling me towards her, and the reality of my situation finally sank in. Sophie had been playing kinky games with her, for fun or for money, and had put me in as a substitute. I pulled back, trying to explain myself.

'No, look, really ... ow! Get off! Look, Miss Chalmers, fuck off, will you!'

She was twisting my arm, trying to get it behind my back, and it hurt. I found myself being frog-marched towards the sofa, still struggling, and with her still babbling incomprehensible nonsense.

'So you're one of those, are you? Are you? Well, you're going to get what you want this time, my girl. Oh yes you are!'

I was still trying to make her see sense as she began to push me down onto couch, but she had my wrist twisted hard up into the small of my back and it hurt like hell. My temper was rising.

'No, please, just stop. Let me explain, will you! Ouch! Stop it!'

'Shut up and bend over, you little bitch!' she spat.

She slapped me hard across my bum and I just snapped.

'Ow! Fuck off, will you! Ow! OK, you mad cow, if that's the way you want it.'

I wasn't brought up in a big family for nothing. This means I can fight. She was trying to force me into a kneeling position on the sofa. I went, suddenly, unexpectedly, jerking my twisted arm free of her grip at the same instant. She gave a squeak of surprise, off balance, and I'd bounced up, grabbing at her hair. She screamed in pain and anger as I twisted it hard into my hand, then yelped in shock as I sent her sprawling onto the couch, face down. I was going to do her, too angry to stop, and determined to give her a dose of her own medicine. My knee went into her back, my hand twisted harder into her hair and she was helpless, squirming in my grip, and begging.

'No, not this. Not ever. No, please. No.'

'Yes!'

'No. Oh God, that bitch Sophie!'

I didn't know why Sophie was a bitch, and I didn't care. There was a big, silver-backed hairbrush on the table, probably meant for my bottom. I applied it to hers, hard, slapping it down on her quivering cheeks to the sound of her anguished wails and the meaty smacks of metal on flesh. She squealed like a stuck pig, and my temper was beginning to give way when she suddenly began to talk again, babbling, and with her voice thick with lust.

'Yes, do it. Beat me, Lucy, beat me hard. Punish me. Harder, please. Make me come, Lucy, make me come!'

I stopped, nonplussed. She was whimpering, limp and defeated, but with her bottom pushed up and her thighs a little open. I could smell her excitement. The catch of her body had come loose, baring her bottom. Her pussy showed too, swollen and glistening with juice. I stood back, confused, unsure of myself, scared by my own reaction and what I'd got myself into.

She'd stopped talking and, with a last, broken sob, she reached back with both hands, one to her pussy as she lifted her bottom and set her knees wide, one to the reddened flesh of a smacked cheek. I realised she was going to masturbate over what I'd done to her, but for all my shock I simply couldn't tear myself away. She was sobbing and clutching at her smacked bottom as she rubbed herself in lewd, abandoned ecstasy, her fingers working in the wet, fleshy folds and grasping at her smacked cheeks.

I just stood there, rooted to the spot, gaping foolishly as the muscles of her legs and bum began to contract. She was showing off to me, no question, revelling in the intimacy of her exposure, presumably because I'd punished her. When she came she was calling my name, over and over, something so intimate I found myself blushing furiously, fidgeting too, with no idea what to say, or how to cope with the situation.

The spell broke as she began to come down from orgasm. I knew I couldn't face her after what had happened and I just fled, out of the door and out of the house. Luckily she'd failed to close the security gates, and I ran on down the lane, not stopping until I was forced to catch my breath, where the lane to her house joined the road. I couldn't imagine her coming after me, but my feelings were utterly confused and I was taking no chances. There was a footpath sign a little way down the road, and I took it, angling across the fields towards the river valley and the sanity of Henley station.

It was only once I was back in London that I began to see the funny side of what had happened, or at least until I began to giggle hysterically. The first thing I did was find a bar and down two double Powers in quick succession. That got rid of the resentful pout I'd been struggling to keep off my face all the way from Henley, and I rang Sophie with the intention of telling her that the next time she dropped me in it with some psycho-bitch lesbian it would be nice to have the situation clearly explained first.

Unfortunately she wasn't answering her phone or her mobile, perhaps in anticipation of my call. I still had most of the day left and no idea of what to do with myself because the incident had left me a bundle of nerves and thoroughly confused. What I really needed was somebody to talk to; somebody who might be able to explain my feelings, or at least understand. I wasn't sure if I wanted to laugh or cry, to feel disgust or elation, to throw up or to find somewhere quiet where I could bring myself to ecstasy under my fingers.

The only two people I could possibly talk to were Sophie and Bobbie. Bobbie was presumably off on an assignment somewhere; but if Sophie wasn't answering her phone, there was still a chance she was in. Somewhat settled by the whiskey, and with nothing better to do, I set off for Camden and her flat. Sure enough, she was there, peering through her spy-hole when I knocked. She opened door immediately, but she didn't look too hot. She was pale and scruffy and clad in a pink bathrobe.

'Lucy? What are you doing? Why aren't you in Henley?'

'I was in Henley. I came back.'

'Why? What happened?'

'Plenty, believe me! You might have told me she was nuts.'

'I'm sorry. I wouldn't have suggested you, only I thought you could handle it, and what happened anyway? Look, come in.'

I went in and plonked myself down on the sofa, the very one Niall Flynn had had us over just a few days before. It seemed like years ago. She went into the kitchen and I began to talk, my tension flowing out with my words.

'I got to Henley, waiting to be picked up, and this woman in a big fuck-off Jag arrives, and she calls you ... anyway, you know that. So off we go, and I'm thinking what a miserable cow she is, and when we get back to her house I get sent upstairs. There's this maid's uniform laid out, you know, like a sexy French maid, and I thought she wanted me to wait on some blokes. I don't mind that stuff, for a laugh, but I'm not dressing up for some old bastards to perve over, not when it's like a power trip.'

'It's just a game, play, that's all,' said Sophie.

'Yeah, I know that now.'

'Sorry. But you must have known, at least, that she was a lesbian? I told you, didn't I?'

'No! I didn't even know she was a woman! Hilary is a man's name too.'

She laughed.

'You sure found out! But seriously, I told you about her, at the Cross Keys, that day we were working in the theatre?'

'No you did not.'

'I did, I'm sure I did.'

'You didn't, Sophie, really. I had no idea at all, not until I walked in on her to find her in just here underwear and a pair of kinky boots!'

'Oh no!'

'Oh yes. I just freaked. I couldn't understand what she was talking about. When I saw her in just this black body stocking I dropped the champagne she'd asked for and she started going on about how I didn't need to smash stuff to get what I wanted, then she just went for me.'

'What happened?'

'I tried to calm her down, but she wouldn't stop. Maybe she thought I was play fighting or something, because she was telling me I was going to get what I wanted. She was really hurting me, too, and I just lost it.'

'What do you mean?'

'Well, she was going on about how she was going to spank me, so I gave her a taste of her own medicine, with this silver-plated hairbrush.'

'You spanked her? You spanked Hilary Chalmers!?'

'Yes.'

Suddenly she was in fits of laughter. As she emerged from the kitchen there were tears in her eyes, of sheer delight, and she threw herself down in an armchair, shaking with mirth.

'What's so funny?'

'You spanked Hilary Chalmers. That is so good! Wait until I tell Bobbie, she'll bust a gut.'

I had to smile, I couldn't help it.

'Explain.'

'OK, she is such a bitch, that woman, and you spanked her. Oh my God! How did she take it? I bet she screamed the fucking house down!'

'No, not really. Well, at first, yes, but then she got horny over it, really quickly. She was begging me for more, sticking her bum up and everything. I stopped, because I didn't know what to do, and she started wanking herself off. She did it, Sophie, right in front of me, everything showing, and I do mean everything!'

'You're joking!'

'I am not. She was wild, clutching herself and rubbing like crazy.'

'Fuck me! What did you do?'

'I ran. I know that sounds pathetic, but I suppose I just couldn't handle it. That's why I came here. I wanted to talk to you.'

She nodded and sat up properly in the chair, hugging herself and shaking her head.

'Oh boy, what a laugh. Sorry, Lucy, I should have said, but I thought you knew, honestly.'

I was less than half-convinced she was telling the truth, but I let it go. What I needed was support, not a fight. She went on.

'This is how it is. She owns Body and Soul, you know, the health food chain, or she did anyway. When Bobbie first started with Super, Body and Soul used to employ temps all the time, and Hilary Chalmers was strictly hands on, always around the offices. She started taking Bobbie on for her personal stuff, and it was obvious she fancied her. Bobbie's well into women, and she went for it. She got a shock when she found out what was expected of her, but she can handle that stuff. So can I, really. So when Bobbie was off one time I stood in, just like I wanted you to. Back then Hilary had this flat in London, but after Body and Soul went public she was loaded and didn't need to do so much. We've been going out to Henley ever since, and when I couldn't go, I thought you might like a slice of the action.'

'Me?'

'Sure. I mean, you went with Bobbie, and you didn't freak when we did Keith that time, so I thought you'd be up for it. She gives serious tips.'

I just nodded, not knowing what to say, whether to feel flattered or angry, amused or upset. Sophie was biting her lip, and obviously thought she'd made a mistake. One thing I was sure of – I didn't want her, or Bobbie, to be less of a friend because I couldn't cope with what they were into. She was waiting for a response, and I forced a smile.

'That's great, Sophie, and I would have done it, only you should have told me. If I'd known, I'd have been OK with it, perhaps better prepared.'

I wasn't so sure, but it was what she wanted to hear. There was another problem.

'Shit, I hope I haven't fucked it up for you.'

She shrugged.

'Maybe, maybe not. I mean, it sounds like she enjoyed what you did.'

'That's for sure, but still ... you don't think she'd complain, do you?'

'To whom? You don't think Maryam Smith knows anything about this, do you?'

'Well, no.'

'To her it's just a premium account. It's funny, 'cos she's well pleased with herself, having the wonderful Hilary Chalmers on the books, businesswoman of the year and all that crap. No, Lucy, Hilary's not going to complain. What she'll do to my arse the next time I see her is a different matter.'

'Do it to her instead.'

'Yeah, easy for you to say. You know something, you're scary. I couldn't do that, not ever. I mean, she's one tough lady, and she's bigger than either of us!'

I shrugged.

'I suppose I caught her by surprise.'

'Yeah, right. Just remind me not to get on the wrong side of you.'

Sophie and I parted friends, better friends than before. I felt I'd been let into an inner circle, something very special. I had to make it clear that I wasn't going anywhere near Hilary Chalmers again, but both of them accepted that, and if anything seemed to be ever so slightly in awe of me for what I'd done. On the Tuesday I was assigned to a cube farm in the back of Paddington Station, cataloguing the files of a company that had been bought out by a rival. It was tedious stuff, with every detail having to be fed into a home grown computer program that was anything but computer friendly, and no body to talk to in my little box of a work station. In contrast, the previous day seemed a distant and thrilling experience. Leanne was with me, but I never saw her, except first and last thing, because lunch consisted of a bloke wheeling a trolley load of dodgy sandwiches around the cubes.

The week seemed to take for ever but, despite the boring work, my excitement was slowly rising. Bobbie and Sophie were always on the phone, and I saw Niall every evening. I got shagged every evening too, because the prospect of Saturday had him permanently horny. Not that I was much different, being nervous and excited. When I met Bobbie for a drink after work on the Friday night my feelings ended up stronger still.

She'd been to Henley, as personally requested by Hilary Chalmers. As with me, she'd been picked up at the station and driven to the house. Once there she'd been told to strip, and had spent the day playing maid and being spanked repeatedly across Hilary Chalmers' knee, and in a variety of rude positions. Three times she'd been made to go down on her employer, and when she'd left she'd been given two envelopes instead of the normal one. The second contained three hundred pounds in cash, for me.

My reservations lasted approximately half a second before I accepted it. After all, why not? It was being offered, and to judge from Hilary's reaction I'd given her quite a thrill. Bobbie had the same, along with her pay and, sure enough, my fee for Monday was a full eight hours at twenty-fours pounds. To cap it all, Hilary Chalmers was apparently worried about me because I'd run off.

I spent Saturday shopping, indulging myself as I had never done before. For once in my life I felt I had money to burn, and I was determined to make the best of it. I went into Knightsbridge first, but the prices were insane and most of the stuff just too stuck-up for me. I'd have just felt silly. Chelsea was better. First I bought a serious pair of boots, knee-high patent leather in gold with block heels, completely over the top. Next was a pair of jeans, black, from one of the best labels, and sold with a set of three bikini-style thongs in bright colours. They weren't going to go with the boots, but a gold dress I saw in a shop window at the top of the King's Road was. It was a perfect match, so short it would be seriously cheeky on me, and two hundred pounds. I bought it anyway.

By the time I got home I was knackered. I knew Mum would have a fit if she found out how much I'd spent, so I sneaked upstairs and put it all in my wardrobe before climbing into the bath. For once the house was relatively quiet, and I had a long soak, lying half-asleep in the hot soapy water. Niall was picking me up, supposedly for a straightforward date, but I couldn't resist my gold outfit. It had tiny straps. A bra would have looked silly with it, so I didn't bother. The material was light, too, and after trying a couple of pairs of knickers and discovering that the line showed through I decided to be really daring and do without. I was only going to have to bend slightly and anyone behind me was going to get a flash of bare bum, maybe more, which felt deliciously naughty.

When Niall came for me I put a coat on so as not to cause comment, then flashed my bare pussy to him as we reached the car. He was already drooling, and if he hadn't had to drive I swear he'd have fucked me on the spot, and sod who was looking on. He nearly crashed on the way into Sophie's, but we made it, to find her and Bobbie already there, dolled up and ready to go. Sophie was in a skirt and top, both tiny, and when I gave her a teasing flash she took her knickers off too. Bobbie was more demure, just, in white slacks that hugged her bum and a big cotton shirt tied under her breasts. Niall couldn't keep his eyes off us, and expected to get down to business straight away, his hands on the buckle of his belt as Sophie kicked her knickers to one side.

'So, ladies, who's first?'

Obviously he'd forgotten all about our agreement. He was also pushing his luck. I wagged my finger at him.

'Oh no you don't. Night out first, nookie later, if we feel like it.'

Sophie caught on immediately.

'Yes, that's right, if we feel like it. We may, or we may not.'

The effect wasn't what it might have been because, as she spoke, she was bending down to retrieve her knickers so Niall could see her bare bum. Bobbie applied a firm slap to the meaty cheeks showing under the hem of Sophie's skirt as she moved for the door.

'Don't worry, Niall, she'll be up for it. She's a slut. Aren't you, Sophie? Lucy's right, though, drinkies first. Come on.'

She opened the door, drawing an astonished look from an old man getting out of the lift who was just in time to catch a peep of Sophie's bare bum. I saw what had happened, and so did Bobbie. Both of us doubled up laughing as she shut the door, then Niall laughed as he too realised. From that moment it was sealed. We were going to bed, the three of us. We were going to have an almighty shagging session and that was that.

We were teasing Niall in the lift, stroking him through his trousers and threatening to get his dick out. He was rock hard and it showed, reducing all three of us to helpless giggles as we started up towards the High Street. Niall had his arms around Sophie and me, with Bobbie walking separately until I put my spare arm around her waist so she wouldn't feel left out. She immediately took a pinch of my dress and tweaked it up, just for an instant, flashing my bare buttocks to the world. I slapped her bottom, but I was up for mischief, and the brief exposure had sent a hot flush across my face and chest.

We went in the first pub we came to, for just one round, then on to the next. I was going to get plastered, and I was going to fuck all night, sod everything else. Niall had Guinness, as usual, and I joined him, starting on the whiskey chasers at the fourth pub. By the fifth my head was swimming, and the four of were in a world of our own, the crowds around us, everybody else, unreal, irrelevant.

We stopped at a place beside the canal to eat huge steaks smothered in green peppercorn sauce, and sticky chocolate pudding. All the while we were laughing and joking, with our conversation growing ever dirtier and more intimate. Sophie was sprawled in a comfy chair, her back to bar, and it wasn't long before she let her thighs slip apart, showing her pussy and eyeing Niall with hot, eager eyes. It was time, no question, before we got too paralytic, and we left, walking rapidly back the way we'd come, hardly speaking, all of us eager to get to the privacy of Sophie's flat.

The moment the lift doors had closed behind us I was kissing Niall, tongue to tongue, his arms around me. I felt his fingers as he bunched up my dress, baring my bottom. Bobbie was giggling as she saw, and I felt her hand touch me, stroking and slapping, Sophie too. I didn't care. I was too busy trying to get Niall's cock out of his trousers without breaking our kiss. He tried to pull back, but I had him pinned in the corner and out it came, already hard, hot and long in my hand. I began to wank him, tugging on it as the girls slapped at my bum cheeks.

I heard the chime of the lift bell, and felt a sharp thrill at the thought of being caught. We reached our floor, and I led Niall out by his cock, laughing crazily as we ran across to Sophie's door. I was playing with him as Sophie groped in her bag for the keys, and I was on my knees as she pulled them out, sucking on Niall's lovely cock.

Somewhere down the passage a door slammed, and we tumbled into the flat together, just in time.

All four of us were laughing, and as Niall slumped into an armchair with his erection sticking up like a flagpole. I went straight down on him. He opened his trousers as I began to suck, and I pulled his briefs down at the front to get out his balls, taking them straight into my mouth. I was kneeling, my head in his lap, feeding on him, my bottom stuck out, and suffused with a glorious warm glow from the girls' slaps.

Sophie went to the kitchen. Bobbie watched me suck, eyes bright with excitement. I threw her a glance as Niall's balls slipped from my mouth, offering her a chance to join in. She took it, squeezing in beside me to lick at him too. Her arm came around me as we worked together, kissing and licking and sucking until he had begun to groan and thrust his hips. I knew he was going to come, and I pursed my lips into a tight hole to let him push in. He grunted and took hold, tugging at his shaft, which slipped from my mouth at the last instant, to spend a fountain of come in our faces.

We were giggling with mirth as we ran for the bathroom, just as Sophie came out from the kitchen with a bottle of wine and four glasses. She saw, her mouth falling open at the sight of our faces, and as I got to the sink her voice floated after me.

'You might have waited for me, you greedy bitches,' she said.

I just laughed.

'You can have the next go, I promise, and it'll take longer.'

Bobbie and I washed and returned to the living room for wine. Niall was still in the armchair, sprawled out contentedly with his cock and balls hanging out. Sophie was perched on the arm of his chair, tickling him with a fingernail, a glass of wine in her hand. I poured myself a glass and went to the sofa, content to watch Sophie tease Niall back into action. Bobbie lay down, her head in my lap. I began to stroke her hair, my body and mind suffused with warm pleasure, drink and sex together, the taste of Niall rich in my mouth, my bottom tingling pleasantly.

Slowly, very slowly, Niall's cock began to respond to Sophie's caresses, first stirring, then stiffening and lengthening. When his helmet had began to push out from his foreskin she took him in hand, wanking gently as he lay back with his eyes closed in easy bliss. My own need began to rise faster. When she reached one lazy hand up to stroke the outline of my breasts I didn't stop her, contenting myself with speaking gently to Niall.

'Niall, open your eyes, watch.'

His eyes came open, sleepy pleasure changing abruptly to a hungry stare as he saw what Bobbie was doing. When he spoke his voice was hoarse and commanding.

'Do it bare, show me.'

I hesitated but Bobbie didn't. Shifting her body a little, she tweaked the straps of my dress off my shoulders and pulled the front down, baring both my breasts, straight into her hands. Niall's tongue flicked out to moisten his lips, his cock now hard in Sophie's grip. My nipples were stiff, and grew stiffer still as Bobbie began to run her fingers over them, until both were aching with need.

Sophie bent down to take Niall in her mouth, sucking on his now straining erection as he watched Bobbie play with my breasts. From the look on his face he was in hog heaven, getting a three-way girlie show that most men would give their eye teeth for. Her fingers found his balls, tickling underneath and his body grew tense. Bobbie's mouth closed on me, sucking one aching nipple, a sensation too nice to let me pull away.

Taking Niall in her hand once more, Sophie climbed onto him, swinging her leg across his lap and tugging her skirt high. I could see every detail, her cheeky bottom spread to show her pussy and her bottom hole, Niall's cock taut and ready, the helmet glossy with pressure. She began to rub him on herself, moving him in to the moist crease of her sex, dipping the head into her, and back, right on her clit.

He could barely take it, his teeth gritted in pained ecstasy, his fingers locked onto the arms of the chair as she used his dick to masturbate. Bobbie had my breasts in her hands, sucking urgently at my nipples, and I couldn't help myself, pushing my chest out into her face. One hand went lower, burrowing between my thighs and I just gave in, opening up to her fingers, even as Niall's patience finally snapped. He grabbed Sophie's bottom and drew her firmly down onto him, fucking her as Bobbie began to masturbate.

Niall was staring, his eyes locked to mine as he bounced Sophie on his erection. She was rubbing herself, gasping and snatching at her pussy as her body slid up and down. I was lost to pleasure, my breasts tight and sensitive to Bobbie's kisses and little nips of her teeth, my pussy already twitching under her fingers as she rubbed me off.

Sophie came, bouncing crazily on Niall's cock with her hands clutching at her pussy and breasts, the long, taut shaft working inside her. It was too much, too rude, too horny, to watch them fuck at such close quarter. She was still gasping and shaking as my own orgasm hit me, and I was clutching Bobbie's head to my chest and pressing her hand to my pussy as my whole body shook and shivered in blinding ecstasy.

Bobbie didn't stop, and I was just too drunk and too high to protest as she got down between my thighs. My body was still trembling in the dying moments of my climax as she began to lick me, and I simply closed my eyes and let her get on with it. Only when she gave a sudden gasp and I felt her head pushed into my body did I look again to find Niall behind her, holding her hips with her slacks and knickers pulled down at the back, his cock deep inside her.

I could feel the shocks running through her body as he began to pump in to her. Her licking grew clumsy, and more urgent still, so hard I was biting my lip, my pussy agonisingly sensitive under her tongue. When my climax hit me it came from nowhere, my body going into sudden spasm, completely out of control, shivering and twitching in ecstasy, out of my head with pleasure.

It only stopped when she did, moving forward to cuddle into me, her body between my open thighs, her head on my chest. Niall has slipped out, and shuffled forward to fill her once again, gasping as he fucked her with his teeth set hard. He was slamming into her bottom, making the neat, pale cheeks quiver with every thrust, until at last he came, snatching himself free at the last instant to spatter her upturned bottom.

I'd collapsed, still as horny as hell but so tired. The moment Bobbie had let go I reached out to pour myself more wine, and drained my glass at a gulp. Niall sat back, sprawled on the floor in blissful exhaustion. Sophie came to us on the sofa, cuddling up beside Bobbie and I. Twice I'd come, and I hadn't even fucked, but I was going to, just as soon as Niall had got his act together.

It wasn't going to be anytime soon. We relaxed, talking and drinking, laughing and swapping filthy stories. Bobbie talked the most, under Niall's prompting, describing lesbian encounters, including Hilary Chalmers. I hadn't realised just how bad she was, going with boys and girls, letting herself be spanked and tied up, all sorts, and loving every moment of it. Niall was impressed, stroking his cock as he listened. Before long he'd begun to stiffen again, and down I went, kneeling between his open legs to lick at his balls.

My bottom was stuck right up, my dress too short to cover me properly. I knew it was asking for trouble from the girls, but I wanted that lovely warm glow I'd felt when they'd slapped me in the lift. Sure enough, I'd barely got to work when my skirt had been twitched up behind. Both of them began to spank me, a cheek each, laughing and calling me a bad girl as Niall's cock gradually began to harden.

I only stopped when the slaps began to really sting, sitting back on my haunches to rub my cheeks. My whole bottom was aglow, deliciously warm, and with Niall's cock now once more a solid pole of flesh, I was ready for my fucking. I took his hand, pulling him up and into the bedroom, where I threw myself down on the bed, my head spinning, my fanny badly in need of cock. My thighs came up and open, my little dress rose to show everything, my arms came wide in welcome and he had mounted me, sliding deep into my body with one easy push.

The girls had come in behind us, Sophie bouncing onto the bed as Niall began to fuck me, giggling as she pulled off her clothes. Bobbie quickly pushed off her trousers and knickers, and was nude from the waist down as she climbed onto the bed. I smiled up at them, dizzy with pleasure as Niall fed his cock in and out of me all the way, withdrawing each time to penetrate me again and again.

He sat up, rolling my legs high, my beautiful dress a dishevelled tangle around my middle, one long gold boot stuck high in the air. Again we began to fuck, and I took my breasts in my hands, letting my pleasure soar, knowing it would be slow and wanting exactly that. My eyes were closed, and when I felt soft flesh brush my forehead I knew one of the girls was going to mount my head.

All I could manage was a soft moan, half protest, half desire, and then her pussy was over my mouth and I was licking, utterly abandoned, utterly wanton. Niall had my legs, holding me firmly as he fucked me, and as I opened my eyes I saw that it was Bobbie who'd sat on me, her face set in bliss as she stroked her breasts through her blouse.

I took hold of her bottom, licking freely at her pussy. Sophie was to my side, naked, thighs cocked apart, stroking herself as she watched. I was lost, as bad as them, eager for my mouthful of another's girl's sex, eager to lick as I was fucked, eager for anything that gave me so much pleasure, that felt so naughty, and so good.

Niall grunted and moved and I was being rolled over as Bobbie dismounted. He turned me easily, his strong hand simply flipping me, bottom up. I scrambled to my knees, offering myself, even as Sophie wriggled down beneath me. His cock and her tongue found my sex almost at the same instant, her thighs came up to wrap around my head and I'd been pulled in to her sex.

He took my hips, thrusting against my warm bottom cheeks as she licked me, and him too. Bobbie moved in beside me, kissing Niall and caressing my bum and back, tickling, stroking, slapping at the flesh of my cheeks. I gripped onto Sophie's thighs, revelling in the taste and feel of her, wanting to enjoy it, wanting to be as rude I could possibly be.

She found my clit with her tongue at the same instant Bobbie slipped a finger in up my bottom hole. My body jerked, a spasm of pleasure close to orgasm, Niall's thrusts grew suddenly harder and, as I started to come, a truly dirty thought hit me. I couldn't stop myself. My hands snatched at Sophie's cheeks, hauling them wide to show the little puckered star between. As I felt my climax about to burst, I imagined what it would be like to fuck her in the ass. I lost all sense of what gender I was, imagining myself having a penis and imagining the brutal earthy sense of taking her; of filling her soft flesh with come. At that moment, as every muscle in my body locked in the most perfect orgasm, I was both man and woman – an entirely sexual entity. As if to celebrate this debauchery, I puckered up my lips, and kissed my friend right on her anus.

7

29 August, 5.10 p.m. – Lucy Doyle wakes to find herself in bed with Niall, Bobbie *and* Sophie.

29 August, 5.11 p.m. – Lucy Doyle goes back to sleep.

I hadn't meant to get up when it was nearly dark, it had just worked out that way. We'd stayed up until dawn, drinking and talking, all four of us stark naked. I could vaguely remember realising that Bobbie was asleep, and listening to Sophie talking about the best places to buy shoes, with the light already growing strong outside the curtains. I could also remember kissing her bottom hole, and more, later, although most of it seemed like a dream.

My feelings were surprisingly clear, nothing like the jumble of emotions I'd experienced after my encounter with Hilary Chalmers. Perhaps it was because I'd been in control, and had known what was likely to happen before we began. Whatever it was, I was content with what I'd none, without a trace of guilt, only a wry self awareness of what I'm really like.

When it comes to sex, I've always liked the feeling that what I'm doing is improper, naughty, something to be disapproved of by the prissy, stuck-up types I've always hated, and the Church. Playing with other girls definitely fell into that category, while Father Jessop would have regarded kissing another girl's bumhole as positively Satanic. It was an amusing thought.

My head hurt, and my whole body ached, but I was

still flying as I rode the tube home that night. Niall had gone much earlier, needing to get to some family do, and I could vaguely remember him cursing as he struggled to get his trousers on in a panic. Bobbie stayed put, intended to go in with Sophie the next day, so I was alone. The family thought I'd stayed with Niall, and Mum gave me her soft smile as I climbed the stairs towards my bed, pride and approval blended with just a touch of worn patience. I smiled back, which was about all I could manage, and went up to strip, shower and collapse.

I still didn't feel too good in the morning, and could have well done without Maryam Smith ringing at eight on the dot to tell me I was back in Paddington. It was all I could manage to shower and throw some clothes on, still half asleep and in no mood to iron my office clothes. Nobody even saw, let alone commented, and for once I was grateful for my featureless cube, because it meant nobody could see me.

There was still the supervisor, a keen young woman not much older than me, but who had a business degree and made it plain that she regarded temps as pond life. She wasn't about, but I was wary of her and did my best not to actually doze off, although I might as well have done for all the use I was. By eleven I'd done two files and desperately needed ten minutes kip. I just couldn't help myself, and slumped forward on the desk, resting my head on my arms, my head full of pleasant, sleepy images of Niall's masculine charms.

Inevitably that was the exact moment the supervisor chose to check up on me, only it wasn't the officious woman. It was Luke. His sharp comment broke off suddenly as I twisted around with an apology already on my lips and we were staring at each other.

'Lucy?'

'Luke? Hi. Look, I'm sorry . . .'

'Don't be. It was wonderful. I haven't been able to get you out of my head ever since . . .'

'Eh?'

'Our time together. It was so good. I have to talk to you, Lucy. Can you do lunch?'

'Oh God, no, not now, Luke. I can barely keep my eyes open. Sorry, nothing against you, but I can't face anything heavy just now.'

'What's the matter? Are you ill?'

'No, tired. I was up all night Saturday, and I still haven't caught up on sleep.'

'How about dinner then, on me?'

'I couldn't, really . . .'

'If you need a kip, just go in my office. There's an armchair, and nobody'll know except me.'

I nodded, pathetically grateful, and let him steer me off among the cubes to an office at the far end of the room. As he'd promised, there was an armchair, a big black one with badly scuffed plastic and the stuffing come out at the bottom. I collapsed into it, my body going slowly limp as he left, closing the door behind him and turning the key in the lock.

By the time I woke up it was late afternoon, with the sun throwing splotches of rich yellow light across the furniture. My mouth felt dry and my body stiff, while I badly needed to pee. Fortunately Luke had thought to unlock the door at some point during the afternoon, and I was able to freshen up and get myself some water and a coffee. I took the coffee back to his office, where he was seated behind the desk, looking through a sheaf of papers.

'Better?'

'Yes, thanks.'

'Up for dinner?'

I nodded. Only a complete bitch would have refused.

'Great. We'll go to *Mise en Scène*.'

'Whatever. I mean, that would be great, thanks. I'm not really dressed the part.'

'That's cool. Scruffy is in.'

'Thanks a bunch!'

He was right, but there was nothing to be done about it beyond retiring to the Ladies for a more thorough freshening-up session. By the time I was finished it was half-five and people were beginning to leave. I hung around in the downstairs lobby, waiting for Luke and hoping he wasn't going to hit on me.

For one thing I was still sore, and I wasn't really up for it anyway. I was kind of sexed-out. He also lacked the manly edge I like, the sense that it's only by a great effort of willpower that I don't get my clothes ripped off and a cock stuck up me on the spot. Niall had it, and Todd Byrne, and Frazer, but not Luke. He was more like a puppy, eager but unsure of himself.

He was certainly nervous, oddly nervous, as we walked down the Edgware Road together towards Marble Arch. It wasn't embarrassment, because he kept coming back to what had happened with Bobbie and Frazer, as if he couldn't get it out of his head. In between he talked films, on which subject he had an exhaustive knowledge and, once we were in *Mise en Scène* and waiting for our drinks, he began to explain the background to the various posters and mementoes decorating the place. I let him talk, happy to listen.

There were three styles, French, American, and Cajun. That meant no decent whiskey, but a double shot of Wild Turkey began to put the energy back in me, with Luke still going on happily about the intricacies of the film industry. He'd ordered wine, a bottle of heavy Californian red, and was drinking like a fish, a good third of it gone before out food arrived. For a while there was silence as we both tucked in, and when he spoke again his voice was more nervous than ever, and he wasn't discussing films.

'Lucy, I really have to say this, but it's not easy.'

'Don't then.'

I gave him a silly smile, praying he wasn't about to tell me he loved me.

'No, I have to. It's been preying on my mind ever since that night, but I can't do it on my own. I need you to be there.'

It sounded like he wanted me to toss him off, and he sounded so pitiful it was going to be hard to refuse. I steeled myself, determined to be polite but firm, and was about to speak when he went on, in an urgent whisper.

'I've got to do it, Lucy. You know, what you said ... with Frazer, or somebody else, a black guy, preferably. I want to suck a man's cock and I want you to make me do it.'

For a moment I was just staring as his face turned from its normal fresh pink to blazing scarlet. Then I burst into laughter. I just couldn't help it, and his expression changed on the instant, to utter misery, as if he was about to burst into tears. He began to rise, stammering apologies, but I reached out to take his wrist, holding him back.

'No, no, don't go. Sorry, I didn't mean to laugh. That was wrong of me. You just gave me a bit of a surprise, that's all, and you sounded so earnest!'

'I am earnest! I can't get it out of my head. Ever since that night I've been thinking about it, fantasising about it, you know. And when I saw you in the office I knew I had to at least ask.'

'You were right to. Everyone should have the right to ask.'

'You'll do it then? Please, Lucy.'

'I didn't say that. I mean, I don't mind, and it was fun. It would have been more fun if Frazer had let you. That's the problem, you see, finding the right guy. You can't force a straight bloke to do this stuff. They freak out.'

'Don't you know anyone who might?'

I thought. Niall would kill him, Todd was a bit of a caveman, but I couldn't see it. I could hardly ask Richard Drake. The same went for the guys at Tilbury, with the possibly exception of Ismael, who was a dirty bastard. Unfortunately I had no way of getting in touch with him and couldn't be sure anyway. I shook my head. Realistically, they were all rampantly heterosexual.

'Not really, no.'

'Maybe if we went to a gay bar? Would you take me to a gay bar, Lucy?'

'A gay bar? I don't know.'

'Sh! Be quiet!'

I was going to demand what gave him the right to tell me to shut up, only to realise that somebody was approaching our table. A shadow fell over me. Luke looked up with an ingratiating grin and I turned to find a tall, bronzed man standing over us. Just from Luke's expression I knew he was somebody senior, but I could have told anyway. There was just a touch of grey in his hair, he carried himself with an easy confidence, and his face suggested that he was used to be obeyed, and promptly. He turned me a smile, and spoke, addressing me but looking at Luke.

'So, Luke, you've been hiding the pretty ones from us, huh?'

Luke gave a light, obsequious laugh and spoke.

'Good evening, Mr King. This is my friend, Lucy, who's working as a temp in the Centrans building. Lucy, meet Mr King, President of KMC.'

'You can call me Charles,' the man responded, a comment very clearly addressed to me and not to Luke.

I smiled politely. KMC was the company I was on assignment to. My immediate instinct was to complain about the rate of pay, the working conditions, the lack of air conditioning and user unfriendly database, but I held my bland smile and let him kiss my hand, thinking what a smarmy git he was. Of course he had to ask.

'So, Lucy, you see a lot of firms. How do you rate KMC?'

Not a sensible question to ask Lucy Doyle.

'As an employer? A little below average.'

Luke cringed. King's eyebrows rose.

'Below average?'

'Yes. Not that I know much, of course, because I'm just doing the Centrans files, but if the database we're using is anything to go by you need some new IT staff.'

'New IT staff, huh?'

'Sure. Somebody who can think at the level of the staff who actually do the work. It's a lot of work for the money too, but I suppose that's a good thing, from your point of view.'

He didn't look best pleased, and then suddenly he was all smiles.

'I like that! You've got guts. Maybe you could pick up a hint or two from Lucy, eh, Luke?'

He ruffled my hair and walked off, chuckling to himself, with Luke muttering under his breath.

'Sure. Let me try a line like that. I'll be deinstalled and my desk'll be on the pavement in seconds flat. Arsehole.'

He sighed and swallowed most of what was left in his wine glass. I went back to my food, a steak 'Monroe' which, for some reason, involved mustard sauce. Luke kept glancing at the bar where Charles King and two other men were standing in a group drinking shorts, but he spoke after a while.

'How about it, then?'

I'd finally worked out why a steak Monroe came with mustard sauce, and had been thinking about transvestites, which led me back to what we'd been talking about quite easily.

'How about what? Oh, right. I don't know. It sounds fun, sure.'

'Say you'll do it, Lucy, please.'

'I'd do it. It's just a hassle finding the right guy. Straight guys won't go for it, and I don't suppose gay guys would want me hanging around. I suppose you could advertise for a bi-sexual black guy on the net somewhere, and then let me know if you hit pay dirt?'

He nodded urgently.

'I could do that, yes.'

I didn't answer immediately because something else had occurred to me. In one of the pubs we'd been in on the Saturday night there had been a message on the wall in the Ladies. Some guy had left his mobile number with an offer to suck him off through a hole in the partition, claiming he had the biggest cock in London. Sophie had been with me at the time, and it had made us giggle, only I couldn't remember which pub it had been.

'So you just want to suck another man's cock, yes?'

'With you watching.'

'Right, but does he have to watch too?'

He looked puzzled.

'Just come with me.'

I took him by the hand, leading him towards the door, only to have my dramatic exit spoiled by a waiter pointing out that we hadn't paid the bill. We were both too dozy to realise, having got carried away thinking about Luke's sexual dilemma. After settling up we caught a cab to Camden Town, with Luke constantly demanding to know what I was up to, with rising excitement, and me refusing to tell him. He wasn't the only one getting excited. I might not have fancied him, but what we were doing was thrilling, and maybe even dangerous. My stomach was fluttering as we climbed out of the cab and as I tried to figure out which pub the message had been in.

We hit fourth time lucky, after four shots of whiskey and four visits to the loo. The message was still there, clear as day, also the joke, 'meet me on Lyme Regis cobb' I'd scrawled underneath it. I copied down the number and rejoined Luke in the bar, where he was sipping nervously at a glass of red wine. Time to tell all.

'I have a number, a guy who says he's got a huge cock. He says he's called Aaron. This is what we do. I call him, and say I'd like to meet. He comes here, we have a few drinks and I take him in the Ladies, where there's a hole in wall. A glory hole, I think it's called. Only you're already in the cubicle, and you suck him instead. Sound good?'

He was shaking as he answered, a wordless noise I chose to take for assent. I wasn't much better myself, my hand shaking as I tapped out the number.

Nobody answered.

I rang again.

Nobody answered.

I bought a second round of drinks, took as long as my patience would allow, and rang a third time.

Nobody answered.

I could have kicked the bastard. There he was, leaving dirty messages in Ladies loos, and he didn't even have the sense or decency to leave his mobile on. I'd been so keyed up, especially when I'd found his number, and I was shaking with reaction. Luke was no better, torn between relief and disappointment, but there was nothing to be done, except try again later.

Or try somewhere else. I was game for anything, just about, and I could remember Ryan making jokes about what went on at Hampstead Heath. I took Luke by the hand, leading him towards a bus stop.

'Right, enough nonsense. You're going to suck cock one way or another.'

'Sh! Lucy!'

I hadn't exactly been subtle, and there were plenty of people around. One girl sniggered as we passed and said something to her mates. A bus passed us, slowing for the stop, and we ran ahead to catch it. As we came into the light I saw just how red Luke's face was, and I was laughing as I threw myself into a seat. The bus lurched forward and Luke had plonked himself down beside me.

'Lucy, please, this isn't something I can really handle.'

'You started it,' I reminded him.

'Yes, but where are we going?'

'Hampstead Heath.'

He knew, because he made an odd little noise in his throat as he swallowed hard. I was enjoying myself, bold, horny, and, OK, pissed too, but determined to succeed. Bobbie was going to be delighted but envious when I told her. And Sophie. I even considered calling them, but I was scared that Luke would lose his nerve and bottle out. He was holding my hand, or rather, holding onto my hand, adding to my feelings of mischief and power.

We got off where the road passed along side the Heath, which made a great dark space beyond the reach of the streetlights. Alone, I wouldn't have gone in, but with Luke I felt OK, for all his nervousness. We found a gate between high hedges that cast black shadows in the dull orange-grey glow of the street lights. I could just about see the path, and a figure coming towards us, setting my heart hammering until I saw it just an elderly woman out walking her dogs.

'Where do you suppose is a good place?'

'I don't know. Look, Lucy, I think we should call it a day.'

'Sh, just relax. It's too late to back out now.'

He went silent, letting me lead him up the path and deeper into the Heath, where just the occasional light made pools in the darkness. There were people about, more than I'd have expected, and at a junction I turned up the hill, in among trees and alongside where a pond showed as a sheet of dull pewter, absolutely still. A man passed us, his face glimpsed only briefly, but he was elderly, nervous – not a good choice, but perhaps out for the same thing as we were.

I felt a little frightened, very excited, my nerves wire tense, but I was determined not to back out. Luke was worse, hanging back and mumbling about the time, and work, and the possibility of rain. Finally he stopped, where another path crossed ours beneath a lamp.

'Shall we go back?'

'No! You wanted this, Luke, and if . . .'

I shut up. Somebody was coming towards us, a man, young, muscular, dressed in an over-tight top, even tighter shorts that left no doubt whatsoever as to his masculinity, and sandals. Luke's attitude had started to get my temper up, and I spoke without thinking.

'Excuse me. This is my boyfriend. He wants to suck someone's cock. He's a gay virgin and he doesn't want to me.' There. I had blurted it out.

The man stopped, surprised, but only for an instant.

'OK. It's fifty.'

'Fifty?'

'Fifty quid.'

'Fifty quid? What, you charge?'

'Yes.'

'Sod you, then,' I said, out of shock more than anything else. 'Come on, Luke, we'll find someone who appreciates you.'

I still had his hand, and pulled him after me, only not very far, because he didn't want to come. The guy, the rent boy, had stopped too, and was looking at us, none too friendly. Luke spoke, stammering, blushing.

'I don't mind paying ... fifty is OK.'

The guy nodded, slow and easy, his mouth moving into a knowing smile.

'Yeah, thought so. And you want your bitch to watch?'

'I am not his bitch! Fuck you!' I yelled indignantly.

'I don't do girls.'

'And I don't do ...'

'But I'll make an exception for you. Two hundred.'

'Jesus!' I exclaimed.

Luke put his hands up.

'Calm down, Lucy, it's OK, really.'

It wasn't, but I bit my lip. The rent boy took Luke's arm, leading him towards where the path disappeared among the trees in absolute blackness. For a moment I hung back, then followed, not wanting to walk back alone. They were talking, mainly Luke, in the same urgent whisper he'd used in the restaurant. My temper was still up, but I wanted to watch. It was something I'd never seen before, something I knew would turn me on.

After just a few yards they went in among the bushes. For a moment I couldn't see a thing, groping through leaves and twisted branches of some bush, before I saw them together in a patch of faint light where a lamp on the far side of the pond illuminated a piece of open, muddy ground. I stopped, watching, my mouth open, my rising excitement pushing down my irritation. The rent boy gave an order: curt, mocking.

'On your knees.'

Luke went down on his knees in the mud, his face working with emotion. With one smooth motion the rent boy had pushed his shorts down, exposing a thick, pale cock sat above a fat ball sac, all completely shaven smoth. Luke swallowed, his eyes fixed to the boy's cock, his mouth a little open. The boy's hand came down, taking Luke firmly around the back of his head. Luke's head was pulled in, the young buck's cock and balls rubbed in his face, and I felt my pussy tighten. The boy snapped out a fresh order.

'Suck it, you little slut!'

Luke's face was squashed against the boy's genitals, his eyes tight shut, his mouth tight shut, before it opened to take in the thick white penis. Luke began sucking with a desperate energy. The boy gasped, biting his lip as if in sudden pain, but Luke took no notice, sucking as if he wanted to eat the cock that had already begun to swell in his mouth.

I was in shadow, well back, almost invisible, and the temptation to touch myself as the boy grew slowly erect in Luke's mouth was just too strong. My hand strayed to my breasts, stroking my nipples through the material of my blouse and bra until they'd grown stiff with excitement. The boy was stiff too, by then, his thick, stubby erection protruding from Luke's mouth. I saw Luke's hand go down to unzip himself, pulling out his own penis which was, unsurprisingly, rock hard.

Luke began to wank, and as he did so he let the rent boy's erection free of his mouth, licking and kissing at the thick shaft instead. He'd quickly grown urgent, and so had I, my hand on the crotch of my jeans, pressing at my clit through the thick material. Luke was going to come, jerking frenziedly as he licked at the boy's balls. I needed it too, my fingers trembling as I pulled at the button of my jeans, just as the rent boy grabbed his cock, jerking hard, to spray come into Luke's face and onto the crown of his head. Luke's mouth came wide in ecstasy, his cock jerked and, as he took the rent boy back in to suck down his sperm, he was coming himself, all over his hand and into the mud beneath him.

My breath came out in a long, slow hiss. I was shaking, badly needing my own orgasm, but it was over, and I couldn't do it, not in front of them. As Luke got up I was fastening my jeans, unsatisfied, and as I stepped forward the rent boy turned to me with a happy grin.

'Good, huh, bitch?'

I nodded, swallowing the insult and ducked down to get some tissues from my bag for Luke. He took them with a mumbled 'thank you' and mopped up quickly. I couldn't help but smile, to see a man do what I'd done myself so often. The rent boy waited patiently, before accepting Luke's money, handing over a card with 'Big Dog' and his mobile number on it, then disappearing off among the bushes with a last remark to say that he could be found in the same part of the Heath most evenings.

We walked back down the hill in silence, holding hands. Luke seemed to need reassurance, and I didn't mind giving it, for all that I was boiling inside and wanted to finish myself off with the image of him sucking on the rent boy's cock in my head. Only when we came out from the trees did the resentment start to boil up. I'd done a lot for him, and I was going to be left high and dry, which just wasn't fair. Maybe I didn't fancy him, but still . . .

'Luke, stop. You're going to have to do something for me. Come in here.'

His answer was a soft noise, a whimper, and as I pushed in among the bushes, he followed. It was pitch black, my emotions were a jumble or lust and fear of being caught, and an odd, sullen resentment for the state he'd got me into. I found a tree, by touch, and put my back to it, pushing my jeans and knickers low. Luke's hands touched me, my shoulders, my breasts, my belly, my hips, and he'd taken hold of my bottom and sunk to his knees, his mouth nuzzling my pussy as I pushed myself into his face.

I shut my eyes, struggling to concentrate as his tongue found my clit, lapping clumsily. Nobody could see, nobody need know; I only had to bring back the images: one man sucking another's cock; one man on his knees in the mud, wanking frenziedly as he licked and kissed another's erect penis. Suddenly nothing else mattered, not the noises around us in the night, not the risk, not the rent boy's snide manner; just that I'd seen Luke go down, not just sucking cock for fun, as I would, but worshipping cock. That was what it had been, dick worship, kneeling at a man's feet in the dirt, using his mouth to worship at another man's erection.

My head was full of images of homosexual lust, of cute boys wanking themselves and rough older men spunking in their faces. The urgent male energy thrilled me, and I thought how wonderful it would be if I could swap gender, if only for a day. I'd probably spend it on Hampstead Heath, looking for gay virgins to fuck and spunk over.

As I came I bit my lip hard, determined not to yell out. I took Luke's head and pulled him in, rubbing my cunt in his face, just as the rent boy had rubbed his cock and balls. I wanted my own sex worshipped in the same rude way as I rode my orgasm to one peak, and then a second as I pushed Luke aside to rub myself, finger to clit in order to get it just right, sighing with contentment as I came slowly down.

That was it, or should have been. I hastily made myself decent and we set off down the path once more. Luke was still quiet, but I wasn't having it, and soon had him grinning shyly as we came out onto the road. It was getting late and I had to get home, so I took my phone out to call a cab, just as it rang. I didn't recognise the number, but answered anyway.

'Hello? I did? Oh, Aaron, yes, I did. Sorry, too late. You'll just have to wank yourself off instead.'

I cut the call off, laughing.

Tuesday morning Maryam rang to say I was on a different assignment, still with KMC, but at their headquarters and on a higher rate. Somehow it didn't surprise me, and nor did the sudden change in expression of the receptionist, from superior to deferential, when I gave her my contact name – Andrew Miller. He turned out to be Charles King's PA, which didn't surprise me either.

What did surprise me was the security, as if I was going to meet some political bigwig and not the boss of a transport company. The lift took me to the twelfth floor, where I was met by Andrew Miller, a blond young man with a crocodile smile who I vaguely recognised from *Mise en Scène*. He took me to another lift, with no buttons but a slot for a card. It whisked us up two more floors, to a hallway comfortably furnished with black leather armchairs, potted palms and what looked like original artworks. There was a single door with a panel of number buttons to one side into which Andrew Miller pressed a code before using his card once again.

As the door slid open I was expecting something out of a James Bond movie, perhaps a big table with expensive but dodgy-looking characters sitting around discussing the latest plan for world domination. What I got was a big, very masculine living-room, done out in black leather and chrome, with a huge picture window at the far end looking out over London. In the centre of the floor was a magnificent rug, woven in tones of black, deep red and old gold. Charles King was seated in one of the armchairs, smoking a cigar.

'Lucy, hi. Good to see you. Not on the rug please, it's a Shahin Dezh, pre-war.'

'Oh, right. Is it expensive then?'

He chuckled.

'About what you'd earn in ten years, and irreplaceable'

'Oh.'

I glanced around the room. Somehow it didn't seem very likely I'd been asked up to do some filing. Carefully avoiding the prized rug, I took a seat near his and crossed my legs, wishing I didn't feel quite so unsure of myself. It was something about him – his power, not physical power so much, for all that he was a big man, but a businessman's power, or a politician's power. Richard Drake had had it, in an easygoing way. Charles King had it in spades. I felt I ought to be attracted to him, as if it was obligatory. He got up.

'Drink?'

'Please, yes. Whiskey, Irish if you have it.'

He raised an eyebrow.

'Not just a pretty face, I see. Redbreast OK for you, or Bushmills Green label?'

'Redbreast, please.'

'You're a Catholic girl, then?'

'They're both owned by Irish Distillers, I just prefer Redbreast.'

'I didn't mean to offend.'

'You didn't. I'm Catholic, yes, but you could say I was lapsed.'

I'd been going to say 'very lapsed', but I bit it back. He'd made a gaffe and apologised, only the apology had been in his words, not his tone. I took my whiskey, a triple by pub standards, wondering if the idea was to get me drunk and seduce me then and there. He'd poured himself a Scotch, a single malt I didn't know, and a measure, if anything, that was even more generous. By the time I was too drunk to know what I was doing, he'd be too drunk to do anything about it.

He went to the window, looking out over the rooftops towards the river and the London Eye. I waited, more than happy to be paid twelve pounds an hour to sit in a leather armchair drinking whiskey. At last he seemed to come to a decision and turned around.

'You're intelligent, Lucy, and bold. I like that in a woman. It means I don't have to dissemble. I find you very attractive, and I'd like you to come out with me on a trip, to Inagua, in the Bahamas, for a week. I have a little villa there. Believe me, it's paradise.'

It was a bit sudden, to say the least. I'd been expecting him to make a play for me, perhaps as simple as getting me drunk, more likely a slower effort; but a trip to the Bahamas was more than I'd bargained for, a lot more. After all, what he was saying was that he wanted to take me to his villa and bonk my brains out, if not in so many words. Finally I managed a response.

'That's ... um ... very generous of you, Mr Charles, but ...'

He raised a hand.

'I know, a little sudden, but why beat around the bush, eh? I didn't get where I am today by beating around the bush.'

He smiled, but it took me a moment to get the joke. I managed a weak laugh as he spoke again.

'Boyfriend? I understand, and I'll respect your decision, of course, but –'

'I'm not attached, not really,' I blurted out.

'No? Good, but I'll tell you anyway, because it's good advice, take it or leave it alone. When you're young, particularly if you're a woman, and trying to make your way up in the world, you mustn't let people hold you back. OK, that boy you've known since school may be goodlooking, and he may be good in bed. Go with him, and you'll be pushing a pram before you're twenty-one.'

I had to nod, because it was exactly what had been going through my head since the moment it had been decided I was Niall's steady girlfriend. He knew how old I was because he'd have seen my resumé from Super Staff, and he was right about the pram pushing. He went on.

'Don't do it, that's my advice, and somehow I don't think you want to?'

Again I nodded, with him still talking.

'Then there's the other way. Make your contacts, network, pull yourself up, until you're in charge. Then you can make your own choices. Marry? Sure, if you want to, when you want to. You're the boss. Now, I'm not going to lie to you, this is no marriage proposal. I've been through three wives and that's my lot. I want to have you. I want to fuck that round little arse of yours.'

He stopped, because I was choking on my whiskey, not with shock, despite what he'd said, but with laughter, because he was trying to shock me right out of my knickers. It was funny. If only he knew ... When I'd finally swallowed the whiskey I'd managed to keep in my mouth I answered him.

'Mr King ... Charles, last weekend I went to bed with

a boyfriend and two girlfriends, all together. Believe me, I can handle it.'

For one beautiful moment there was shock on his face, and then he composed himself. He gave a light laugh.

'I like you, Lucy, I really like you. You've got guts. Say you'll come with me?'

'I'll think about it, OK?'

'Fine, take your time. I'm a busy man, Lucy, so . . .'

His hand had gone to the front of his trousers, and my heart jumped at the thought of him simply getting his dick out and demanding it be sucked. I'd have done it, too, because after acting so bold I'd have felt a right prat backing out. He merely extracted a wallet as he continued.

'Here's a little something for your wardrobe and, if you decide not to come, well, that's the way it is. Here.'

He was holding out a sheaf of notes. I knew the game. If I took it, I was obliged, really no different to the boys who reckon standing a girl fish and chips entitles them to being tossed off on the way home. He didn't know me. Some of those boys had got my knee in their balls. Rather more had got their hand jobs, but that wasn't the point. I do as I like, and I took the money.

'Thanks, that's very generous.'

'You're welcome. Drop back this afternoon, say three o'clock? Show me what you've bought.'

In other words, he wanted a strip show, or maybe it was just my dirty mind. I finished my whiskey and left feeling quite pleased with myself but not one hundred percent sure about his offer. For a start there was Niall, who was not going to be best pleased. Then again, eventually I was going to have to point out that he didn't own me, if only when I went off to uni. Mum wasn't going to approve either, which meant I'd get it in the ear from Mary too. If anything that made me want to go more.

More important was the question of whether I wanted to. Charles King was fairly attractive, if a bit old for me, and not entirely my type. I'd enjoyed his openness, and would have sucked his cock if he'd demanded it, but he was just a bit too arrogant. Yet I'd coped easily with Richard Drake. I'd coped with the mad lesbian Hilary Chalmers, sort of. Why not Charles King?

There's a big, big difference between Watford and Inagua. For a start, I could pronounce Watford. There was a good train service to Kilburn too. I'd be in Inagua for a whole week, just the two of us together and no escape. Yet if it did work it would be a wonderful break, and with uni in September perhaps my last chance for a decent holiday in several years. Certainly I wouldn't be able to afford it as a student, and maybe the offer would never come again?

At the very least it made sense to let him shag me first. That way I'd find out in good time if he expected to tie me up, or bugger me, or dress me as a French maid and spank my bottom, *à la* Hilary Chalmers. It was a bit mercenary of me, maybe, but it made sense. No doubt after a little fashion show with my new clothes he'd be well up for it.

I was thinking about it all the way to Oxford Circus, but had quickly lost myself in a shopping frenzy, the second in a few days, and both courtesy of older, rich types desperate to get into my knickers. For all my pride I had to admit to the temptation because, just a few weeks before, the idea of spending a hundred quid on a bikini that barely covered my embarrassment would have seemed outrageous. I bought two, one green, one blue, and tops and shorts and sandals, and a new bag, and a huge picture hat I could only possibly have worn on a sun-drenched beach.

Having just slightly overspent his money, and treated myself to lunch at Fortnum and Mason, no less, I made my way back, still undecided. Once again I had to go through the routine of receptionist, Andrew Miller and security lift before being admitted to the presence of Charles King and, once again, he was seated in his armchair smoking a cigar. I had to work.

'Do you actually do any work, or do you just have minions rushing around?' I asked him.

He gave a low chuckle.

'Oh yes, I work. I direct, which is my job. While you've been off shopping I've arranged the sale of the Centrans building, where you were working, at a tidy profit I might add, maybe seven million, once the final figures are in. Oh yes, I work.'

'Oh, right. Anyway, I've got some great gear, beach stuff mainly. Look at this hat!'

I took it out, posing in it as if for a photographer. He watched, puffing on his cigar with a small, indulgent smile on his face.

'And sandals, sun cream, beach towel, stuff, stuff, stuff ... and these great bikinis. They're *La Madeleine*, I hope you don't mind? Because there's no change.'

'I didn't expect any.'

'Good.'

He had to ask me to try one on. He was sure to ask me to try one on. He knocked out the tip of his cigar into an ashtray.

'You know we'll be in the middle of the hurricane season, don't you?'

'Oh. No I didn't.'

'Don't worry. One's just gone through, and we'll be clear. Assuming you're coming, that is?'

'I'm still not sure.'

He merely shrugged, very casual. I'd expected him to make a move, after the way he'd boldly informed me he wanted to fuck me, and as I straightened up with the two bikinis I was feeling rather at a loss.

'Do you like them?'

'Absolutely. One of the best designers, I always think.'

So much for subtlety.

'Don't you want to see it on?'

'Of course, on the beach below my villa. Here in London you're fine just as you are.'

I smiled, still unsure of myself. To all intents and purposes I'd offered to strip, and he'd turned me down. Yet he wanted to 'fuck my little round arse'. He was still talking.

'I wonder if you realise just how beautiful you are, Lucy? When you look at yourself in a mirror, what do you see?'

'Myself. Do you mean naked?'

'Not necessarily. I'll tell you what you see. You see your own perception of yourself and, far be it for me to claim to know what that is, beyond the obvious; the red of your hair, the delicacy of your face, the physical lines of your body. What you don't see, but I do, is how you look out on the world. There's a fire in you, of real determination and pride, but underneath that there's a touch of insecurity. To a man like me that combination is hard to resist.'

'Why bother?'

His smile grew broader and he shifted in his chair.

'So bold, yet so young. Now an older woman, she would either slap my face and walk out, or come to me, but you, you're unpredictable.'

I shrugged, dropped the bikinis back into their bag and walked towards him. He may have actually thought

I was going to slap his face, because I swear he flinched as I reached him, but his arm came around me as I curled myself into his lap.

'Come on, then.'

My hand had gone to his chest, but I didn't linger, moving down to his trousers and rubbing over the expensive suit material. I wasn't ready, not quite, but as I undid his zip and pulled his cock free, catching the male scent, I knew I soon would be. He let me do it, sitting back and smoking his cigar as I brought him gently to erection, stroking and teasing at his cock until it had grown in my hand. As I did it he was holding me, his hand around my waist, then higher, to tickle the nape of my neck and send shivers down my spine.

I'd been going to wank him off and fantasise a little, the way Bobbie liked, to see what he said when he was about to come. A clever idea, I thought, but with his fingers teasing the sensitive skin behind my ears and the feel of his cock in my hand, my little scheme was quickly giving way to raw lust. He was soon hard, and he had a nice cock, a really proud one, curving up from his belly, rock hard and a good size too. As his fingers began to move down my spine I gave in, bending down to take him in my mouth, sucking and licking at his erection as the heat in my pussy picked up.

He never said a word, still smoking and watching me suck him as he teased me, his hands finding my bottom only when I was thoroughly ready. I moved a little, letting him get at me. My skirt had been lifted, rucked up to show my knickers: hardly sophisticated, not even very dignified, but I no longer cared. Still sucking, I quickly opened his trousers and pulled his balls free, treating myself to a lick before climbing up, onto his lap.

His hands closed on my hips, taking a firm grip and turning me, to let him see my bottom. I pushed it out, eager to show off, stroking my breasts as he held me, his cock pushing to the gusset of my knickers, ready to do its stuff. His thumbs pushed into my waistband and my knickers were being eased down, very slowly, in full appreciation of my arse as I was stripped.

Bare, I settled down onto him, teasing my breasts as I wriggled my bottom onto his hard cock. There was something very rude about my naked flesh against his tailored suit. He took hold once more, lifting me under my bum, his cock head now in my crease and against my cunt, and then in me. I couldn't help but sigh in pleasure as I was filled with cock, and I was immediately wiggling and gyrating against him, revelling in the feel of him inside me. He gripped my hips, bring my wild squirming under control, to let me know I was being fucked, firm and steady, by a man in control. My bare bottom was in his lap. I was getting fucked, just the way he'd wanted.

As I rode his cock I quickly stripped, tugging the buttons of my blouse open and flipping up my bra to get my breasts bare. He immediately took them in hand, squeezing them and teasing my nipples until I was moaning and working my sex on his cock. A hand came lower, onto my pussy, and I was being masturbated as we fucked, my thighs wide, my knickers taut between them, his fingers rubbing in my crease.

It was so dirty and wrong to be doing this in his office. I loved the fact that I had impressed him to this extent; had made this powerful man hard in his pants for me. I thought about him thinking about me, having fantasies over me and wanking off to porn mags. But now it was real. He was getting what he wanted, and that turned me on – the fact that I was pleasing him. Making him stiff and about to shoot his load. With this thought, I came, crying out in ecstasy as I writhed on him, my pussy full of his cock, my breasts bouncing wildly to the motion of my fucking, my bottom squirming against him. He groaned, his grip tightened and I knew this was the moment. As he let go, he leant over to whisper in my ear, 'You dirty little tart, Lucy. You're going to get a lot more of that, my darling.' I was in a state of bliss, my scheming completely forgotten.

I didn't promise to go to Inagua, despite an unexpectedly nice fucking. He didn't press the point, contenting himself with telling me he was leaving on the Friday and would appreciate an answer reasonably soon so that he could, if necessary, invite somebody else. That was at least honest, which was a refreshing change after having to play games with Niall. It was also irritating, because I genuinely wasn't sure what I should do.

On the tube home I was still trying to work it out, and even tossed a coin, at the exact moment the train went over some points, so that I dropped it and was forced to grovel on the floor to get it back. It had caught in a groove on the floor. I got off at Kilburn Park, intent on a quiet drink in the Duchess, a tatty, old-fashioned pub just down the road from Father Jessop's parochial house. I chose it because none of my friends would be there and I wanted to work things out for myself, but I'd no sooner got to the bar that somebody called my name – Todd Byrne.

He was sitting on his own, a pint in his hand, his shirt two buttons undone, his legs splayed carelessly apart to show an impressive bulge in his work-worn trousers, a bugle I had rather enjoyed twice before. Setting my thoughts of Inagua aside for the time being, I went to join him, cradling my whiskey as I spoke.

'How's it going? You're definitely OK with the job then?'

'Oh yes, he'd not do that to me, not Father Jessop. Known me too long.'

'He did it to me.'

'He can't fathom women, that one. Makes him uncomfortable.'

'Yes? I thought he was jealous.'

'Perhaps that too. But you've been doing all right for yourself? That's a powerful lot of shopping you've got there, for sure.'

'Oh, yes. Getting sacked was the best thing that's ever happened to me! I should thank you, I suppose.'

'You can thank me anytime you happen to be passing, Lucy Doyle!'

He laughed and went on as I found myself smiling and blushing ever so slightly.

'I'm not serious. You're with that fellow Niall Flynn? You're to be married, I hear?'

His words were like a sting.

'You hear wrong. I've been seeing Niall, yes, but I've no plans for marriage!'

'Is that the way of it, then?'

'It is, and if I've a mind to pay you a visit, I will!'

He took a thoughtful swallow of his pint. I was seething, and I had to know.

'Who told you me and Niall were getting married?'

'Davy Miles, if I remember right.'

'The barman at Gogarty's?'

'That's the fellow.'

His smile hid laughter, and I could just imagine what else Davy Miles had told him. I sighed. My phone went. Todd went back to his pint as I answered.

'Hello? Yes. Aaron. No! And I don't care how big it is! Jesus, give me a break will you.'

I'd cut the connection, and the last sentence was addressed to empty air. Todd was looking puzzled as I quickly turned the phone off, but he kept his thoughts to himself. I drained my whiskey, wondering why life had to be so complicated. Todd spoke again.

'So, if you've a mind, you'd be very welcome?'

It was an invitation, and I very nearly accepted. My mood wasn't right, but if I had not been expected home for my tea I'd have gone for it anyway, perhaps after a few more drinks. As it was, I stood up, made a polite apology and stepped around the table to kiss him, full on mouth, just to show I really meant it, which was the exact moment Niall's father and elder brother chose to walk into the bar.

8

31 August, 6.05 p.m. – following a hasty departure from the Duchess, Lucy Doyle decides she is going to Inagua.

What I should have done was stand my ground. Easy to say.

Not so easy to do. Besides, I could hardly point out to Mr Flynn that since I had actively participated in allowing his son to shag two of my friends it was only fair that I be allowed to snog who I pleased without criticism. He wouldn't have understood.

On the Wednesday morning I made a hasty exit from the house, keen to postpone the inevitable confrontation with Niall. I was still at the KMC headquarters, which presumably meant a day, or part of a day, with Charles King, and with any luck the rest of it shopping.

He was in Edinburgh, leaving me at a loose end. Knowing that Leanne was still slaving away in the cube farm, and that the others were all working too, I felt it was only fair I do something other than loll around in Charles King's penthouse. Andrew Miller was more than a little surprised by my attitude, but gave me a work station and something to do, justifying sets of figures, which I suspected was a pointless task as there were no mistakes.

It kept me busy, though, along with surfing the net for info on Inagua, which turned out to be one of the remotest islands of the Caribbean. I also passed on my acceptance of his offer to Charles King, and during the course of the day I received three texts:

Keith – would I like to go to the cinema with him?

Luke – he was desperately in love with me and wanted me to take him to a gay bar.

Aaron – when did I want to come and suck his big, black cock.

I turned Keith down as politely and gently as I could, saying I'd love to come but my boyfriend wouldn't approve. He was the sort of boy it's impossible to be nasty to, not counting tying him up and spanking him, of course, which isn't nasty ... not really. He was also the sort of boy who does nothing for me sexually whatsoever.

With Luke I was rather more pointed, telling him that he wasn't in love with me at all, but merely in lust, and then only because I was willing to help him fulfil his fantasies. I also told him I might be willing to play in the future, just as long as he didn't make any demands on me. It was quite abrupt, and I felt a bit of a bitch afterwards, because it was really what I wanted to tell Niall.

My reply to Aaron was going to be very pointed indeed, but I was halfway through it when my instinct for mischief got the better of me. He was a pushy bastard, and incredibly full of himself, claiming that once I'd been with him I'd never want another man again, so I decided it would be fun to take him down a peg or two. I sent back a seriously purple text, offering to suck him off and let him do anything he wanted to me, and that I'd meet him where two paths crossed next to the lowest of the Hampstead bathing ponds. I then sent a text to Big Dog the rent boy, purporting to come from Aaron and suggesting the same meeting place, before blocking both numbers.

I also sent texts to Sophie to say I was going to Inagua, and Bobbie, the same, plus a request to crash at her flat. It was cowardly, because I knew I had to speak to Niall sooner or later, but to know what you should do and to actually do it are two very different things. Bobbie accepted happily, suggesting we meet at a pub in Goodge Street, near where she was working.

The evening was odd, fun, but with the thought that I should be on my way back to Kilburn to face the music constantly nagging at the back of my mind. Bobbie was openly jealous of my chance to go to Inagua, and extremely supportive of my decision to go. We talked for hours, about men, especially Niall, work, life, shoes, sex and more. Apparently Charles King had a reputation for seducing office girls, and for helping those who accepted his advances with their careers, although it made no difference to my indecision. When we finally decided to go to bed it seemed the most natural thing in the world to get in with her, to cuddle, and to gently tease each other to orgasm, as I described watching Luke suck the rent boy's cock.

In the morning I knew I had to act. Bobbie was up early, with an assignment in Croydon, and by half-past eight I was sitting in a café sipping hot black coffee and convincing myself that the series of lies I was about to tell were white ones. That done, I made for home, to pack and inform Mum that I was off to the Caribbean for a week to work as PA for a non-existent Ms Andrea Miller.

Next on the list was Niall, down at his garage. I was sure he'd have found out about me kissing Todd Byrne, and I was fairly sure he'd be angry, however hypocritical that was. All the way there I was telling myself I'd have to lay down the law and tell him just how things really stood. What I actually did was answer him back with a sharp retort, pointing out that, had it not been for Todd, Father Jessop would have made my life difficult for a long time to come. After a few heated words he accepted what I was saying; we ended up kissing and cuddling, and would have done it on the floor if the garage had been even slightly less busy. I also told him I was off to the Caribbean with Ms Andrea Miller, stressing the Ms, and agreed to go out with him and stay over.

That evening he was surprisingly tender, almost soppy, and also as horny as hell. After a meal and a few drinks he had me in the living-room, in the bathroom and twice in bed. By the morning I was tired, sore and more conflicted than ever, but still determined. I was going, and that was that.

I was up at six, home at half-past, and out of the house with my bags by seven. It was hot, and after lugging everything to the KMC building I was very glad indeed of Charles King's company limo. From then on it was a breeze, limo to Heathrow, business class seats to Freeport and an internal flight to Matthew Town. The last leg took us over the tip of Great Inagua, an expanse of rugged hills and flats in shades through dusty grey-green to brilliant emerald, set in bright blue sea with the shallows picked out in paler tones. Just to look at it made me want to strip off and leap into the sea, and when we got out of the plane and the heat hit me the urge grew stronger still.

There was a car to meet us at Matthew Town, driven by a boy who looked about sixteen, with the darkest skin I've ever seen and a big, cheerful smile. I returned it, my eyes on the sleek, bare muscles of his chest, just as his were on me, but Charles barked an order and he busied himself with our cases before I could introduce myself.

From the airport we drove out along the coast, with the sea to our right, the most wonderful rich blue with whitecaps scattered across it as far out as I could see, a fretful surf breaking on the beach and large lizards basking on the sun-baked rocks.

Charles's villa proved to be over half-an-hour's drive down the coast, and it was even more remote than I'd imagined. The road had long given way to a track, and an even rougher one led down to where the house perched above a tiny cove of perfect white sand. I got straight into my bikini, while the boy, Sam, was still unloading the car. I slapped about a gallon of factor 25 on my pale Irish skin, trotted happily down to the water, and plunged in.

Just hours before, and it seemed like no time at all, I'd been lugging my bags down the Kilburn High Road, and now I was floating free in cool, sunlit water. It was pure bliss, a truly wonderful moment, and made all the better because I knew that a good girl would have been processing files in the Centrans building, and very good girl would have been making tea for Father Jessop. I was a bad girl, I intended to continue being a bad girl, and I was swimming in the Caribbean, and if I had to spend the rest of my life with every miserable po-faced git I came across looking down their noses at me, it would be worth it.

My solitary idling lasted a good while before I was brought back to earth, at least partially, by the arrival of Charles. He was dressed in black swimming trunks and sunglasses, his upper body and legs quite bare, and nicely muscular, attractive, for all the touch of grey in his hair. I was lying in the shallows, letting the little waves rock my body back and forth, and smiled up, grateful for the opportunity he'd given me and glad to be in his company. He returned my smile, his eyes moving lazily down my body.

'You see, this is where your bikini was made for.'

I rolled over and crawled a little way out of the water to flop myself down on the sand beside him. He was wrong. My bikini was made for some fashionable beach, where everyone would know it was a *La Madeleine* and be suitably envious as well as admiring what it showed of my figure, which was just about everything. Here, there was no reason to show off, and no reason to tease. I told him.

'No. This is where I can go stark naked without a care in the world.'

As I spoke I'd tweaked open the fastening of my bikini top. I pulled it free, lifted my bum to push the bottoms down off my hips, kicked them away, and I was naked – deliciously, uninhibitedly naked. Charles gave a pleased chuckle as I lay back down, my eyes closed, in a state of sleepy bliss. For a moment there was silence save for the gentle lapping of the waves, before Charles spoke again, just as his fingertips found the nape of my neck.

'You're right, of course, although it could never be wrong for you to be naked.'

My answer was a low purr as he began to caress my neck. He wanted to have me, no question, and that was just fine, so long as he took his time and didn't expect me to do anything active. I stayed as I was, my eyes closed, my head resting on my folded arms, my body slowly warming in the late afternoon sun. He didn't speak, his caresses slow and gentle, but growing gradually firmer as he began to massage my back. It was so soothing, making me sleepier still, at first, until the even, steady rhythm of his pushes gradually began to turn me on.

Still I didn't move, enjoying the sensation as he rubbed up and down, from my neck to my midriff, to the small of my back, a little lower each time, so that before he'd even touched my bottom I wanted to push it up for his touch, and for his cock. When his thumbs at last began to press down on the first swell of my cheeks I thought he would do it, sure his cock had to be hard and his lust rising to the point where he'd be unable to hold himself back.

To my surprise he skipped my bottom, moving down to my legs instead, first my feet, then my calves, and my thighs, until they'd come apart, showing my wet, eager pussy from behind. Still he stroked and caressed, gently squeezing my flesh, completely unhurried. I wanted mounting, fucking, good and hard, and to be made to come on his cock the way he brought me off the first time.

I began to lift my bottom, more by instinct than choice, to show myself behind and make an invitation of my pussy. My breathing was already deep, and deeper still, a low panting as he finally took the hint and began to mould the flesh of my bottom, squeezing my cheeks and pulling them wide to stretch my bottom hole open. He was behind me, between my open thighs, everything on view to him, and on offer. I thought I'd get his cock at any moment, thrust hard into me, but it was his tongue that touched my flesh, and not my sex, but higher, pushed firmly onto my anus.

My breath came out in a gasp and I was wriggling my bottom in his face, utterly uninhibited in my need. It felt so good, and if I was a little scared that he might try to bugger he, the pleasure of being licked was just too good to even think about making him stop. As he pulled back I was sobbing with need and apprehension, but I wanted to at least let him try. My bum stayed up, and when his cock settled between my open cheeks I was biting my lip, only to have the full, hard length eased in to my pussy.

I stayed in that position as he used me, my bottom pushed up to meet his thrusts, my fingers grasping at the sand in my ecstasy. He was up on his arms, as if doing press-ups into me, then abruptly right on top of me, his hands under my chest to grasp my breasts, his belly slapping hard on my bottom as he rode me in a flurry of pushes, jerking himself free at the last second, to come over my bottom.

Even as his sperm spattered down on my flesh I was reaching back, eager to masturbate, one hand under my belly, one hand behind, rubbing in what he'd done on my bottom. I was gasping with lust, too far gone to care about anything except my pleasure as I rubbed on my clit, my fingers down between my bum cheeks, touching the rude little hole where I'd been expecting him to put his cock. I came in a heaving, shuddering climax.

Only one thing spoilt that first, glorious fuck. I was plastered with wet sand, and got straight back into the sea to wash it off, catching a movement on the balcony of the villa as I stood up. Realising the boy Sam must have been watching, and rather pleased with the idea, I made a joke of it to Charles. His response was to march up to the house and bawl the poor boy out, with a vengeance, calling him a dirty Peeping Tom and worse. I thought it was a bit harsh, and as soon as I'd got my bikini on I went up myself, intending to intervene.

By the time I got there it was all over, and Charles apologised, both for his temper and the fact that Sam had seen me naked and watched us fuck. I assured him I didn't mind, and got a brief lecture on the jealous male which left me wishing I had Mike and Ismael there to have me from both ends.

After a delicious dinner of grilled fish, barbecued yams and rice he had mellowed out again, and so had I. We sat up, watching the sunset and long after, sipping rum as he expounded his philosophy of life, which was basically that, with one life to live, any sane person should squeeze out every last drop of pleasure they could. It seemed a little selfish, but I didn't say anything, content to let him have his way.

The night was hot and sticky, but with a huge fan rotating directly above the bed it was at least bearable. Charles liked his positions, especially those that let him enjoy my bum. After going doggy, I mounted myself backwards on him so he could watch his cock slide in and out between my cheeks, then with him on top of me the same way we'd done it on the beach. Afterwards I was left wet with sweat as well as come.

We walked down to the sea, swimming together naked in the phosphorescence, with only the faint lights from the villa and the moon to see by. By the time we'd got out we were both fit for nothing but to lie in a sleepy, half-contented haze until tiredness finally caught up with us.

The next day was more of the same: lazy, hot, with nothing to do but eat and shag and swim. I wanted to go nude all the time, because it felt right, and because I'd never before in my life had the chance to just be naked without anybody minding. Unfortunately somebody did mind – Charles, because Sam was about and he had friends who were likely to drop in unannounced when they discovered he was on the island. I didn't make an issue of it, but stayed in my bikini and a light wrap.

Some of the friends arrived that evening. They consisted of two Americans, Paul Castellani and Dan Bergman – one a small, precise top-flight New York lawyer, the other a big, loud businessman from Forth Worth. Both teased Charles about me, which was quite funny, and left me in the mood for a good, hard fucking once they'd gone home. I even asked to have my bottom smacked, but Charles was too rough, with none of the skill Bobbie and Sophie had shown.

The next day we went fishing on Dan Bergman's boat, which was not a success. I felt slightly queasy all day, without ever actually giving in to sea-sickness, while they seemed to take it for granted that I'd play the role of waitress and general galley slave while they sat harnessed in their chairs. When they did catch something, a marlin, I just felt sorry for the poor thing. It had been an exhausting day all round, and Charles barely managed to get it up that evening before falling asleep.

By the next day I felt I was losing track of time. Nothing seemed hurried, nothing really seemed to matter and, if in the back of my mind I knew that this was an illusion from being under a rich man's wing, I could see no reason not to enjoy the effect. I was coming to understand Charles's character too, and that he wasn't really so very different from Niall. Both were like lions, only comfortable as top male, easy with women, but naturally aggressive to other men. As he humped me one more time that night I was again wishing I had a nice cock to suck while he did it, and lamenting the pride that stopped my desire becoming reality.

In the morning Dan Bergman rang to suggest another fishing trip, this time for shark. I declined, preferring to laze at the villa and perhaps explore a little, citing my queasy tummy as an excuse. Charles accepted my choice without making too big a deal out of it and, for the first time, I was left to my own devices. As the noise of the car faded, the villa was left in silence, made all the more intense by the occasional cry of a bird and the faint murmur of waves.

My first thought was that at last I could go naked, and Sam wasn't about. So I stripped nude, except for sandals and sun block, first to swim and laze on the beach, then, when it began to get really hot, indoors. It felt good, pleasantly naughty and unfamiliar, doing ordinary things but stark naked. Even reading a book in one of the big wicker chairs in the main room added to my gently climbing sense of arousal.

By lunchtime I was on a slow burn, allowing my feelings to pick up with the sure knowledge that when Charles came back and put me on my knees for a seeing-to my climax would be truly glorious. I began to pose, thinking how he'd like to see me, bent a little to show off the curve of my back and the flare of my bottom cheeks, across the table with my feet set wide and my bum lifted for rear entry, crawling on the floor with everything flaunted in totally uninhibited display.

I stayed nude as I ate a big paw-paw for my lunch, with the juice running down between my breasts as I spooned the pulp out. My hands got sticky too, and I ended up rubbing the juice into my breasts and teasing my nipples erect before pulling them to my mouth to lick off the sweet stickiness. By then my arousal was coming up towards boiling point, and as I stood on the veranda caressing my breasts and thinking dirty thoughts, I knew there was no way I could wait for Charles.

Walking quickly to the bedroom, I turned the big fan on, triggering what seemed a deliciously cool down-draft of air. I climbed onto the bed, crawling, imagining Charles behind me, or any man, watching, his cock stiffening in his hand as his eyes feasted on my bare bottom and he imagined what he could do to me. Face down on the bed with my bum a little lifted, I reached back to stroke myself, letting my fantasy develop.

He'd be rock hard, staring as I touched myself, my thighs open, as they were, my cheeks spread to show every rude detail between. I'd be teasing my pussy, tickling my bumhole, just as I was, bringing my pleasure very, very slowly up towards ecstasy. Four hours or more I'd been naked, my need slowly rising, and I wasn't spoiling it. I told myself I wouldn't touch my clit until I quite simply couldn't help it.

I rolled on my back, my eyes closed as I began to play with my breasts and my bottom, using my fingertips, and nails, to take myself higher and higher. The sun block was by the bed and I dribbled some onto my chest, rubbing it into my breasts until my nipples were so taut they'd begun to ache. More went between my bottom cheeks, to allow me to slip a finger in up the tiny hole between, a deliciously rude sensation. I slipped my thumb into my pussy, thinking how it would feel if instead of my fingers I had two cocks inside me, and a third in my mouth.

Two men had been wonderful, what would three be like? How impossibly full would it feel to have cocks in pussy and up my bottom at the same time? For that matter, how would it feel to take a cock up my bottom at all? Dirty? Improper? Maybe too painful ... or maybe not. My finger felt nice, and as I slipped a second in, nicer still.

I could hear my own soft moans as I masturbated, a reaction I had little control over. My feelings were too high and still rising. I thought how I'd have to take my three imaginary men, mounted on top of the first with his cock in my me, leaving my bottom spread in a thoroughly rude pose, the little hole my fingers were working in spread to the second's cock. Up he'd go, pushed deep, to fill me to my head, and the third would pop his in my mouth to let me suck. There were no men, but I wanted to get into the position to come, so flipped myself over onto my knees.

... to catch a movement on the veranda outside. I froze, my heart hammering for just an instant as Sam darted away from the window through which he'd been watching me. Then I was running for the bathroom and a towel, burning with blushes. He'd seen; he had to have seen, everything, including me putting my fingers up my bottom. It was hideously embarrassing, and left me feeling sexually vulnerable too, imagining him bursting in on me and thinking I was fair game for anyone.

He wouldn't dare, I was sure, but I was shaking badly as I quickly washed and threw a robe around myself. The only thing I could think of to do was act as if nothing had happened, maybe stick my nose in the air, because I could just imagine him with his ever-present grin, but now knowing, very knowing.

Only when I'd got control of myself again did I dare to step out of the bathroom, to find him standing in the doorway. I nearly jumped out of my skin, and might have screamed, only he looked more frightened than I felt, and was babbling immediately.

'I'm sorry, miss, I'm truly sorry. Don't tell Mr King, will you? Please don't tell Mr King. I'll lose my job, I will, so please, please don't tell. I didn't mean to watch. I didn't.'

I put up my hands and he went quiet. My heart was still hammering, but my fear had vanished. He was no rapist, nothing like it, just a frightened boy, not frightened of me as such, but of his bullying employer who was my lover. King was such a pig to him, and would undoubtedly sack him on the spot. I tried to reassure him.

'Relax, will you, I'm not going to tell Charles. I wouldn't do that.'

'No? Really not?'

'No, not ever. Why would I? Look, you just scared me, that's all, standing out on the balcony like that.'

He nodded, shame-faced and apologetic. I didn't really know what to say, beyond a completely ridiculous desire to point out that I didn't usually stick my fingers up my bottom when I masturbated.

'I, er ... let's have a beer, OK?'

'I'm not allowed.'

'Yes, but I am, and Charles is off fishing with his Septic friends.'

He gave me another puzzled look.

'Septics ... septic tanks, Yanks, Americans. It's rhyming slang, a way some people talk in London. Apples and pears. Septic tanks.'

He was looking at me as if I was nuts, then slowly the grin returned to his face. I went to the fridge and took out a pair of cool bottles, then to the freezer, where Charles kept the glasses ice cold. I filled both and took them out onto the veranda, with Sam following, still rather hesitant. He took his beer, but kept glancing around as he drank it, as if expecting Charles to materialise out of thin air. I'd felt sorry for him from the start, but never realised he was quite so frightened.

It was hard to know what to say at first, beyond asking questions about his life and the island. His responses were guarded at first, but he gradually loosened up, and we were laughing together by the time we'd finished our second beer. I felt more than a little odd, edgy, to think what he'd seen, and maybe because I'd been getting pretty close to orgasm when he'd caught me.

By halfway down the third beer I'd decided I was going to give him the treat of his life. I needed it, for one thing, and he was attractive, in a boyish way, while the size of the bulge in his shorts had suggested interesting possibilities, and he seemed to be erect half the time. He wanted me too, and would enjoy it all the more for me being Charles's lover.

When I went to fetch another beer I loosened my robe a little, to allow the edges to fall open as I sat down, showing him quite a lot of thigh and maybe more. He responded with furtive glances, evidently believing it was accidental, but as we continued to talk, he began to swell in his shorts. I let my thighs slip a little further apart and gave him a glance from below half-lowered eyelashes. Still he sipped his beer, trying not to be too obvious as his eyes flicked repeatedly between my legs.

I stretched and settled back in my chair, not bothering to rearrange my robe, which now lay half open, showing the inner curves of my breasts and at least hinting more forbidden delights. Still he sipped his beer and cast furtive glances.

I adjusted my position yet again, allowing my robe to fall open, displaying one breast and the full swell of my mound. He swallowed his beer at a gulp and made a hasty and embarrassed adjustment of his cock, which was rock hard.

I did no more but stood up, took him by the hand and led him into the bedroom. Once in there, I sat on the bed, pulled down his shorts and took him in my mouth, sucking eagerly as I held onto his firm, smooth legs.

He never said a word, looking down at me in amazement as I sucked and licked at his cock, took his heavy balls in my mouth, and rubbed my face against him. Even when I shrugged off my robe and took him between my breasts he stayed silent, staring wide-eyed as I folded his jet-black cock into the creamy pale flesh of my cleavage. He might have been shocked, but he wasn't backward, soon sliding about in my cleavage with my nipples rubbing on his flesh, until it was just too much for me.

I lay back, pulling him on top of me, my breasts still held together around his lovely dark cock. He was long, but quite narrow, with a fleshy purple head that just needed kissing and licking. Soon I was giggling and trying to kiss and lick at his knob as he continued to rub against my breasts. He'd have done it in my face, maybe, but I wanted more, and pushed him down as my thighs came wide in invitation.

He didn't need any more encouragement, and mounted me, grinning as he filled me. I took my breasts in my hands, playing with myself as my fucking began, and hoping he'd take his time. It felt so good, and I wanted him to come with him inside me, perhaps even up my bottom, if I dared.

I did. He was easy, no threat, somebody I'd never see again, and somebody who'd take it slow. My voice came urgent and broken as I pushed gently on his chest.

'Stop, Sam, I want to turn over.'

For the first time since I'd taken his cock in my mouth he spoke.

'Yeah, great, I love your ass, in that bikini.'

'And bare, yes? I know you were watching.'

'Bare, yes, on the beach, and when you dress, in white panties.'

'You've been watching me dress? You dirty little sod!'

His answer was a big, toothy grin, and I'd rolled over, offering him my bum. He took hold of my cheeks, kneading them, pulling them wide and mumbling about what a beautiful bottom I had and how much he wanted to fuck it. His cock found my pussy hole and he was in me, pushing hard, to rob me of breath, until I forced myself, sure he'd spunk at any moment.

'Lovely, thank you, Sam, thank you, but would you ... oh God, just put it up my bum, please?'

I could hear the embarrassment in my own voice, and when he didn't answer for a moment I thought I might have put him off. Then his cock was being drawn slowly from my pussy hole, his thumbs had spread my bottom cheeks wide, my anus was showing to him, and I knew I was to be buggered.

'Gently, Sam, slowly ... don't hurt me.'

He didn't speak, but I felt his cock head push to my bumhole and my mouth had come open against the bed sheets. I felt myself start to open, quite easy, my hole slippery with sun block and my own juices and, for the first time in my life, a cock was being introduced to my bottom hole. It did feel rude, deliciously improper, filling my head with lovely, dirty images of how sluttish I was as he eased it up. There I was kneeling in the nude on white sheets, copper-coloured curls spread out, as a beautiful young man took my anal virginity.

Only when his balls met my empty pussy did I know he was all up. I was gasping and clutching the sheets as he began to move inside me, and I'd reached back for my clit, knowing I had to come over my first ever buggering.

'Do it, Sam, nice and slow, and you can slap my bottom, if you like. Spank me, like I'm naughty.'

I was letting him bugger me on Charles's bed. He was hesitant, patting my cheeks as he moved himself slightly in my bottom, but he'd soon got the idea, slapping and laughing with delight as I played with myself. I was going to come, in moments, spanked and buggered on

Charles's bed. My clit was burning under my fingers as I rubbed, and his balls were pushing on my empty pussy, reminding me over and over of exactly where his cock was, deep up my straining bottom hole.

When it hit me I screamed the house down. It was just such an utterly, wonderfully rude thing to be doing, and the feeling when my body went into contractions on his cock was something else, taking me up to a long, glorious peak with my fingers working urgently and my bumhole tightening over and over on his intruding cock. He gasped, jamming himself in as deep as he could go. The knowledge that he'd come too brought me up to a second, higher peak, with my fingers locked in the bed sheets, my mouth wide, my toes curling, and my screams of ecstasy echoing around the room and startling the birds from the trees.

Sam was still pumping into me as I collapsed in a heap on the bed, and he stayed there, on top of me, still joined, holding me to him as we both went slowly limp. I could have lain there for ages, maybe until he was ready again, because it still felt nice, and it would have been good to be held and kissed a little before a second, equally thorough session. He was going to pull out, but I took hold of his hand, my voice a sigh as I spoke.

'No ... do me again, when you can. Shit! Move!'

He'd heard it too, and he didn't need telling, the growl of an engine, which could only possibly be Charles's car. Sam tired to pull out, which hurt so much I had to tell him to slow down, wasting precious seconds as Charles's tyres crunched on the gravel outside. As the engine died, as we caught voices, Charles, and Paul Castellani and Dan Bergman, Charles again.

'Lucy! We're back. Fetch some beers, would you?'

My teeth were gritted in pain as Sam finally pulled free, hopped back, tripped over his lowered shorts and went flat on his face on the floor. I was already scrambling for my robe, which was on the floor, leaving me in an unutterably lewd pose as Charles's footsteps sounded on the wooden stairs.

'Lucy?'

'Hi, Charles. I'm up here. Give me a moment, will you?'

'What's the matter?'

I'd got my robe, and I'd pulled it on, albeit inside out, as Sam lurched out onto the balcony. Charles appeared, but I was sitting on the bed in my robe, dishevelled, sweaty, but alone. Sam was gone, and dashed for the steps down to the garden, straight into Paul Castellani and Dan Bergman as they came around the corner.

The aftermath was horrid, shouting and screaming, accusations and threats, ending with me throwing my things together as Charles stood to one side in cold anger. Sam had run for it, with both Americans in angry pursuit, if not for long. They'd returned, puffing and full of righteous indignation for what Sam had done, for what I'd done.

I didn't even bother to answer their reproaches, walking away in near blind fury. Charles tried to call me back as I reached the gates of the villa and got a V-sign for his trouble. Thinking they might follow in the car I took off cross-country, through rocky scrub land that quickly left my legs scratched and the dress I'd thrown on badly torn around the hem, which only made me more angry.

Finally I came out onto another track, hot, sweaty and bedraggled. I'd begun to calm down, and was wondering what I should do beyond my immediate need, which was to get out of the sun and quench my thirst. There was a shack visible some way ahead, the corrugated iron roof shimmering in the heat haze, with a green sign next to it. I made for it, praying it was a bar of some sort, which it was.

The owner didn't seem particularly surprised to see me, and let me have some badly needed water. Sitting in the shade of an awning with my bags around me, feeling utterly fed up, I tried to take stock.

I was not going back, no way. My pride wouldn't let me crawl to Charles, not if it meant I had to swim back to England. I had my passport, but no money, or tickets. I could call home, but it was going to take a lot of explaining, and if the truth came out I would, never, ever, hear the end of it. I could call Bobbie and ask her to wire me some money. She'd understand and help, although I had no idea how to go about it, and would obviously need to get to Matthew Town first.

For the moment it was the sensible thing to do; get to Matthew Town, where I could get official help, or maybe work in a bar until I had the money for a flight home. Anything, so long as it didn't involve Charles King, or risk my family and Niall finding out what had really been going on.

Getting a lift was easy. A battered truck pulled in for petrol, driven by an old man and stacked with watermelons under a tarpaulin. I asked if he was going to Matthew Town and he agreed to take me, not even asking for petrol money. He talked non-stop all the way, and demanded a kiss when we arrived, our destination a fruit wholesalers. I gave it willingly, and got a watermelon as well as my lift.

It was only a little way down to the water, where there was a smart hotel complex, then an open beach where a rickety pier extended into the sea. I went to sit on the pier, removing my shoes and dangling my aching feet into the water as I ate my melon and thought over my predicament. My anger had died down, but I still wasn't going back to the villa. Charles King could rot before he'd have the satisfaction of me crawling to him.

The best bet had to be to find somebody who could give me advice, perhaps a more experienced traveller. Certainly I should avoid going to the authorities if I possibly could, because that would mean explanations which, in the long run, were sure to lead to trouble. I wondered what a chambermaid or bartender was paid in the huge white concrete hotel along the beach. Probably not very much. It was better to wire Bobbie for help.

In the UK it would be evening. Being mid-week, she'd probably be in. I got up and started along the beach. The hotel seemed as good a place to call from as any, but I looked a complete ragamuffin. I needed to change, something that was hardly going to attract attention on a beach. Digging into my bags, I found a white cocktail dress I'd brought in case Charles took me anywhere formal for dinner – an idea that now drew a bitter laugh to my lips.

Outside the hotel the beach was crowded, but on my side of a low fence there were only a few stragglers, none of whom were taking any notice of me anyway. Quickly peeling off my dress, I slipped it on and extracted my bra through the side. A moment with a mirror and hairbrush and I no longer looked as if I'd been dragged through a hedge backwards, although I still felt sticky and uncomfortable. It would have to do, and I made for the hotel.

The lobby was a huge, airy space, with cool air blowing down in a refreshing curtain immediately inside the door. I paused for a moment, enjoying the wonderfully fresh feel after the stifling heat outside, before walking across to the reception desk. A middle-aged man with a paunch hanging over a pair of vivid green and yellow shorts was managing to hold the attention of both the girls in banana-yellow uniforms, trying ineffectually to chat them up, and both turned as I approached.

I explained that I was stranded and needed to call someone to wire me some money; that I didn't have any on me but would gladly pay the appropriate charges when I did, and asked if I could contact a friend in the UK. They were sympathetic, but had to consult the manager, who proved to be a cow.

No, I couldn't make a call without paying at the time.

No, it didn't matter that I had no money and needed to make the call before I could pay for it.

No, this was a hotel, not a charity. I should go to the police station in town.

In the end I left before she could instruct the two yellow-uniformed heavies who'd begun to hover to throw me out. Feeling thoroughly fed up, I went outside, to sit on my bags by the roadside. There were other hotels, or it might even be an idea to try a private house. Eventually I'd succeed, probably once I found a man to ask.

I was about to move on when the big American in the colourful shorts approached me, his red face split by a big, dirty grin, his hand extended in welcome.

'Hi, I'm Harry. You say you're stranded, clean out of money?'

'Yes.'

He sank down on his haunches, nodding and beaming.

'How much d'you need?'

'I'm not sure. Just enough for my airfare, but I couldn't possibly ask –'

'Uh, uh, stop right there. You ain't asking nothing, missy, not for free. You just come up to Harry's room for an hour, or maybe two, and I'll pay your air fare, and maybe a bit over. You know, I'm looking for some female company on this little holiday of mine. My wife back home, she don't like the heat too much. But I love it, and the local honeys too.'

He let out a jovial belly laugh, devoid of all embarrassment or shame. He was brash and boisterous and it was obvious what he meant, blatantly obvious, and I was left gaping at his sheer nerve, too taken aback even to kick him in the balls. He took my silence, and my expression, for rejection, and stood up with a shrug.

'You just think about my offer then, missy, and if you change your mind, I'm in five-seven-two, that's suite five-seven-two.'

He gave a final nod, let his gaze linger on my chest for a moment and made for the hotel. I watched him walk away, full of outrage and shock that he could have suggested such a thing, and so casually. And yet it would be so easy, a quick shag, something I'd done many times for the fun of it, sometimes just because I was drunk and some guy was persistent, so why not for money? I shook my head, amazed that I could even think such a thing.

He was overweight, crude, as old as my Dad.

But younger than Charles King.

Although not as good looking, or wealthy.

Not that wealth ought to matter.

Yet he was seriously sleazy.

And letting Sam bugger me wasn't?

I bit my lip, trying to find a really, really good reason not to do it. The disapproval of my family didn't matter, or at least, it was theoretical disapproval, because I was hardly going to tell them. I guess that was a bit of the old Catholic guilt creeping in. I'd always been told as a little girl that God could see everything – a shameful thought that still reminds me of what a sinner I am, if I think about it too much. If anything it helped weaken my resolve. Nor did I care what Niall would think, while

I was sure both Bobbie, and Sophie even more, would not only understand, but support my decision. I was going to do it.

He was halfway back to the hotel, sauntering in the evening light. I got up before I could lose my nerve, hurrying after him with my bags bumping on the ground. A passing tourist gave me an odd look, which I ignored, despite the uncomfortable feeling that she was able to read my mind, thinking, look at that Irish slut. If only her family knew what she was doing.

'Excuse me, Harry. Hang on a minute,' I shouted.

He stopped and turned. I was wondering just what the hell I thought I was doing as I caught up with him, but it didn't stop me.

'I've changed my mind. OK?'

He gave me his big, sloppy grin.

'I thought you looked a sensible girl.'

'Yeah, right. My air fare, OK, and enough to get me to the airport, and from Heathrow back to London.'

'You're on, baby,' he said, expansively, as if he was the new Austin Powers or something.

His hand closed on my bottom as he steered me through the door. A twinge of resentment caught me, but I didn't speak out. He'd paid to touch, and there was no use complaining.

I felt odd as we crossed the lobby, ascended in the lift and walked down a long corridor to his suite. I felt detached, as if I wasn't really there, but observing another girl going to her fate. Once in the room he wasted no time as he asked me to pose for him, teasing with my dress, showing off the seat of my knickers, playing peek-a-boo with my tits, sticking out my bottom and slowly unveiling my cheeks, before finally going nude.

By then his shorts and sandals were off and his cock

was a hard pink pole in his hand. He was so eager, almost bursting, which made it very, very easy to take charge. I took him by the cock, led him into the showers and went down on him as cool water cascaded over our naked bodies. He was sighing with pleasure as I sucked him, and to my surprise he was complimenting me, on my hair, my waist, my tits, my bum, even my accent.

When the time came to 'do the nasty', as he called it, I stood up and put my hand against the wall with my bottom stuck out towards him and the water trickling down between my cheeks. He gave a grunt of satisfaction at the sight, put his cock to me, and then deep up my pussy. I got my fucking, braced against the wall with my bum cheeks jiggling to the thrusts while he grunted and puffed his way to a noisy, gasping orgasm, pulling out at the last second to do it over my bottom.

An hour later I had a flight booked on his credit card and a hundred dollars in my pocket. Two hours later and we were discussing Dublin over a gourmet meal washed down with White Star Moet champagne. Three hours and I was giving him a genuinely affectionate peck on the cheek outside the hotel. Four, and I was at the airport. Five, in the air, on my way back to London.

I felt good. Not saintly good, but good all the same. I congratulated myself on my resourceful attitude. After all, I'd done what I had to do. It didn't make me a bad person. It didn't make me immoral. It made me strong.

9

10 September, 7.57 a.m. – Lucy Doyle is woken by the telephone.

10 September, 7.58 a.m. – Lucy Doyle prepares to be sacked, again.

I'd escaped Inagua, but it was rather a case of out of the frying pan and into the fire. As I touched down at Heathrow I was rather wishing I'd stayed, perhaps for the full two weeks until I was due to go up to uni, even if it did mean being merrily porked round the islands by Dirty Harry.

For one thing, I wasn't supposed to be back, and there would have to be explanations. For another, although I'd squared things with Niall, Todd Byrne was still an issue, along with Luke, Keith, Richard Drake, Hilary Chalmers, maybe even Big Dog the rent boy and Aaron of the big black cock. Thirdly, there was Super Staff, because I couldn't see Charles King just letting it go.

Sure enough, when the phone rang before eight on the Friday morning it was Maryam Smith and she wanted me in at the office without delay. I went, wondering what she knew and what to say. King would hardly have told her the truth, but he could well have made up some outrageous story, and at best it would be my word against his. Very likely I was going to get the sack, but all I could think of was to keep quiet and hope for the best.

I bought a doughnut in the Edgware Road, killing time before going up and wondering if just possibly the whole thing was a false alarm, as before. It wasn't. Mrs Smith was behind her desk, stern-faced and leafing through my file. She waded straight in.

'Miss Doyle. Good morning. I regret to say that a complaint has been made against you.'

'Yes?'

My tone was supposed to be surprised and aggrieved. It came out as guilty. Hers was sharp as she went on.

'Mrs Henshaw at the Tilbury Bond . . .'

Relief washed over me, closely followed by consternation. If King hadn't complained, it was only because he was still in Inagua and probably thought I was too.

'She cites that your work rate for the last afternoon you were there was thirty percent below target throughout, and that no reason was given for this lapse. We expect better than that at Super Staff, Miss Doyle.'

'Oh, er . . . right.'

'Is that all you have to say?'

'Sorry?'

'Don't you wish to explain yourself?'

I'd been thirty per cent below target whatsit because I'd been servicing the entire warehouse and security staff, but I didn't expect she'd consider it a good excuse.

'I didn't feel very well. You know, time of the month.'

'Then you should have reported to the medical room. Complaints can not be taken lightly, Lucy, and I'm afraid I will have to give you a first formal warning.'

She pushed the document towards me, a triplicate form.

'Please sign and take the yellow copy.'

I signed, feeling slightly numb and wondering how it would be once Charles King got his hooks into me. Mrs Maryam Smith filed the other two copies with brisk, economical motions, one in my file, one in a tray, then turned to her computer, speaking again.

'You're with Ms Hilary Chalmers again today. There at least you seem to have made a good impression.'

'Er, thank you.'

She printed out my paperwork and I took it, along with the First Formal Warning, which I gave the same treatment as Bobbie had given hers the first morning I'd been there. Had it really been just a few short weeks? It felt like eternity.

I wasn't completely happy about meeting Hilary Chalmers again, for all the impression I'd made on her. No doubt she was going to want to seduce me into playing her kinky games once again, and I wasn't really up for it. My experience with Charles King was too raw to allow me to feel good about the whole employer/temp relationship thing. It's also a little embarrassing to meet a woman you last saw masturbating with her spanked bum stuck up in the air.

Not that I was going to refuse. She was generous and, with uni coming up and the likely termination of my employment when King got back from Inagua, I needed every penny I could get. So I told myself I'd be polite and friendly, doing what was asked of me up to a point – that point being getting my own bottom spanked.

To my surprise it was nothing like that at all. Her attitude had changed completely; she was polite, respectful, almost worshipful. With her being twice my age I found it all a bit hard to take in, unlike the expensive lunch she bought me at the Elephant Inn. She'd been so confident before, but now she was nervous, saying she needed to talk to me and suggesting a walk in the nearby woods.

What she asked of me genuinely shocked me.

* * *

I came back from Henley with five hundred pounds in cash in my pocket and what can only be described as a shopping list of perversions. It was all a bit beyond me, and I was wishing she'd asked Bobbie instead, but apparently the fact that I'd had the guts to turn the tables on her made me the 'ideal person'. What she wanted, in general and to use her own words, was, 'to be brought down from high to low, wholly and unconditionally'. What she wanted in detail was enough to make my stomach tighten.

Fortunately, she wanted both Bobbie and Sophie in on the act, which was just as well, as I badly needed to consult them. I got the chance on the Monday, at some telecom company in the East End on a big decruitment drive, employing temps to fill in for the redundancies in their fault control department before moving the whole she-bang to Bangalore.

Both of them thought Hilary's request was hilarious, and were more than happy to help. I was a little taken aback by their sheer glee in her coming humiliation, but then, they'd both been spanked by her, and I hadn't. There were other, less simple, things to organise too, and we agreed to meet at a convenient pub to discuss it after work.

Fault control was the best job I'd had other than the private ones. In essence it was simple, and boring, but there were just too many opportunities for mischief to be ignored. People would ring in to 'report' a fault with their equipment, or, more accurately, to complain about a fault with their equipment, because, more often than not, they'd worked themselves into a fine temper before ringing. We were then supposed to fill in a fault log and pass it on to the engineers.

The reality was very different. None of the callers knew who we were or where we were, but the great majority had somehow got it into their heads that we were personally responsible for their woes, even those who'd spilt coffee on their equipment, which was by far the commonest fault.

I was between Sophie and Kanthi, which was just asking for trouble. At first it was annoying, with people shouting at me and demanding to speak to the chief engineer or even the MD, but after I'd lost my temper with one man and called him a slimy ball of turds things got better. His explosion of wrath as I put the phone down on him left me smiling and the girls clapping and cheering. After that it was a riot, with Sophie and I trying to outdo each other in winding the callers up, and Kanthi egging us on in delight.

Bobbie was at another desk, but soon caught on and joined in, until at last one of the engineers realised what was going on and told us to stop. He wasn't angry, though, more amused, as he and his colleagues had to put up with the same foolish aggression when they went out on call. I kept right on anyway, because with Charles King sure to do his worst and uni coming up, it no longer mattered.

We gathered after work at a pub called the Golden Eagle, already high on our day's mischief and up for more. Given what we were supposed to do to Hilary Chalmers, we could hardly discuss it in front of Kanthi, who would have been shocked, but none of us were mean enough to send her away. Keith was there too, playing a sort of weird musical chairs in his efforts to sit next to me and repeatedly trying to pin me down about when he could take me to the cinema, which he seemed to regard as a necessary prelude to sex.

In the end the three of us had to pretend we were tired and moved on, although we'd at least decided that the best place for Hilary Chalmers' self-imposed degradation was Sophie's flat. It was actually getting late, and with the pubs full of wagging ears and all three of us supposed to be back at work for eight the next morning, we decided to call it a day for real.

I was still thinking about it on the way home, and the next day on the way in. Bobbie, in particular, understood what Hilary wanted well enough to help me over my feelings of unease and, after a lunchtime chat, I was as keen as they were. The main problem was that we needed a man, a dirty bastard, but somebody who'd do as he was told. Niall was out, because there was just no way he'd let me, or Bobbie and Sophie, stay in charge. There were three possible alternatives:

Big Dog the rentboy, in that he worked for money and so would presumably take orders, but he was probably too aggressive and maybe too gay for our needs.

Luke, who would certainly do as he was told but was really too mild to make a proper job of it.

Aaron, who might be ideal but would need checking out.

It was supposed to happen on the Saturday, which didn't give us much time, while to contact a complete stranger for sex was something that needed to be done very carefully. It was also something that carried a delicious thrill, now that I had a reason, something both girls agreed on. We decided to go together, and to bring Luke along for safety. Mild he might be, but he was a big lad and could keep us safe.

That evening, with trembling fingers and both the girls pressed close, I retrieved Aaron's number and sent him a text on Sophie's phone, because I hadn't forgotten about the phoney meeting I'd set up by the ponds on Hampstead Heath. He responded immediately, hardly surprising with three girls calling to discuss 'possibilities for his huge cock'. We'd meet the next night, Wednesday, at the pub in Camden Town where he'd placed his advert.

Once we'd done our dirty deed I went back to Niall's. I'd promised to cook for him, on demand, one more little sign that he was getting too possessive. Once again I told myself that I'd talk it through with him, and once again I just ended up getting fucked, this time bent over the table after we'd eaten, with my knickers down behind and my tits in a plate of half-finished spaghetti Bolognese.

He wanted to take me to Gogarty's on the Saturday night, and I had to tell him I'd already promised to go out with the girls, citing an imaginary hen party as my excuse. He argued a bit, saying I should put his needs first, but then abruptly changed his mind and made me kneel on the bed for a spanked arse and another fucking to make up for his missed evening. Afterwards he told me I could expect spankings to be a regular part of our relationship, to 'keep me in line'.

Nobody keeps Lucy Doyle 'in line', but nobody. I was rather getting to enjoy having my bottom spanked, especially with a good rough shagging to follow, but that was sex, pure and simple. The next morning I was in a fine state of conflict, sexually satisfied but thoroughly resentful. On the way in I was thinking of how I could bring things to a head, which seemed inevitable.

I was at a different workstation, and didn't get a chance to speak to Sophie until the evening, and then only once we were on our way to Camden after getting rid of Keith. She disagreed.

'Don't worry about it. You're off to uni next week, three hundred miles away. Play it cool, and my bet is Niall'll have a new girlfriend within a month.'

Bobbie agreed, and I could see it made sense, for all that it hurt and once more left me wishing he'd be more reasonable about our relationship. I'd have gone on about it, and probably worked myself into a fine state, only Luke was waiting outside Camden Town tube, looking more than a little unsure of himself.

'So what's the deal again?'

I chose to answer, despite having explained.

'It's simple. We're going to meet this guy Aaron, because we need him to do us a favour. You're here in case he's a nutter but, as a special treat, if he's into guys you get to suck his cock.'

Luke went instantly pink, glancing to Bobbie and Sophie, both of whom were trying not to giggle. I put up a reassuring hand.

'Don't worry, they know, and they love the idea.'

Luke's response was a grimace, but he tagged onto us as we started down the High Street. Whatever he was like personality wise I was very glad of his presence, but still nervous as we pushed in to the pub. It was crowded, mainly people my age out on the town, and a few older, in street clothes or work clothes, drinking and talking, some perhaps on assignations, but few like us.

We ordered drinks and propped ourselves against the far wall, near the door to the loos. All four of us were tensed up, Luke the most, and rightly so with any number of possibilities for the end of the evening, ranging from a punch-up to taking Aaron's big black cock in his mouth. Sophie and Bobbie were holding hands, eyes bright with expectation.

In the space of an hour, three single black men came into the pub, and each time my heart jumped. Sophie had a red ribbon in her blonde hair for Aaron to spot us, but it made her well cute, and all three of the men gave her a long glance, Bobbie and me too. None approached us, but when the fourth guy came in, I knew we'd found our man.

He was a good six foot four, lanky but muscular, with short dreads and tats on his bare arms, but none of that mattered. What did was his expression and the way he held himself, just bursting with confidence, and a lewd, mocking sexuality. Here was a man who could send girls messages demanding his cock be sucked, and laugh off the refusals. Sophie had seen too, and gave a sharp intake of breath. He saw her, pointed one finger and started towards us. I swallowed, my stomach churning, very glad that he didn't know I was the one who'd sent him up onto the Heath to meet a rent boy. He spoke as he came close.

'You're Sophie, yeah? And Lucy and Bobbie. And you, you're the minder. Me, I'm Aaron, but I guess you know that.'

Luke responded with a gruff nod, trying to look tough. Aaron made an easy gesture.

'That's cool. So, you all want a portion, or you want to watch Sophie do the business?'

It was a bit abrupt, but I managed to come back, determined to at least try and keep control.

'It's a bit more complicated than that.'

'Anything you like, girl.'

'OK. Do you want a drink? We need to find a table, maybe upstairs.'

I went for the drinks, taking Bobbie with me, and the others made for the stairs. She spoke first.

'He's cute, a bit of a poser, maybe, but cute. I'd have him.'

'Right, but how about for Hilary?'

'We'll see. Not if he gets pushy, though, because he's a big guy.'

'He is, isn't he? What about on the night, we won't have Luke?'

'Maybe we should. He could stay in the kitchen or

something, but I'm not sure he could do much if Aaron turned nasty.'

'No.'

I bit my lip, feeling a little scared but too excited by the possibilities to back out.

'We'll just have to make sure this evening. Make sure he knows it's cock-sucking only and see how he reacts.'

Bobbie nodded and I turned to catch the attention of one of the bar staff. Once we'd got the drinks we made our way upstairs to a much quieter bar where Sophie, Luke and Aaron were seated around a table. Sophie was talking animatedly, and laughing, Aaron listening, Luke hanging back. I put the drinks down.

'So, what's up?'

Aaron answered me.

'My cock,' he joked. 'Just as soon as we're back at this little miss's flat.'

I glanced at Sophie, who returned a mischievous smile. It was all going a bit fast.

'Fine, no problem, but what we really want you to do is come along on Saturday afternoon, with the three of us, but for another woman ... an older woman, who wants a ... a specialist service.'

'What's that?'

I glanced to where a group at a nearby table had their ears flapping our way.

'Nothing you can't handle, I'm sure.'

'There's nothing I can't handle, girl.'

I had to answer him. He was just too cock-sure.

'How about being whipped and buggered?'

'Hey, I ain't no freak!'

'Fine, it's nothing like that, just checking out your limits. Look, I'll explain.'

I leant close, to whisper in his ear, and had the satisfaction of watching his expression change slowly from arrogance to surprise. When I sat back I was smiling, but also hoping he wasn't going to lose his nerve. He took a swallow of his vodka Red Bull and nodded.

'I can do that, yeah, just so long as I get some action. You girls into stuff like that, then?'

'Not really ... well, maybe. Sometimes.'

We continued to talk, Aaron very brash and amused, taking our attraction to him for granted. He really was arrogant, and I could see him making a girl go through with it if she tried to back out, leaving me more than a little uncertain. Bobbie and Sophie had no such qualms, happily stoking his vanity by admiring the admittedly impressive bulge in his jeans, even stroking it. That was all he could take, downing his third vodka Red Bull as he stood up.

'We've got to go, or there's going to be an explosion.'

Sophie's response was to nuzzle his crotch with her face, purring happily. They linked arms as we left the pub, Bobbie on his far side, which left me with Luke, as happy to watch as they were to suck his cock. It was easy for him, no pressure, and he was well full of himself, his arms around both of them before we were halfway down the High Street, and his hands on their bums before we'd got to Sophie's flats.

I was wondering if he was going to object to Luke, but he simply ignored him, groping and kissing the girls, pinching my bum too, as we got out of the lift. In Sophie's flat there was no hesitation. He sat down in the centre of the sofa, let his legs slide apart as the girls got down to either side, and flopped his cock out of his trousers. He was big, very big, thick and black and veiny, and only half stiff, with the pink tip of his helmet just poking out from a meaty foreskin.

Sophie went straight down, taking him in her mouth even as she pulled out his balls. Bobbie watched for just a moment, before joining in, the two of them licking on his rapidly expanding cock shaft as he watched with an amused expression. I quite wanted it in my own mouth, and I knew exactly what would be going through Luke's mind because, when it came to cocksucking, Aaron had to be his ideal.

Aaron looked up at me suddenly and pointed to his cock.

Why not? I went down on my knees between his open legs, my arms around Bobbie and Sophie as I buried my face in his crotch, licking at his dark, heavy balls. I wanted my breasts out while I did it, maybe my bum bare too, to tease him, to see if he'd break the agreement I knew Bobbie had made. And if I got fucked, well ... I got fucked.

My fingers went to my shirt, tweaking my buttons open. He watched as I opened my blouse and tugged up my bra. I paused briefly, to heft my breasts in my hands, showing off to him, before going back to licking his balls and the shaft of his cock. Bobbie was no better, her hand down her trousers, playing with herself as she enjoyed his erection, or Sophie, her top and skirt quickly pulled up to show her knickers and bra. His hands had been on the back of the sofa, but now settled on the girls' bums.

He was pushing it, but I was too high to care, playing with my breasts as the three of us licked and sucked and kissed at his lovely big set of cock and balls. Soon I'd pulled my skirt up, showing my knickers, then my bare bum, surely an invitation? He held back, cool and easy as the three of us worked on him, but suddenly something seemed to snap. He pushed up and I was sent sprawling, my legs wide, my pussy spread, his body on top of mine, his cock jammed deep as I gasped in shock and he was fucking me, furiously hard, and calling me a tart and tease as I grunted and panted underneath him.

Luke did nothing, just watched open-mouthed as I was fucked on the floor. Bobbie and Sophie reacted, jumping in to pull on his shoulders, too late, as he finished off, spunking deep inside me before pulling free to milk out the last of his come over my mound. I was panting, dizzy with sex, too horny to stop myself as my fingers went to my clit. There was a sour, knowing grin as Aaron stood up, watching me masturbate over what he'd done.

The girls saw, and let go of him, watching as my fingers worked in my crease, wet with his come, bringing myself up, higher and higher as I replayed over and over the way he'd just thrown me on the floor and fucked me, until I came, crying my ecstasy out loud to the room.

When we met again, after work on the Thursday, we had serious trouble deciding what to do. As Sophie argued, and I had to agree, it had been a bit much to ask of Aaron, or any red-blooded male, not to fuck me. On the other hand he hadn't even bothered to ask, or apologise afterwards, simply assuming that because I'd taken my knickers down I was up for it. I had been, of course, but that wasn't the issue.

Bobbie argued that up until that point he'd been very well behaved, although apparently he'd had his fingers up both their snatches by the time he'd lost it. Therefore, as long as we were game to satisfy him, everything would be OK. Sophie agreed, but I wasn't quite so sure, and at the least wanted a reliable man around – a man who wouldn't prove to be completely and utterly useless, as Luke had.

The thing was that Luke had been completely over-awed by Aaron, basically because he had really wanted to be down on his knees and sucking cock, preferably with the three of us laughing at him while he did it.

That was all very well, but entirely useless for our purposes. I needed a man I could trust, a real man, and I could only think of one possibility – Todd Byrne.

Maybe I'd have given up on it, but the more I thought about it the more deliciously improper it seemed. After weeks of being expected to kow-tow to executive types it was going to get a lot of frustration out of my system. I needed the money too – five hundred each – because, despite my good wages, I'd actually managed to spend more than I'd earned over my time as a temp. Still I might not have done it, but Friday morning tipped the balance.

I got the call I'd been expecting all week, from Maryam Smith. She didn't even want me in at Super Staff. I was sacked, and that was that, no explanation, no nothing. It had to be Charles King's doing, perhaps threatening to take his business away if I wasn't fired, perhaps making up some outrageous lies about me, perhaps even telling the truth, or a twisted version of it. Whatever, it left me seething.

It wasn't fair, to get me thrown out of a job just because I'd bruised his precious ego, and that was what it was, nothing more. I'd had every right to have sex with Sam, or anybody else I wanted, any way I wanted. Maybe, just maybe, he'd had reason to be angry, but to take my job away was right out of order.

I was going to go in and tell Maryam Smith where she could stick her job, but by the time I'd got to the Edgware Road I'd realised it was pointless. It wasn't even really her fault, and she almost certainly didn't know the truth. Charles King was the one to blame, but what could I do? I went drinking, from pub to pub, downing Guinness with whiskey chasers and plotting ever more fanciful revenges. The only even vaguely sensible one was to let the warehouse boys at Tilbury Bond have me anyway they liked in return for beating him to a pulp, and that was just going get me arrested. I was in my fifth pub when it hit me, the perfect revenge, calculated to hit him where it hurt but not to land me in jail.

My bladder was on the point of bursting as I made for the KMC building, but I hung on, my legs crossed and my toes wiggling on the bus, and my thighs pressed firmly together as I stood in front of the receptionist. My voice was full of contrition as I asked if I might be allowed to see Mr King, and when Andrew Miller came down to ask what I wanted I told him I'd come to apologise.

Up we went, through the security system and into the presence of the great Charles King, his face set in smug condescension, as I stepped into the centre of the office, pulled the gusset of my knickers aside and emptied the full contents of my bladder all over his priceless Persian rug.

It was nearly two hours before I got out of the KMC building, which was how long it took for Charles King to calm down enough to realise that having a nineteen year-old girl accusing him of demanding that she pee in front of him was not going to be good for his reputation.

My line was simple. I'd offered to apologise. He'd demanded a filthy act to humiliate me before I got a sound fucking, and in my fear and confusion I'd agreed, failing only to realise that I wasn't supposed to go on the carpet. He ranted and raved, but finally he had to accept that when the questions started it would be poor, tearful little Lucy Doyle who was believed, and not big bad Charles King, who'd seduced more office girls than he'd had hot dinners.

I left.

It felt good, really good. My fists were clenched in

triumph as I walked out through the lobby with my head held high. Only when I was out in the street did the reaction of what I'd done hit me. I was shaking so violently I had to sit down. Then there were tears. Then laughter. I was choking the laughter as I walked, thinking of his face as I'd let go all over the rug, his speechless outrage and his wild, impotent fury. All the way home my mouth was constantly twitching into a wicked smile. I'd already decided to ask Todd Byrne to be our minder on the Saturday, and I was in just the mood to have some of my excess energy fucked out of me.

He would still be at work, at the Parochial House but, after the carpet incident, the thought of running into Father Jessop didn't really bother me. I got off at Kilburn Park and walked to House, singing happily to myself as I went. There was no sign of Jessop, but Todd was there, clipping a hedge, his muscular torso naked and damp with sweat. He grinned as he saw me.

'Hi, Todd, you said to call. Got a moment?'

'For you, always. Come inside?'

'Sure.'

I followed him into his hut, watching the muscles on his back play as he went. Just the smell of him was getting me horny, never mind how he looked and the knowledge of what he could do to me, while the great head of energy I'd built up by confronting King was rapidly turning sexual. He was grinning as he spoke.

'So, what can I do for you?'

We both knew the answer, and Hilary Chalmers could wait.

'What you do best, Todd. I really need it.'

He didn't need telling twice. As I stepped close he'd taken me in his arms, kissing my mouth even as he fumbled up my skirt and my fingers groped for his fly. A moment later my knickers were down at the back and he was growing in my hand as he fondled my bottom, our mouths working together as we readied each ourselves for sex.

I went down on him before he was fully hard, wanting to feel him swell in my mouth, and to taste him. He held my head as I sucked, leaving me on just long enough for his cock to grow rigid before lifting me under my arms, pushing me hard against the door, ripping my knickers free of my thighs and plunging deep into me. Immediately I was gasping and panting in breathless ecstasy as he fucked me, my legs splayed wide, my breasts bouncing. He stuck his fingers into my shirt and tore it wide open. He was grunting as he did it, crude and animal, with his sweat-slick, hairy chest rubbing on my nipples and his coarse trousers right on my pussy, splaying my sex lips to touch my clit.

And I was gasping my head off as I came, totally unable to control myself, bucking and squirming in his grip, shudder after shudder running through me until, with a final bestial grunt, he jammed himself to the hilt and let it go inside me, looking me in the eye with a cheeky, dirty expression on his face and a curl to his lip like the bad boy he was.

He gave me a last kiss before lifting me off his cock and lying me down in a chair, heedless of my dishevelled state and ruined clothes. Several buttons were gone, although my knickers were beyond hope – a mangled damp mess that reeked of pheromones. By the time I left he'd agreed to come along on the Saturday, with the understanding that once he'd done his bit he could take me to bed. That was fine, because I was going to need it.

Hilary Chalmers rang me Saturday mid-morning to ask if everything was as it should be. I told her it was, fairly confident that nothing could go wrong. She would be arriving at Paddington on a one-twenty train, which I was supposed to meet. From then on every detail was carefully arranged, with Bobbie, Sophie, Aaron and Todd each playing their part. I could still think of a dozen ways it could go wrong, but there was nothing to do but keep my fingers crossed.

I took a mini-cab to Paddington, just in time to watched the one-twenty pull in, disgorging its passengers, including Hilary Chalmers in a white designer suit, expensively cut and accessorised to the nines, as if she was off to a garden party at the Palace. Her haughty stare was everything I remembered as she saw me, and I responded with a polite and servile dip of my head, greeting her respectfully as I reached to take her bags.

'Good afternoon, Ms Chalmers,' I said in a rather forced sing-song voice that we both knew was put on.

She didn't trouble to respond, but walked briskly towards the cab rank with me staggering behind. My mini-cab was waiting, the hulking driver with his eyes fixed firmly in front, chomping on something highly calorific. I held the door for Ms Chalmers and loaded her bags into the boot before climbing in myself, next to the driver. A single, cold word came from the back.

'Knightsbridge.'

It took a moment to get free of the station traffic, and then we were up the ramp and away, turning left, and then left again. Only when we'd joined the pack of traffic in the Marylebone Road did Ms Chalmers speak up, her voice full of impatience.

'This is not the way to Knightsbridge.'

'No, it isn't.'

I pressed the central locking, which closed with a satisfying click. Again Ms Chalmers spoke, now angry, commanding.

'Whatever are you doing? Turn this car around this moment!'

'I don't think so. Left here, Aaron.'

He turned, up into the jumble of small streets east of Marylebone Station, both of us ignoring Ms Chalmers' protests until we'd pulled in beside a square, with a row of ornamental cheery half overhanging the car. It was our first risky moment, and I was glancing around as Bobbie and Sophie piled into the car either side of our posh client.

'Right, you stuck-up bitch, it's pay-back time!' said Bobbie, who grabbed our victim as Sophie struggled her knickers off under her skirt and forced them into Ms Chalmers' open mouth, reducing her protests to a feeble mumbling. A brief fight and her stockings had been pulled off and used to lash her wrists and ankles, leaving her helpless and dishevelled, her skirt rucked up so high the front of her expensive silk knickers showed, her blouse torn to show the curve of one plump breast.

As Bobbie and Sophie began to strip Chalmers of her jewellery and rifle her bag for her money and cards, Aaron was pulling out into the road. We'd done it, unobserved, and my pounding heart slowed a little as we picked up speed. Ms Chalmers was still struggling as we looped around Regent's Park and down to Camden Town, tugging furiously against her bonds and mumbling through Sophie's knickers.

The girls just laughed at her and began to torment her, pulling her jacket open and tweaking her big breasts, pinching her squirming thighs and the soft curve of her belly. I watched, enjoying myself as she wriggled and twitched under their pinches, and occasionally reaching out to nip at where I could get at the soft flesh of her breasts.

We made Sophie's towerblock, the next risky bit, pulling into the underground car park and stopping in the gloomiest corner. I got out first and ran to the lift, signalling the others to follow me as the doors slid wide to reveal an empty interior. Ms Chalmers was dragged from the car and across to me, her perfect leather shoes scraping on the rough concrete. I'd held the door, and was already pushing the buttons for Sophie's floor as they bundled her into the lift.

All it needed was for somebody to stop the bloody thing before we'd reached Sophie's floor, but our luck held and nobody did. Sophie ran to open her door, the rest of us following with the squirming Ms Chalmers supported between us. We made it, and dropped our victim to the floor, Sophie crowing in triumph.

'Got her! Stick her in the bathroom, Aaron, and let's have a drink to celebrate.'

Bobbie answered.

'You're on. Hang about, and I'll use some of the bitch's money to buy some champagne, the best!'

Ms Chalmers was hauled into the bathroom and dumped on the tiled floor by Aaron as Bobbie left. I collapsed down on the sofa, extremely glad we'd got away with it. We were now safe, and could indulge ourselves at leisure. Todd was in the kitchen, munching a sandwich, and greeted me with an indulgent wink. I kissed him, allowing my hand to stray to his crotch for just a moment, but pulled back as he found the curve of my bottom.

'Later, anything you like. This is fun!'

He shook his head in mild deprecation for my behaviour, patted my bottom and let me go. Aaron was back in the room, the bathroom door closed.

'You are three mad bitches, you know that!' Todd shouted through his sandwich.

There was laughter in his voice, and Sophie joined in, bouncing down in a chair. Aaron sat too, legs well splayed, his cock a prominent bulge in his trousers. I checked my watch to be sure I had my timing right and settled back, no longer worried but with a pleasant, tingling excitement growing inside me.

Bobbie was soon back, with a half-case of vintage champagne she'd managed to lug all the way from the High Street. Sophie fetched glasses and we began to drink, toasting each other and the success of our scheme in the full knowledge that Ms Chalmers could hear every word we said. Sophie was particularly pleased with herself.

'This is going to be good, so fucking good. When I think of all those spankings . . .'

'And that hairbrush of hers! She'll regret using that, oh yes.'

'She'll regret it all once we're done with her, and not just the beatings, but every little snotty remark.'

'Every order, in that nasty way she speaks.'

'Every put down.'

'Every demeaning task, everything. More champagne, Aaron, Sophie?'

We drank, and drank some more, four bottles over an hour, to leave my head swimming and my bladder tight. Knowing what I was going to do, the inspiration for my revenge on King made me feel increasingly naughty, and when the time was up I was more than ready for Hilary Chalmers. I drained my glass.

'Let's go.'

Aaron had Sophie's blouse open, and had been toying idly with her breasts, but she detached his groping hand. Both stood, Aaron having to adjust his erection first, and I shook my head in mock vexation.

'Tut, tut, you'd better let that go down first.'

He gave a loose shrug, pulled his zip down and hauled it out, a thick pole of hard brown cock meat extending vertically from his fly. I felt my tummy tighten, remembering how he plunged it into me.

'OK, that's good, I suppose. Get your balls out too.'

Out they came, left bulging beneath the tower of his erection, a sight to delight any rude girl, and terrify a prissy one, or a middle-aged lesbian, perhaps. I went first, pushing open the bathroom door, to find Hilary Chalmers as we'd left her, bound and gagged on the floor, her designer skirt rucked up to show the crotch of her white silk knickers, her torn blouse a little open to reveal the heaving flesh of her ample chest, her eyes fixed to Aaron's straining erection. I gave a curt order.

'Get her bare.'

I went to the bath, to pick up the big wooden bath brush Sophie had bought the day before. Bobbie had come in last, the silver hairbrush from Hilary's bag in her hand. Sophie squatted down, grinning as she ripped Hilary's blouse wide open and tugged the bra cups down to spill out heavy, firm breasts. Hilary had begun to squirm again, and make little whimpering noises through her gag, but it made no difference. She was rolled onto her front, her skirt pushed up around her waist, her knickers dragged down to her thighs, and her bottom bared – two pale, meaty cheeks trembling in her anticipation. Aaron clicked his tongue in satisfaction at the sight, making me chuckle as I spoke.

'Right, Chalmers, first off, a good spanking, a dose of your own medicine. One hundred smacks.'

Bobbie stepped forward, placing one sharp, heeled boot in the small of Hilary's back and immediately bringing the hairbrush down on the bare, quivering nates with a meaty smack. I joined in, applying the bathbrush, unable to restrain a grin as Hilary's flesh cheeks bounced and wobbled to the smacks, the white flesh quickly turning red.

Sophie counted the smacks, her pretty face twisted into an expression of malicious glee. As the count grew higher, we spanked harder, turn and turn about, until Hilary was writhing her bottom in her pain, her muscles twitching and her bottom pushing up and down to hint at the rude details between her cheeks, and at the lips of her glistening sex. We gave no attention to her muffled pleas for mercy, dishing out the full one hundred strokes to leave her shivering on the floor, her bottom flushed deep red, a muscle in one thigh twitching uncontrollably. I stood back.

'I hope that's taught you a lesson, Chalmers. That's how it feel to be punished like that, you vicious bitch. Feels good, does it, like you tell us it should? Feels good to be stripped and humiliated and spanked, Ms Chalmers; spanked on your bare arse?'

Her only answer was a muffled sobbing. I stepped closer, pulling up my skirt.

'OK girls, Aaron?'

Aaron wasn't OK, his cock was absolutely rigid. I shook my head and stepped across Hilary's prone body, straddling her legs.

'Turn over, bitch, or you get another hundred.'

She obeyed, rolling to look up at me, her eyes full of emotion and lust as they met mine. Bobbie climbed into position, and Sophie was splay-legged above Hilary's head and waist. Both had their skirts rucked high, Sophie bare, Bobbie in lacy white knickers, which she pulled aside, leaving Hilary staring up at a bare pussy. I tugged my own gusset aside, pushing my belly out a little, above where Hilary's lowered knickers left the plump mound of her cunt showing between her thighs. There was panic in her eyes and she began to squirm again as I spoke.

'OK, bitch, have some champagne, second hand!'

I let go, my pee spurting out onto her body, to splash on her pussy mound and her belly, soiling her knickers and thighs from a dizzy height. Sophie laughed to see, and let go her own stream, full on Hilary's breasts, and lastly Bobby, right in the face. I couldn't help but feel mean, peeing all over her, but I knew from what Sophie had told me that she really got off on being humiliated and, odd as it seemed, she may even reward us for it. She was an odd creature, Hilary Chalmers; a most unusual beast – a female pervert, in fact. I got off on it, too. It was impossible to deny the sadistic glee bubbling up beneath my pity, or the delightful sense of naughtiness. No one was being hurt. It was all good, dirty fun.

We let her have it all, laughing like drains. She was incensed, squirming on the floor, then rolling over to protect her face, but succeeding only in making sure her hair got a fair share. By the time we'd finished she was in an agony of emotion, writhing in her bonds, her big breasts squashing out on wet floor, her glistening red buttocks working in her anguish, to show the rude pink hole between and the lips of her sex. I stepped back.

'You're on, Aaron. Now for the finalé. He's going to sort you out.'

Chalmers went wild, wriggling in the puddle beneath her, her breasts and belly splashing in it as she struggled to free herself, her naked bottom bucking furiously. Sophie bit her lip in excited anticipation as Aaron sank into a squat, his huge dark cock held in his hand. He reached forward to feel for her sex and announced to everyone how wet she was.

I was staring as he did it, my tummy fluttering and a hot rush between my legs, watching him crudely finger-fuck her – this hulking great geezer having his fill of posh totty. She let out a single, bitter sob as Aaron took himself in hand and then positioned himself to push it slowly in to the tune of her muffled gasps.

My hand had gone between my thighs as I watched her getting fucked, remembering how it had felt myself, and unable to hold back. I sat on the bath, legs wide, staring as I rubbed myself through my knickers, until Bobbie and Sophie sat down beside me to enjoy the live sex show. Bobbie's hand slipped between my thighs and into my knickers. I didn't stop her, but returned the favour, to both of them, the three of us toying with each other as we watched Hilary Chalmers getting it on the floor.

At that moment I wanted it myself, to be treated as we'd treated her, snatched off the street by three vindictive girls, tied and gagged, my bottom stripped and spanked, laughed at as they pissed all over me, and finally given to a man, to be shagged senseless as they masturbated over what they'd done to me.

I felt my body go tight, Bobbie's fingers rubbed harder, and I was coming, my eyes glued to where Aaron's thick black cock was moving in and out between Hilary's well spanked, glistening wet bottom cheeks. I held it for ages, my fingers still working in the girls' knickers, until Bobbie snatched her hand away and pressed mine to her pussy, coming with a low moan.

Sophie was pulling on me even as Bobbie finished, and I could guess what she wanted. I went down as they cuddled together, to press my face to her fanny, licking as she took me by the hair. Her legs were wide open, her belly pushed forward, and found myself kissing her bottom hole, too high to think twice. She gave a pleased purr as my lips pressed to the tiny, puckered ring, before pulling me firmly onto her as Bobbie began to suckle on a breast.

Behind me Aaron was starting to grunt, and Hilary's

little muffled cries had taken on an urgent, desperate quality. I licked harder, full on Sophie's clit, and a moment later her thighs were tightening around my head and she too was coming. Only when she let go of my hair did I pull back, twisting around to watch the climax of Hilary's treatment.

Aaron was nearly there, tight lipped and grunting with effort as he drove his cock into, again and again. I moved close. My hand slipped in under Hilary's belly to find her clit, and I was masturbating her, everything but my task pushed from my mind as I gave her what she had asked of me – orgasm at the deepest, most emotional moment of her fantasy, when the man we'd chosen to shag her was coming.

Her whole body was shivering as it went through her, quite simply the longest orgasm I'd ever witnessed, starting before Aaron came to his own grunting, puffing climax, and continuing long after he'd shot his load. I only stopped when she'd gone completely limp and turned her head to look at me, her face full of exhaustion, gratitude, and bliss.

I'd done it, all of it, without a hitch. Even Aaron had played his part to perfection. I'd come too, more excited than I'd expected, although it didn't mean I wouldn't be indulging myself with Todd later on. He'd been watching from the door, and while he looked more than a little bemused, there was no escaping the implication of the bulge in his trousers. I gave him a friendly squeeze and a kiss.

'Right with you, just let us clean up a bit.'

He nodded and went to pour himself a glass of champagne as we began to clear up, taking turns in the shower, soaping each other and getting nice and clean. Hilary was absolutely delighted, positively bubbling over with pleasure and looking totally relaxed. She was calling me her angel, which seemed a bit incongruous after what we'd done, but I didn't mind. I didn't mind the amount of money she slipped into my hand later, either, a cool grand in fifty-pound notes, which was going to make an awful lot of difference to me at university.

There was only one bottle of fizz left, so Hilary sent Bobbie for more, with instructions not to spare the expense. We'd just about finishing cleaning up, and I was bunging those clothes that had a chance of being saved into the washing machine when the doorbell went. Sophie was in her bedroom, getting dressed, so I went, expecting Bobbie with the champagne.

It wasn't.

It was Keith, holding a bottle of cheap white wine, his voice full of forced merriment as he spoke.

'Hi, Lucy, Keith's here, so now it's party time!'

I hesitated, just too long, wondering what to say, and he'd pushed inside. With everyone sitting around drinking champagne I could hardly deny it was a party and I wasn't telling the truth in a hurry. I didn't want to hurt his feelings either, even if it was crass of him to turn up uninvited just because he knew we'd be getting together. Yet what could I say?

Sophie emerged from the bedroom, now in a red PVC cat suit that left her breasts bare, clearly up for more.

'Keith!'

He was staring, open mouthed. The look on her face changed from surprise to annoyance as she covered her breasts.

'What are you doing here?'

I heard the lift chime and quickly went to the open door in case it was a neighbour.

It wasn't.

It was Luke, and with him Big Dog the rentboy, one in denims, the other in leathers, including tight, abbreviated shorts. I quickly pulled the door to, then changed my mind, not wanting them inside, but not wanting them outside either.

'Come in, quick. What are you doing, here?'

'Aaron's here, yeah?'

'Yes, but . . .'

I hustled them inside and shut the door. Sophie was talking to Keith, who looked as if he was about to cry. Aaron stood up, grinning. Todd stepped forward, throwing a questioning glance at me. I raised my hands in exasperation as Big Dog spoke, jerking his thumb towards Luke.

'Hi bro, this is my bitch, like I promised, and this . . . this is the bitch who sent you up the Heath.'

They were looking at me, and I knew how they'd found out, through Luke. Aaron gave a slow nod, the friendliness suddenly gone from his face. I raised my hands, babbling, even as Todd stepped towards us.

'It was a joke, that's all, Jesus!'

The bell went. This time I checked, looking through the peephole and half expecting to find Maryam Smith, Father Jessop, Charles King, Old Uncle Tom Cobley and all.

It wasn't.

It was Bobbie, and I quickly let her in, grabbing the bag of champagne bottles from her hand in desperate hope of defusing the situation.

'Come on, everyone, champagne all round!'

Hilary spoke up.

'I really don't think . . .'

'Look, you little bitch, I want to know what the game is,' said Aaron, who would not take kindly to being made to look a fool.

'Yeah, little bitch is right,' said Big Dog.

Todd jumped in.

'You call her that again, you dirty poof...'

Bobbie was calling for calm. The room dissolved in noise, everyone talking at once, voices rising with anger. I put my hands up, struggling for anything that would just make them shut-up. The bell chimed. I went, grateful for the interruption, and expecting an irate neighbour.

It wasn't.

It was Niall. Dressed as Superman.

'Hi, Perky, I'm your stripper.'

I began to stammer, wondering how in hell to explain Aaron and Big Dog, Luke and Todd.

'I ... we ... er ... we've already got a stripper ... strippers.'

'You've got other blokes in there?'

He pushed the door wide, too strong for me to do anything. I turn to face the room as he stepped in, biting my lip in an agony of embarrassment. He froze, staring at Todd.

'So it's true! You bastard!'

Todd turned on him, massive fists coming up. Big Dog snatched the moment, swinging a punch in. Todd caught it and pushed, sending the rent boy sprawling on the floor and closed with Niall in a flurry of fists. The girls were shouting, Keith was in tears, Aaron was yelling abuse. Hilary Chalmers gave an angry exclamation, rounding on me as I back for the open door.

'And where do you think you're going?' she said, haughty voice back in place.

'Er, university. Bye.'

And with that, I ran, my wild red hair flowing behind me.

Visit the Black Lace website at
www.blacklace-books.co.uk

**FIND OUT THE LATEST INFORMATION AND TAKE
ADVANTAGE OF OUR FANTASTIC FREE BOOK OFFER!
ALSO VISIT THE SITE FOR . . .**

- All Black Lace titles currently available
  and how to order online
- Great new offers
- Writers' guidelines
- Author interviews
- An erotica newsletter
- Features
- Cool links

**BLACK LACE — THE LEADING IMPRINT
OF WOMEN'S SEXY FICTION**

**TAKING YOUR EROTIC READING
PLEASURE TO NEW HORIZONS**

LOOK OUT FOR THE ALL-NEW BLACK LACE BOOKS – AVAILABLE NOW!

All books priced £7.99 in the UK. Please note publication dates apply to the UK only. For other territories, please contact your retailer.

PEEP SHOW
Mathilde Madden
ISBN 0 352 33924 1

Naughty Imogen likes to watch. When her boyfriend Christian is out at work she spends her evenings spying on the neighbours through binoculars and viewing her secret porn collection. Most of all, though, she likes to go online and pretend to be Christian while she chats up men on a Manchester gay dating site. But when her latest virtual beau and borderline obsession Dark Knight asks for a photograph, her voyeuristic games become complicated. Suddenly Christian is being drawn in to her sleazy thrills without his knowledge. Imogen's getting more eye candy than she ever dreamed of, but at what price? **A potent and dark modern erotic novel that explores sexual anonymity in the heart of the urban landscape.**

RISKY BUSINESS
Lisette Allen
ISBN O 352 33280 8

They come from different worlds, but their paths are destined to cross. Liam is a working-class journalist fighting a passionate battle against environmental injustice; Rebecca is a spoilt rich girl used to having whatever, and whoever, she wants. They are thrown into a dangerous intimacy with each other when Liam – on the run from an irate enemy – is forced to hijack Rebecca's car. Using his rugged charm, he manages to access her true sexuality – something no man has ever done. The usually cool Rebecca is forced to make a choice between her sophisticated but bland lifestyle and the exciting but unpredictable world offered by her charismatic captor. **A freewheeling story of what happens when posh meets rough!**

UNDRESSING THE DEVIL
Angel Strand
ISBN O 352 33938 1

It's the 1930s. Hitler and Mussolini are building their war machine and Europe is a hotbed of political tension. Cia, a young, Anglo-Italian woman, escapes the mayhem, returning to England only to become embroiled in a web of sexual adventures. Her Italian lover has disappeared along with her clothes, lost somewhere between Florence and the Isle of Wight. Her British friends are carrying on in the manner to which they are accustomed: sailing their yachts and partying. However, this serene façade hides rivalries and forbidden pleasures. It's only a matter of time before Cia's two worlds collide. **Literary erotica at its best, in this story of bright young things on the edge.**

Also available

THE BLACK LACE SEXY QUIZ BOOK
Maddie Saxon
ISBN O 352 33884 9

- What sexual personality type are you?
- Have you ever faked it because that was easier than explaining what you wanted?
- What kind of fantasy figures turn you on – and does your partner know?
- What sexual signals are you giving out right now?

Today's image-conscious dating scene is a tough call. Our sexual expectations are cranked up to the max, and the sexes seem to have become highly critical of each other in terms of appearance and performance in the bedroom. But even though guys have ditched their nasty Y-fronts and girls are more babe-licious than ever, a huge number of us are still being let down sexually. Sex therapist Maddie Saxon thinks this is because we are finding it harder to relax and let our true sexual selves shine through.

The Black Lace Sexy Quiz Book will help you negotiate the minefield of modern relationships. Through a series of fun, revealing quizzes, you will be able to rate your sexual needs honestly and get what you really want from your partner. The quizzes will get you thinking about and discussing your desires in ways you haven't previously considered. Unlock the mysteries of your sexual psyche in this fun, revealing quiz book designed with today's sex-savvy woman in mind.

Black Lace Booklist

Information is correct at time of printing. To avoid disappointment check availability before ordering. Go to www.blacklace-books.co.uk. All books are priced £6.99 unless another price is given.

BLACK LACE BOOKS WITH A CONTEMPORARY SETTING

☐ SHAMELESS Stella Black	ISBN 0 352 33485 1	£5.99
☐ INTENSE BLUE Lyn Wood	ISBN 0 352 33496 7	£5.99
☐ A SPORTING CHANCE Susie Raymond	ISBN 0 352 33501 5	£5.99
☐ TAKING LIBERTIES Susie Raymond	ISBN 0 352 33357 X	£5.99
☐ ON THE EDGE Laura Hamilton	ISBN 0 352 33534 3	£5.99
☐ LURED BY LUST Tania Picarda	ISBN 0 352 33533 5	£5.99
☐ THE NINETY DAYS OF GENEVIEVE Lucinda Carrington	ISBN 0 352 33070 8	£5.99
☐ DREAMING SPIRES Juliet Hastings	ISBN 0 352 33584 X	
☐ THE TRANSFORMATION Natasha Rostova	ISBN 0 352 33311 1	
☐ SIN.NET Helena Ravenscroft	ISBN 0 352 33598 X	
☐ TWO WEEKS IN TANGIER Annabel Lee	ISBN 0 352 33599 8	
☐ PLAYING HARD Tina Troy	ISBN 0 352 33617 X	
☐ SYMPHONY X Jasmine Stone	ISBN 0 352 33629 3	
☐ SUMMER FEVER Anna Ricci	ISBN 0 352 33625 0	
☐ CONTINUUM Portia Da Costa	ISBN 0 352 33120 8	
☐ FULL STEAM AHEAD Tabitha Flyte	ISBN 0 352 33637 4	
☐ A SECRET PLACE Ella Broussard	ISBN 0 352 33307 3	
☐ GAME FOR ANYTHING Lyn Wood	ISBN 0 352 33639 0	
☐ CHEAP TRICK Astrid Fox	ISBN 0 352 33640 4	
☐ THE GIFT OF SHAME Sara Hope-Walker	ISBN 0 352 29935 1	
☐ COMING UP ROSES Crystalle Valentino	ISBN 0 352 33658 7	
☐ GOING TOO FAR Laura Hamilton	ISBN 0 352 33657 9	
☐ THE STALLION Georgina Brown	ISBN 0 352 33005 8	
☐ DOWN UNDER Juliet Hastings	ISBN 0 352 33663 3	
☐ ODALISQUE Fleur Reynolds	ISBN 0 352 32887 8	
☐ SWEET THING Alison Tyler	ISBN 0 352 33682 X	
☐ TIGER LILY Kimberly Dean	ISBN 0 352 33685 4	

To find out the latest information about Black Lace titles, check out the website: www.blacklace-books.co.uk or send for a booklist with complete synopses by writing to:

> Black Lace Booklist, Virgin Books Ltd
> Thames Wharf Studios
> Rainville Road
> London W6 9HA

Please include an SAE of decent size. Please note only British stamps are valid.

Our privacy policy
We will not disclose information you supply us to any other parties. We will not disclose any information which identifies you personally to any person without your express consent.

From time to time we may send out information about Black Lace books and special offers. Please tick here if you do <u>not</u> wish to receive Black Lace information. ☐

Please send me the books I have ticked above.

Name ....

Address ....

....

....

....

Post Code ....

Send to: Virgin Books Cash Sales, Thames Wharf Studios, Rainville Road, London W6 9HA.

US customers: for prices and details of how to order books for delivery by mail, call 1-800-343-4499.

Please enclose a cheque or postal order, made payable to Virgin Books Ltd, to the value of the books you have ordered plus postage and packing costs as follows:

UK and BFPO – £1.00 for the first book, 50p for each subsequent book.

Overseas (including Republic of Ireland) – £2.00 for the first book, £1.00 for each subsequent book.

If you would prefer to pay by VISA, ACCESS/MASTERCARD, DINERS CLUB, AMEX or SWITCH, please write your card number and expiry date here:

....

Signature ....

Please allow up to 28 days for delivery.